018

REKI KAWAHARA ABEC BEE-PEE

SWORD ART ONLINE
Alicization Lasting

SAO
SWORD ART ONLINE

"I'm back, Asuna."

Kirito § A boy who appeared in the Underworld as a "Lost Child of Vecta." The battle against Administrator left his mind an empty husk.

"You gotta stop it with takin' all the juiciest, most heroic scenes..."

§ **Klein**
Leader of the Fuurinkazan guild. Longtime friend of Kirito's. Logged in from the real world to help save the Underworlders.

§ **Asuna**
A rapier-wielding girl who logs in to the Underworld using Super-Account 01, Creation Goddess Stacia, to rescue Kirito.

"...Welcome home, Kirito."

"Kirito...!!"

§ **Silica**
A beast-tamer in *SAO*. Logged in from the real world to help save the Underworlders.

"Well, I guess he hasn't lost his edge or his sense of abandon..."

§ **Lisbeth**
A master macer in *SAO*. Logged in from the real world to help save the Underworlders.

"I will now devour your feelings, your memories, your mind and soul... your everything."

Gabriel § After dying while using Super-Account 04, Dark God Vecta, he logged in as his character Subtilizer to pursue Alice, the Priestess of Light.

"Let's go, Gabriel!!"

"Alice, this is the way...
This is the path that leads
to the Underworld!!"

"Which would mean that this
address points to..."

Yui § Originally a mental health counseling
program from *SAO*. The greatest top-down
A.I. in the world.

"In other words, this is how we can go—I mean, get back. To that world...to *my* world..."

Alice § An Integrity Knight of the Underworld. The Priestess of Light, whose fluctlight broke through its own limitations.

Battle for the Underworld Status Map
Final Stress Test, Day Two

Eastern Gate

Integrity Knight
Fanatio

Integrity Knight
Deusolbert

Ravine
Created by
Asuna

TEAMING UP

Orc Battalion
Chief Lilpilin

Dark God
Vecta

Integrity
Knight
Sheyta

Pugilists
Guild Champion
Iskahn

Earth
Goddess
Terraria, Leafa

**IN
BATTLE**

American Players
as Dark Knights

**IN
BATTLE**

Asuna

Chinese/Korean
Players as Dark
Knights

CAPTURED

Kirito
(Empty)

PoH

Human Army
Decoy Force

**Real-World
Reinforcements: Klein,
Lisbeth, Silica, Agil, etc.**

Integrity Knight
Renly

Subtilizer

Sun Goddess
Solus, Sinon

DEFEATED

Student
Ronie

Student
Tiese

PURSUING

Integrity Knight
Alice

World's End Altar

Illustration: Tatsuya Kurusu

SWORD ART ONLINE
Alicization Lasting

VOLUME 18

Reki Kawahara

abec

bee-pee

YEN
ON

NEW YORK

SWORD ART ONLINE, Volume 18: ALICIZATION LASTING
REKI KAWAHARA

Translation by Stephen Paul
Cover art by abec

This book is a work of fiction. Names, characters, places, and incidents are the product of the author's imagination or are used fictitiously. Any resemblance to actual events, locales, or persons, living or dead, is coincidental.

SWORD ART ONLINE Vol.18
©REKI KAWAHARA 2016
Edited by Dengeki Bunko
First published in Japan in 2016 by KADOKAWA CORPORATION, Tokyo.
English translation rights arranged with KADOKAWA CORPORATION, Tokyo, through Tuttle-Mori Agency, Inc., Tokyo.

English translation © 2020 by Yen Press, LLC

Yen Press, LLC supports the right to free expression and the value of copyright. The purpose of copyright is to encourage writers and artists to produce the creative works that enrich our culture.

The scanning, uploading, and distribution of this book without permission is a theft of the author's intellectual property. If you would like permission to use material from the book (other than for review purposes), please contact the publisher. Thank you for your support of the author's rights.

Yen On
150 30th Street, 19th Floor
New York, NY 10001

Visit us at yenpress.com
facebook.com/yenpress
twitter.com/yenpress
yenpress.tumblr.com
instagram.com/yenpress

First Yen On Edition: January 2020

Yen On is an imprint of Yen Press, LLC.
The Yen On name and logo are trademarks of Yen Press, LLC.

The publisher is not responsible for websites (or their content) that are not owned by the publisher.

Library of Congress Cataloging-in-Publication Data
Names: Kawahara, Reki, author. | Abec, 1985– illustrator. | Paul, Stephen, translator.
Title: Sword art online / Reki Kawahara, abec ; translation, Stephen Paul.
Description: First Yen On edition. | New York, NY : Yen On, 2014–
Identifiers: LCCN 2014001175 | ISBN 9780316371247 (v. 1 : pbk.) |
    ISBN 9780316376815 (v. 2 : pbk.) | ISBN 9780316296427 (v. 3 : pbk.) |
    ISBN 9780316296434 (v. 4 : pbk.) | ISBN 9780316296441 (v. 5 : pbk.) |
    ISBN 9780316296458 (v. 6 : pbk.) | ISBN 9780316390408 (v. 7 : pbk.) |
    ISBN 9780316390415 (v. 8 : pbk.) | ISBN 9780316390422 (v. 9 : pbk.) |
    ISBN 9780316390439 (v. 10 : pbk.) | ISBN 9780316390446 (v. 11 : pbk.) |
    ISBN 9780316390453 (v. 12 : pbk.) | ISBN 9780316390460 (v. 13 : pbk.) |
    ISBN 9780316390484 (v. 14 : pbk.) | ISBN 9780316390491 (v. 15 : pbk.) |
    ISBN 9781975304188 (v. 16 : pbk.) | ISBN 9781975356972 (v. 17 : pbk.) |
    ISBN 9781975356996 (v. 18 : pbk.)
Subjects: CYAC: Science fiction. | BISAC: FICTION / Science Fiction / Adventure.
Classification: pz7.K1755Ain 2014 | DDC [Fic]—dc23
LC record available at https://lccn.loc.gov/2014001175

ISBNs: 978-1-9753-5699-6 (paperback)
       978-1-9753-5700-9 (ebook)

10 9 8 7 6 5 4 3 2 1

LSC-C

Printed in the United States of America

"THIS MIGHT BE A GAME, BUT IT'S NOT SOMETHING YOU PLAY."

—Akihiko Kayaba, *Sword Art Online* programmer

SWORD ART Online
Alicization Lasting

Reki Kawahara

abec

bee-pee

CHARACTERS

UNDERWORLD

《 Human Empire 》

》》 Rulid Village

Kirito: Lost Child of Vecta. Visitor from the real world.

Eugeo: Kirito's best friend and battle companion.

Alice Zuberg: Eugeo's childhood friend. Broke the Taboo Index's laws.

Old Man Garitta: Sixth-generation carver of the Gigas Cedar. Eugeo's predecessor.

Gasfut Zuberg: Alice's father. Village elder.

Sadina Zuberg: Alice's mother.

Selka Zuberg: Alice's little sister. A holy woman in training.

Azalia: Sister at the church where Selka lives.

Orick: Eugeo's father.	Donetti: Villager.
Celinia: Eugeo's elder sister.	Jana: Child at the church.
Nigel Barbossa: Owner of the village's biggest farm.	Arug: Child at the church.
Doik: Head guard—the calling all the village children want.	Ivenda: Herbs master.
Zink: Man-at-arms. Doik's son.	Ridack: Farmer outside the village.

》》 Zakkaria

Vanot Walde: Owner of Walde Farm.

Triza Walde: Farmer's wife.

Teline Walde: Daughter of Vanot and Triza Walde.

Telure Walde: Daughter of Vanot and Triza Walde.

Kelgam Zakkarite: Liege lord of Zakkaria.

Egome Zakkarite: Participant in the Zakkaria tournament.

》》 Centoria

Volo Levantein: First-seat Elite Disciple at the Imperial Swordcraft Academy.

Sortiliena Serlut: Second-seat Elite Disciple. Kirito's mentor.

Golgorosso Balto: Third-seat Elite Disciple. Eugeo's mentor.

Sadore: Craftsman. Fashioned the Gigas Cedar branch into a sword.

Azurica: Manager of the primary trainee dormitory at the Imperial Swordcraft Academy.

Raios Antinous: Primary trainee, then Elite Disciple. Son of a noble house.

Humbert Zizek: Primary trainee, then Elite Disciple. Son of a noble house.

Muhle: Primary trainee. Cultivator.

Ronie Arabel: Kirito's page, primary trainee.

Tiese Schtrinen: Eugeo's page, primary trainee.

Frenica Cesky: Primary trainee. Friend of Ronie and Tiese.

》》 Central Cathedral

Administrator: Pontifex of the Axiom Church. Analyzed and learned all of the Underworld's system commands. Birth name: Quinella.

Cardinal: Master of the cathedral's massive library, isolated in space. A copy of Administrator. Birth name: Lyserith.

Charlotte: Cardinal's giant spider familiar. Observes Kirito on his journey.

Bercouli Synthesis One: Commander of the Integrity Knights.

Fanatio Synthesis Two: Vice commander of the Integrity Knights.

Deusolbert Synthesis Seven: Integrity Knight. Apprehended Alice for breaking the Taboo Index.

Sheyta Synthesis Twelve: Integrity Knight. Known as "Sheyta the Silent."

Dakira Synthesis Twenty-Two: Integrity Knight. Served under Fanatio. She, Jace, Hoveren, and Geero were the Four Whirling Blades.

Renly Synthesis Twenty-Seven: Integrity Knight. Youngest of the elite knights.

Linel Synthesis Twenty-Eight: Apprentice Integrity Knight, disguised as a sister-in-training.

Fizel Synthesis Twenty-Nine: Apprentice Integrity Knight, disguised as a sister-in-training.

Alice Synthesis Thirty: Integrity Knight. Priestess of Light and possessor of a limit-broken fluctlight.

Eldrie Synthesis Thirty-One: Integrity Knight. Serves under Alice. Birth name: Eldrie Woolsburg.

CHARACTERS

Eschdor Woolsburg: Eldrie's father. General of the Imperial Knights.

Almera Woolsburg: Eldrie's mother.

Chudelkin: Prime senator. Wields the most power after the pontifex.

Operator: The girl who carries people between the fifty-first and eightieth floors of Central Cathedral.

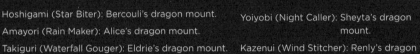

Hoshigami (Star Biter): Bercouli's dragon mount.

Amayori (Rain Maker): Alice's dragon mount.

Takiguri (Waterfall Gouger): Eldrie's dragon mount. Amayori's brother.

Yoiyobi (Night Caller): Sheyta's dragon mount.

Kazenui (Wind Stitcher): Renly's dragon mount.

《 Dark Territory 》

》》 Forces of Darkness

Vixur ul Shasta: Commander of the dark knights brigade. Dark general. Bercouli's rival.

Lipia Zancale: Dark knight. Shasta's lover.

Dee Eye Ell: Chancellor of the dark mages guild.

Sigurosig: Chief of the giants.

Fu Za: Head of the assassins guild. Birth name: Fuelius Zargatis.

Lilpilin: Chief of the orcs.

Lenju: Princess knight from a clan distantly related to Lilpilin's.

Rengil Gila Scobo: Head of the commerce guild.

Iskahn: Tenth champion of the pugilists guild.

Dampa: Iskahn's right-hand man.

Yotte: Smaller female pugilist.

Furgr: Chief of the ogres.

Hagashi: Chief of the mountain goblins.

Kosogi: The next chief of the mountain goblins after Hagashi.

Kubiri: Chief of the flatland goblins.

Shibori: The next chief of the flatland goblins after Kubiri.

Ugachi the Lizard Killer: Flatland-goblin captain who tried to trespass into the human lands.

Aburi: Ugachi's subordinate.

Morikka the Foot Harvester: Orc general who attacked Rulid Village.

《 Gods 》

Stacia: Goddess of Creation. Super-Account 01. Has the power of landscape manipulation.

Solus: Sun Goddess. Super-Account 02. Has unlimited flight and wide-ranging annihilation attacks.

Terraria: Earth Goddess. Super-Account 03. Possesses unlimited regeneration.

Vecta: God of Darkness. Super-Account 04. Has the ability to alter memory.

REAL WORLD

Kazuto Kirigaya: The hero of *SAO*. Kirito the Black Swordsman.

Suguha Kirigaya: Kazuto's adoptive sister. Magic warrior in *ALO*.
                 Player name: Leafa.

Midori Kirigaya: Kazuto's mother. Publishing-industry editor.

Minetaka Kirigaya: Kirito's father.

Asuna Yuuki: *SAO* fencer. Kirito's girlfriend.
             Player name: Asuna.

Shouzou Yuuki: Asuna's father. Former CEO of RCT.

Kyouko Yuuki: Asuna's mother. College professor.

Yui: World's greatest top-down AI.

Rika Shinozaki: *SAO* blacksmith.
               Player name: Lisbeth.

Keiko Ayano: *SAO* beast-tamer.
             Player name: Silica.

Shino Asada: *GGO* sniper.
             Player name: Sinon.

Andrew Gilbert Mills: *SAO* armory owner.
                      Manager of Dicey Café.
                      Player name: Agil.

Ryoutarou Tsuboi: *SAO* Fuurinkazan guild leader. Player name: Klein.

CHARACTERS

Sakuya: Lady of the sylphs in *ALO*.

Alicia Rue: Lady of the cait siths in *ALO*.

Mortimer: Lord of the salamanders in *ALO*.

Eugene: General of the salamanders in *ALO*. Mortimer's brother.

Chrysheight: Kikuoka's avatar in *ALO*.

Siune: Member of the Sleeping Knights.   Jun: Member of the Sleeping Knights.

Tecchi: Member of the Sleeping Knights.   Yuuki: Leader of the Sleeping Knights.

Talken: Member of the Sleeping Knights.

Nori: Member of the Sleeping Knights.

Takashi Hirono: Japanese VRMMO player.

Atsushi Kanamoto: Johnny Black, formerly of Laughing Coffin.
                  Put Kirito into a coma.

Shouichi Shinkawa: Death Gun. Red-Eyed Xaxa, formerly of Laughing Coffin.

Kyouichi Shinkawa: Death Gun. Shouichi's little brother. Shino's former classmate.

Subtilizer: Winner of the fourth Bullet of Bullets, defeating Sinon.

》》 Rath

Seijirou Kikuoka: Lieutenant colonel moonlighting in the Virtual Division
                  of the Ministry of Internal Affairs. Manager of Rath.

Takeru Higa: Project Alicization lead developer. Last student of Shigemura
             Research Lab at Touto Technical University, Electrical Engineering
             Department.

Nakanishi: Naval lieutenant. Rath staff.

Natsuki Aki: Rath nurse and sergeant first class.

Hiraki: Chief researcher at Rath's Roppongi office.

Ichiemon: Electroactive Muscled Operative Machine #1.
          First prototype robot for housing artificial fluctlights.

Niemon: Second prototype robot for housing artificial fluctlights.
        A major improvement on Ichiemon.

Yanai: Rath staff. Spy. Formerly a researcher and giant slug at RCT Progress.

Akihiko Kayaba: Developer of *SAO*. Graduated from Shigemura Research Lab.

Rinko Koujiro: Kayaba's former lover.
                Scientist at California Institute of Technology.
                Graduated from Shigemura Research Lab.

Nobuyuki Sugou: Former employee of RCT Progress.
                   Graduated from Shigemura Research Lab.

Wol-Saeng Jo: Korean VRMMO player.
              Player name: Moonphase.

Myeongwang: Korean VRMMO player. Moonphase's online friend.

Helix: Korean VRMMO player. Moonphase's online friend.

》》 *Ocean Turtle* Assault Team

Gabriel Miller: Agent of private military contractor Glowgen Defense Systems.
                 Leader of the assault team going after Alice's lightcube.
                 Dark God Vecta. Subtilizer in *GGO*.

Alicia Clingerman: Gabriel's childhood friend.

Ferguson: COO of Glowgen DS.

Dario Ziliani: Captain of the Seawolf-class nuclear submarine *Jimmy Carter*.

Vassago Casals: Member of the assault team going after Alice's lightcube.
                Former leader of Laughing Coffin. Player name: PoH.

Critter: Member of the assault team.
          Glowgen DS's cyber-operations specialist (hacker).

Brigg: Member of the assault team. Back from the Middle East. Likes fighting.

Hans: Member of the assault team. Back from the Middle East. Flamboyant.

Chuck: Member of the assault team.

CHAPTER TWENTY-ONE

6

"I...will never...! For...give...you......"

Krsh!!

A second sword pierced Klein's back.

More tears flooded from Asuna's eyes. It was a wonder that she had any left.

Despite being pinned to the ground by the blades, Klein continued to scrabble at the soil. Over him loomed the one-time agitator in the black poncho—the former leader of Laughing Coffin, PoH.

"Oh, man, I can't watch this. You should've stayed put like the small fry you are. This is what happens when you mess with the big dogs," he chided, spreading his hands and shaking his head. In a moment, he spoke to the red knights standing behind Klein in a language Asuna couldn't recognize. One of the players nodded and raised yet another sword.

The third blade gleamed, ready to eliminate the last of Klein's remaining HP.

"Hajimaaaaa!!"

A scream that sounded like Korean emerged from a lone red soldier who raced through the crowd from the rear. He made it just in time to block the downward strike with a blade of his own.

—◠◠◠—

No way…Why does it hurt so much?

Wol-Saeng Jo, under the player name Moonphase, slumped to the ground and braced himself against the agony of having his back sliced by the man in the poncho.

Wol-Saeng's AmuSphere was supposed to be able to transfer only a tiny amount of physical pain signals to the brain. In *Silla Empire*, the game he was used to playing, even an enormous dragon crushing your avatar's head in its jaws produced nothing more than a slight numbing shock.

But Wol-Saeng felt like stove burners were being pressed against the skin of his back. And yet, the pain of suffering the same physical blow in reality would probably be even worse. Wol-Saeng considered himself somewhat of a VRMMO veteran, and even he could barely react in time to the black-poncho man's speedy attack with the thick, heavy kitchen knife. If he suffered that kind of blow in real life, it would probably be instantly fatal or, at the very least, painful enough to knock him unconscious. That meant this was still nothing more than virtual, simulated pain, but that realization didn't help him very much. Unbearable pain was still unbearable, no matter the source. He wished he could log out immediately, circumstances be damned.

Instead, Wol-Saeng curled into a ball on the dark earth and endured.

After all, he couldn't accept the story he had been told:

Supposedly, Japanese hackers had attacked a test server belonging to a new VRMMORPG under development by a team of American, Chinese, and Korean gamers and were killing the testers within the server. And now those testers needed help from outside players to stop the Japanese barbarism.

At least, that was the message going around on social media to get them to dive in. They saw scenes of a group of Japanese players attacking another group of what appeared to be Americans.

But was the video really depicting what the messages claimed it did?

To Wol-Saeng's eyes, the Japanese players were the desperate ones, and the Americans looked more like players in a game. Thanks to thousands upon thousands of Chinese and Korean "reinforcements," the tide of battle had turned, and now the Japanese were powerless—but the discrepancy of their attitudes remained the same. Even with their gear destroyed and HP nearly gone, they were desperate to do *something*...Not to destroy, but perhaps to protect something?

Indeed, just moments before, a woman speaking fluent Korean had emerged from the pack of Japanese players and said:

You are being lied to!! This server belongs to a Japanese company! We are not hackers! We are connected legitimately!! ...Those were Americans, who were brought here under false pretenses, just like you! You're the ones who are being used as tools of sabotage!!

She had called herself Siune. Something in her tone had resonated with Wol-Saeng; he had made his way over to her through the combat and asked, *Do you have any means of proving what you've told us?*

One of Siune's companions was about to say something in Japanese when the man in the black poncho slashed Wol-Saeng across the back, knocking him to the ground.

Everything after that happened in the blink of an eye, and it was entirely one-sided. The Japanese group was overwhelmed by the crimson soldiers, the majority of the former logging out from HP loss, with less than two hundred survivors being stripped of their weapons and rounded up.

The man in the poncho appeared at the front line again, seemingly to make a victory speech—but instead, he did something quite unusual:

He had one player, who was sitting in a wheelchair and clutching two swords, wheeled forward from the Japanese rear guard and began to speak to him in fluent Japanese.

Once again, Wol-Saeng felt that something was wrong.

What did it mean for someone to be in a wheelchair in a virtual game?

In *Silla Empire*, which Wol-Saeng was most familiar with, localized leg damage could cause a Crippling Debuff, which affected your ability to walk, but you eventually recovered with magic, medicine, or time. If a player couldn't walk long enough that he needed a wheelchair, it wasn't really a game anymore.

Plus, the young man in black seemed to have some kind of mental disability. He gave no reaction to the poncho man's speech and simply sat there when the wheelchair was shoved. He almost seemed like an empty husk of an avatar, like a rag-doll body belonging to a player who wasn't logged in.

Eventually, the man in the black poncho grew annoyed, put his foot on one of the wheels, and kicked the chair over. Wol-Saeng gasped, forgetting the pain in his back. Even the other Koreans around him seemed a bit stunned by this.

The young man toppled onto the ground, where he finally performed some kind of voluntary action: He reached for the white sword, one of the two he'd been cradling. He used his left hand, because his right arm was missing from the shoulder down, Wol-Saeng now realized.

But he couldn't reach it. The aggressor had lifted the sword up, just a bit out of reach, the way an adult might pick on a helpless child. The young man strained, not getting off the ground, reaching for the object, but his tormentor grabbed his arm and yanked him upward. He yelled something at the helpless young man and slapped him a few times on the face.

Suddenly, there was a new voice shouting. One of the apprehended Japanese players, a man wearing samurai-like armor and a bandana around his head, attempted to grab the aggressive man in black.

But one of the Korean players behind him raised his sword and drove it deep through the samurai's body. That had to have hurt even more than Wol-Saeng's injury, but the Japanese warrior tried to keep crawling forward until a second sword prevented his advance.

The man in the black poncho gave the skewered samurai a twisted smile. He issued an order in Korean to the red knights: "Kill him. He's just in the way."

One of the knights obeyed and raised a third sword.

It was impossible to sit back and watch any further. There was no guarantee that Siune's explanation was the truth, but at the very least, the way this man would kick over a wheelchair was revolting—and the earnest desperation in the samurai's actions carried the conviction of one trying to protect his friends.

Wol-Saeng didn't have a particularly positive image of Japan. Beyond the history and territorial arguments between the countries, there was an insular nature to the island nation, a derisive kind of arrogance, as if to say that *they* were the only East Asian country worth caring about. The fact that The Seed Nexus was open to Europe and North America but closed off to Korea and China was an excellent example of that attitude.

But...

Japan as a whole did not represent every single individual from Japan. Going back to pre-VRMMO PC-gaming days, there were a few titles with international servers where you could play with people around the world. He'd had bad experiences with Japanese players, but also many good ones.

Wol-Saeng felt disgusted by the actions of the man in the black poncho, and he wanted to believe in Siune and the samurai man. Not because they were Japanese or Korean. It was just his personal conscience telling him this was right.

The instant he moved, more blinding pain stemming from his back shot through his head, but he gritted his teeth and got to his feet. Then he drew his sword, took a deep breath, and...

"...*Hajimaaa!!*" ("...Stoppp!!")

...rushed forward, yelling with as much force as he could muster.

Wol-Saeng's default avatar had average stats and felt slow and heavy compared to his agile *Silla Empire* character, Moonphase.

But throughout whatever bonus effect it was, he now raced across the wasteland like the wind and just barely succeeded in blocking the sword meant to end the samurai's life.

"What…what are you doing?!" demanded the Korean attacker, his voice a mixture of shock and, much more so, anger. Wol-Saeng wouldn't have been able to communicate if it had been a Chinese player, so he knew he had to make use of this good fortune and state his case.

"Don't you think there's something strange about this?! The battle is already won! What reason could there be to torment and torture these people?!"

His compatriot was briefly silent. His eyes traveled to the samurai below, then to the youngster tossed from the wheelchair nearby. Behind his visor, his eyes blinked frequently in surprise. Now that the fervor of battle was waning, this player, too, was slowly realizing the wrongness of what was happening. The force pushing against his blade began to soften.

But before Wol-Saeng could say anything else, a sharp cry issued forth from the crowd around them.

"*Baesinja!!*" ("Traitor!!")

"Kill him, too!!"

With the anger of his fellows spurring him on, the red knight put more strength back into his sword arm. But the next words to be spoken came as a surprise.

"Wait! Let's hear him out!"

"He's right—the guy in the poncho's going too far!"

Other Korean players in the crowd were arguing on Wol-Saeng's behalf now. Those little fires spread across the mass of players, dividing the crowd into hard-liners who demanded the slaughter of the remaining Japanese and moderates who preferred to wait for a proper explanation before any action was taken. That same dynamic spread to the Chinese players, too, and even more angry shouts— these indecipherable to Wol-Saeng—echoed across the wasteland.

How was the one man seemingly in charge going to contain this chaos? Wol-Saeng spun around to find out.

The one who'd started all this was standing over the one-armed youth from the wheelchair, spinning his large, thick dagger in his fingers. Shaded beneath his hood, his mouth was wide and twisted.

It took a while for it to be apparent that he was not gnashing his teeth in anger but stifling laughter. A cold sensation ran up Wol-Saeng's back, strong enough to numb his pain.

There was no way the man in the black poncho had anything to do with any game made by Chinese, Korean, or American developers. In fact, the existence of such a game seemed suspicious at this point. Whoever he was, there was real blood and pain in this battle, and he was trying to get players of various countries to fight…and kill one another. That was his only goal.

Though it sounded as if it came from another person's mouth, Wol-Saeng felt the Korean word for "demon" pass through his lips.

"……*Angma*……"

———

Vassago Casals was born to a Hispanic mother and a Japanese American father in the Tenderloin, a lower-class neighborhood in San Francisco.

In America, baby names that seemed likely to limit the opportunities of the child, who didn't have a choice in the matter, were often rejected at the stage of the birth certificate. That was the only reason his mother had named him Vassago instead of Devil or Satan. Vassago, the prince of hell, was a name with only minor recognition, so the city clerk accepted the name, none the wiser.

There was only one reason a mother would give her child the name of a demon, and that was because she never wanted him—because she hated him.

He didn't know how his parents had met, nor did he want to, but as far as he understood, it was a monetary relationship. The pregnancy wasn't planned, and his mother wanted to abort him, but his father forced her to go through with it. That didn't mean that he loved the son who was born; he checked in every now and then on the child's health but never even brought so much as a gift. About the only thing he ever gave Vassago was the ability to speak Japanese.

It was only when Vassago was around fifteen years old that he finally understood why his father had forced his mother to give birth and then had made only the bare minimum of child support payments.

That was when he was told that there was a child with congenital kidney failure on his father's side of the family—and they wanted *him* to be a donor. He had no choice in the matter. But Vassago gave his own condition: He wanted to live in his father's country, Japan. Once he had donated a kidney, his father would have no use for him, so the status of his financial support would be in limbo. If he had to stay in the slums and deal drugs to survive, he knew where that story would end—so he preferred to start over in a new country entirely.

His father accepted, and in exchange for his left kidney, Vassago received a passport and airfare. He left for Japan without saying good-bye to his mother. When he arrived, fate was even crueler than he could have realized.

By Japanese law, international adoption involved complicated paperwork and stringent requirements, and even if the adoption process was successful, children above the age of six were not automatically given the right to stay in the country. Vassago had no choice but to live outside of the law from the moment he arrived.

So he wound up in the care of a Korean crime syndicate. Because he could speak English, Spanish, and Japanese, they provided Vassago with a fake ID and trained him to be a hit man.

Vassago completed nine successful jobs in the five years before he turned twenty. The tenth job was something he could never have imagined.

His job was to reach and kill a target that could never be found in the real world—the target was in a virtual world instead.

When it was first described to him, he didn't know what it meant. Only when he was given an explanation of the *SAO* Incident, which had arisen just a few days earlier, did it make sense to him. The target was a victim of the Incident, stuck at home under strict security, never to emerge. If they waited for the deadly game to kill him, there was no telling when that would happen or if he might survive and escape eventually. But if they could get into the same game and kill his character, the NerveGear would kill him in real life.

That still left three major problems to solve.

For one, Vassago the hit man would not be able to leave the game until it was beaten. If he died in the game, he was dead for real. And Vassago himself could not attack the target. If anyone got their hands on a game log of who attacked whom, they could potentially trace back the assassination attempt.

The price the syndicate offered to complete this near-impossible mission was astonishing. Vassago thought it unlikely that he would actually get it, even if he succeeded, but he didn't have the right to refuse either way.

Nearly all the unused NerveGears had been confiscated by police, but somehow, the syndicate acquired one. As long as he had the *SAO* software and the will to go in there, neither the police nor the software company could prevent him from logging in. The only real question after that was his character name. Vassago had never played a video game, and he wasn't sure what to go with at first. Deciding to keep it in-line with the name of the prince of hell his mother had given him, Vassago chose the handle PoH.

Vassago's first experience with virtual reality altered his personality—it set him free. He saw his long-forgotten father and distant relatives in the other Japanese players and was keenly reminded of just how much he loathed *all* Asian people.

He would kill his target, since that was his job. And along the way, he'd kill as many other people as he could.

It was with this thought in mind that Vassago founded the biggest guild of murderers in *SAO*, Laughing Coffin, and took many, many lives in total, not just that of his original target. When the guild got too big and he grew tired of running it, he had it clash headlong with the game's elite players to wipe it out so he could engage directly in the job of killing those he'd identified as the greatest targets of all: the Flash and the Black Swordsman. Not long after that, the game was beaten, releasing them all.

When he returned to the real world from the game of death, Vassago felt not joy but emptiness and disappointment. He knew that he would never again experience the dream come true that was Aincrad, so he chose to return to America in search of a similar experience. He murdered the boss, who was reluctant to pay what he'd promised, made off with the money, and crossed the Pacific. Over in San Diego, he found a place in the cyber-operations wing of a private military contractor.

In VR combat training against the National Guard and the Marine Corps, Vassago's *SAO*-honed skills shone brilliantly. He was promptly chosen to be an instructor, but the stable life and income that came along with it did not satisfy him.

One more time. I want to go back there, just one more time. Back to that false world of truth, where everything is digital, bringing true human nature to the surface.

For all his wishing, Vassago finally found himself in the Under-world, a terrifyingly real virtual world, where he came across the Flash and the Black Swordsman again. It wasn't a miracle; it had to be considered fate at this point.

For some reason, the Black Swordsman had undergone some kind of change in mental state, but Vassago knew that if he killed enough people around him, he'd wake up again. It was exactly because the Black Swordsman was that kind of man that Vassago was drawn to him in the first place. It was such a singular desire that Vassago would be happy to kill himself once he'd killed the swordsman.

First, he'd lure the Chinese and Koreans in with false information, then have them slaughter one another en masse. He'd never expected that impromptu story to hold up under scrutiny for very long anyway. More than a few of them were skeptical of the situation already and were arguing with the more fervently patriotic members of the crowd. Once that tension reached its peak, all he needed to provide was a little spark.

Not far away, the Korean he'd given a good punishing was still stubbornly trying to argue with his compatriots. If he shouted to them to cut that man's head off and slaughter all the cowards, the patriots would surely be driven into a bloodlust and draw their swords.

"Just you wait, man...I'll get you up and on your feet in no time," Vassago whispered to the empty-eyed swordsman in black on the ground nearby. Belatedly, he realized that something in the young man's profile reminded him of the glimpse he'd gotten of his half brother just before the kidney-transplant surgery. Something sharp surged in his chest.

First, he'd kill the Black Swordsman and the Flash to log them out, then disengage himself. The next step would be to find wherever the two of them were on the *Ocean Turtle* and kill them again with the utmost relish.

Only imagining that moment could temporarily ease the dull ache in his left side that had been with him since having his kidney stolen when he was fifteen.

Beneath the hood, he grinned and muttered to the young man, "If you keep spacing out, everyone's gonna die. C'mon—you gotta wake up soon."

He took slow, deliberate steps, twirling the Mate-Chopper around in his fingers.

—◦◦◦—

Scritch.

Asuna heard the dry sound of boot soles scraping on parched ground, even as her soul threatened to leave her ears.

Scritch, scritch. It was mechanical, artificial, and yet rhythmic, almost dancing. That was something she'd heard several times before in the old floating castle: the footsteps of Death.

She moved her head to the side and saw, twenty yards away near where Kirito lay, the silhouette of the man in the black poncho stalking toward her.

But it wasn't actually Asuna he was walking toward—it was Klein, two swords stuck through his back. The samurai seemed to be staving off death through willpower alone, and now the man was going to finish the job himself.

Or so she thought at first, but soon she sensed this wasn't correct, either.

Near Klein, two knights in red armor were squabbling in Korean. In fact, all around the army of thousands surrounding the surviving Japanese players and Underworld warriors, violent arguments were breaking out.

It was probably the players who still believed PoH laying into those who had figured out it was all a lie. At this rate, it was going to take only a minor trigger for the former to draw their swords on the latter. Once that happened, the built-up hatred between the Chinese and Korean players would probably be the next thing to explode. PoH was heading over to stop them from…

No…

No. Oh no.

He was heading over to *start* the fire himself.

Just the same way he had when he leaked the location of his own murdering guild's hideout to the frontier group so they could launch a bloody battle to wipe the guild out.

It wasn't clear what he stood to gain by halving the power of the force at his command. The only thing she knew for sure was that something terrible would happen.

As he strode forward, PoH gave instructions in Korean. The two knights holding Klein down turned on the one who'd failed to execute him, sweeping aside their momentary hesitation and grabbing his arms.

The Grim Reaper in black flipped his knife and snatched it out of the air again with a loud smack.

He was going to execute the "traitor" and display his head

to the crowd, driving those Chinese and Korean players who believed him to betray their skeptical companions.

She couldn't allow him to do that. In terms of the ultimate goal of protecting the Underworlders, preventing the red knights from killing one another probably wasn't what she should worry about. But even half of them was still at least ten thousand—and when they were done, they would be even more furious and hateful and would be seeking to channel those feelings toward the Japanese and the Underworlders.

More importantly, the Chinese and Korean players who were in danger of being killed were the ones who were beginning to see the truth...the ones who believed what the Japanese players told them. She couldn't give up and allow them to suffer this painful fate.

She had to move. Had to stand, draw her sword, and stop the execution ordered by PoH.

But her hands and feet wouldn't obey. With each breath she took, the plethora of wounds all over her body ached and sapped her willpower.

......*It's no use.........I can't get up.*

Asuna could only exhale weakly, her knees stuck to the dusty ground.

Her back arched slowly. Dirty, bedraggled hair slid down over her shoulders, blocking her vision.

Tears filled her eyes, and she tried to shut them against the approach of Death's footsteps.

And then...

It's all right.
You can make it, Asuna.

Someone's voice was in her ear, soft but clear.

Someone's hands squeezed her shoulders, gentle but strong.

Warm light flooded into her body—into her heart. A fresh gust of air blew all her pain away.

*   *   *

Stand up now, Asuna.

Stand to protect what you truly care about.

Her right hand twitched, slid across the surface of the earth, and grabbed what lay there: the handle of Radiant Light, the rapier belonging to the Goddess of Creation.

When she raised her head, the Grim Reaper in black had a blade that gleamed bloody crimson held high above him. The pinned-down red knight tensed with terror. The furor around them seemed to vanish momentarily, all eyes trained upon that merciless edge.

Asuna held her breath, gritted her teeth, and put all the strength she still had left into her legs.

She pushed off the ground.

"Raaaaaaaaah!!"

With a bloodcurdling scream, she drew back the rapier. Brilliant-white light shone from its tip. The basic fencing sword skill Linear was one she'd performed thousands of times, if not hundreds of thousands.

PoH's reflexes were sharp enough that he noticed the surprise attack.

"Oh—," he grunted, leaning backward. She thrust her hand straight for the darkness of the hood, which was now moving away from her.

There was a small bit of feedback in her arm. One lock of curly black hair flew into the air, and a few droplets of fresh blood sprayed from dark skin.

He dodged it!

The Underworld was no different from Aincrad in that there was an unavoidable pause after a sword skill. Asuna was frozen for a brief, fatal instant—and PoH's knife came rushing straight for her torso.

But at the same time, she focused her mind on the ground under PoH's feet.

A faint rainbow of light glowed there and vanished. She used the power of Stacia to generate a little bump of earth, just inches tall, under his feet.

Despite being the smallest possible manipulation of the terrain, it felt like lightning struck her brain. And for that heavy price, the dark reaper lost his balance, and his knife did nothing but rip her dress a little.

"Rrgh…!"

Free from her paralysis, Asuna pulled back the rapier again.

"Whoa!" PoH's poncho swung up into the air as he raised his knife to block it.

The divinely quick thrust and the powerful slice met in midair, creating a mixture of white and crimson sparks. Asuna put all her strength behind her weapon, trying to push through PoH's blade.

"What…do you want?" she demanded, her voice hoarse.

With a smirk and a snarl, PoH said from beneath his hood, "Isn't it obvious? The one in black…the one I first tried to kill on the fifth floor of Aincrad and never could. He's the only one I really want."

"…Why do you hate Kirito so much? What did he ever do to you?"

"Hate?" PoH repeated, affronted. He leaned in closer and whispered, "I thought you, of all people, would understand how much I truly love him. In this world full of assholes, he's the only person you can unconditionally believe in. He never broke down, no matter how much I tormented him. Never gave in to temptation, no matter how much I invited him. He always brought me hope and joy. That's why I can't stand that he ended up like *that*…while I wasn't around. I'm gonna be the one to wake him up. And I'll kill anyone I need to in order to make that happen. Thousands…Millions."

As the personification of death exhaled these words, they became a black miasma that clung to Asuna, sapping her will to fight.

"Hope…? Joy…? As if you had any idea…of how much he had to endure because of you!" she snapped back, but the point where their weapons met and scraped sparks into being was slowly, slowly tilting back toward her.

In fact, it wasn't just that Asuna's willpower was weakening. PoH's wicked Mate-Chopper was trembling like a living creature in his hand, growing slightly thicker and larger with every passing second.

PoH noticed her shock. A smile emerged from the darkness beneath his hood.

"I finally figured out how this world works, too. In here, spilled blood and spent life converts straight into energy. Just like how the Priestess of Light burned up the Dark Army with that huge-ass laser beam."

Asuna had been given an explanation of the core system of the Underworld, too, before she dived in. These "spatial resources," as they were called, couldn't be used without complex commands or weapons that absorbed them from the air. But even if the Mate-Chopper's enlargement was an effect of spatial resources, PoH hadn't spoken any commands, and the knife itself had to be a converted item from his *SAO* character data. It couldn't be equipped with the Underworld's resource-absorption function.

PoH continued, reading Asuna's thoughts.

"This dagger, the Mate-Chopper, was designed so that every time it kills monsters in Aincrad, its stats go down, and the more you slice up players—other people—the higher its stats get. But if you kill an obnoxious number of mobs, eventually the curse is supposed to wear off, and the weapon transforms into some special katana with a similar name. Obviously, I wasn't interested in that. The point here is that the way its strength grows as it slashes human beings still works in the Underworld. The lives of the Americans you people killed, and the Japanese the allied Chinese and Koreans killed, swirl around this battlefield. If the Chinese and Koreans kill one another after this, there will be even more life in the air."

As the Grim Reaper whispered, his Mate-Chopper creaked and groaned, growing larger. Asuna's Radiant Light, top-level GM equipment, seemed unable to withstand its pressure. All the sound in the background faded away, leaving Asuna with only her breath and her pulse in her ears.

PoH's very presence seemed to weigh on Asuna, as though the evil weapon's effect also applied to his height.

"Once I suck up every last one of those lives, I'm going to kill all the artificial fluctlights in this entire world, from end to end. I'm not just talking about those pathetic people trembling behind you—I mean all of them: the monsters in the dark lands and the humans from the dark empire. However many thousands of people that is, I'm sure he'll wake up in response to it. *If* he is the Black Swordsman I believe in."

A cold gust of wind rustled his leather hood, revealing the eyes underneath for a brief moment. They were red and dimly glowing.

A devil. He was not human, but a true devil.

That was the true nature of PoH. The mask of the cheerful agitator he wore in Aincrad and the mask of the harsh commander he wore here were both just that: lies. In truth, he was a cold, cruel agent of vengeance who sought only to inflict pain, to torment, and wipe out all traces of humanity…

The strength went out of Asuna's knees. Her rapier creaked in its struggle, and the knife's blade edged closer to her throat.

"Don't worry. I won't kill you yet. I'm just going to make sure you can't interfere anymore. You need to be around to watch… when he wakes up and dies in my arms."

The Mate-Chopper was close to twice its original size now. Radiant Light issued a high-pitched scream, and a fine crack ran through its length.

With her right knee having fallen to the ground, Asuna watched a black mist spilling from the hood covering her eyes. Through the darkness shone only the thick steel blade and her crimson eyes.

Just before Asuna completely lost all strength, someone's small hand touched her back, providing support.

*   *   *

It's all right.
I'll always be at your side.

A pure-blue light shot from the center of Asuna's chest, piercing the darkness.

In the reflection of the flat surface of the Mate-Chopper, Asuna could see pristine white wings extending from her own back.

All the sound came back—the clamor and chaos of the battlefield mixing in again, along with the voices of her friends.

"Asuna!! You can do it, Asuna!!"

"Asuna!! Asunaaaaaa!!"

"Get up, Asuna!!"

"Asunaaaaa!!"

Lisbeth. Silica. Agil. Klein.

And not just her closest companions. She could also hear the surviving *ALO* players, like Sakuya, Alicia, and Siune and the other Sleeping Knights, as well as the soldiers from the Human Guardian Army, like Renly, Tiese, Ronie, Sortiliena, and the many other guards and friars, all chanting her name.

Thank you, everyone.

Thank you, Yuuki.

I can still fight. Your hearts united give me strength.

"I won't give in…I will never allow myself to succumb…to someone like you…who is only capable of hatred!!" she screamed. A surge of white light issued from her being, jolting PoH backward.

Asuna returned to her feet and drew back her rapier hand. Waves of pale-purple light reminiscent of the color of thyme flowers emerged from the weapon, coloring the entire world.

"Hrrrng…!!"

The reaper attempted to stand his ground, but that just left him wide open to attack.

Asuna activated the Original Sword Skill she'd received from Yuuki, the Absolute Sword.

Five attacks from the upper right, lightning-fast thrusts in a diagonal line.

Five attacks from the upper left, another line of glowing points intersecting with the first.

"Gaaah…" PoH gasps were flecked with bright blood, but his giant knife still glowed red. If he caught her flush with a direct counterattack, it would easily wipe out what health she had remaining.

But Asuna's onslaught wasn't over.

"Raaaaaaah!!"

She focused all her remaining energy into the tip of the rapier for the last—and biggest—attack, right at the intersecting point of the two lines.

It was the end of the eleven-part OSS, Mother's Rosario.

A purple flash like a shooting star penetrated PoH's chest. The black-clad personification of death flew high into the air and came crashing down heavily a good distance away.

Asuna fell to a knee again, having spent all her mental strength. Inside her head, she said once again, *Thank you, Yuuki.*

She did not hear a response this time. Perhaps it was only ever a phantom hand and phantom voice created from Asuna's memories. But given that this was a world built out of memories, that meant it was no illusion.

Normally, the OSS Mother's Rosario shouldn't be usable. Even if Higa and Kikuoka implemented the sword-skill system from the original *SAO*, it was Asuna the undine from *ALO* who'd inherited Mother's Rosario. Stacia-Asuna hadn't been converted from that character and wouldn't contain the data of that skill.

Yet, the OSS executed properly, visual effects and all. If that was the power of Asuna's imagination bringing it to life, then the encouragement from Yuuki coming back from her memory was real, too. Memories never vanished.

PoH's avatar was still lying prone on the ground. But it was impossible to imagine that he had taken an eleven-hit combo skill with GM equipment and survived. Unlike the other players,

he was connecting with the STL, so even if he died, his body wouldn't disintegrate. It would remain here for a time, like those of the humans and the darklanders from the Underworld.

She got to her feet, using her rapier for support, then turned to check on Klein. He still had the swords in his stomach, but the three players keeping him captured had taken their distance, and like the fourth knight who'd rushed to intervene, they watched her in disbelief.

Asuna wanted to go to Kirito as soon as possible, but first she headed for Klein to remove the swords and heal his wounds. But no sooner had she taken a step or two than she sensed a faint rumble through the earth.

She held her breath and turned around again.

PoH was on the ground, completely immobile. But the Mate-Chopper, still in his hand, emitted an eerie light with swirls of red and black. In fact, it seemed that the air of the entire battlefield was slowly rotating around the knife.

"Oh no…it's absorbing the sacred power!!" shouted Sortiliena, who stood at the front of the human army.

Asuna gritted her teeth and started to move toward the malignant blade so she could destroy it once and for all. But before she could get there, the Grim Reaper in black rose to his feet, as though pulled upright by the floating weapon.

The front of the poncho was greatly damaged, exposing his figure and his tight leather suit. There was a huge hole in his chest where the final blow of the OSS had struck, through which the background behind him was visible.

The Underworlders exclaimed in fright when they saw PoH standing despite his entire heart having been blasted out of his chest. Even the Chinese and Koreans were unnerved by it, and *they* assumed this was just another VRMMO world.

Most likely, the Mate-Chopper was absorbing the tremendous amount of spatial resources in the air and converting them into HP for PoH. But even with that assumption in mind, Asuna couldn't stop herself from trembling.

PoH was diving through The Soul Translator. He had to be feeling the exact same level of pain as he would in the real world. Asuna felt mind-obliterating pain from being pierced through the side with a spear. She couldn't imagine what it would feel like to have an enormous hole blasted through the middle of her chest.

But the god of death just grinned with blood dripping from his lips—and bellowed in a voice loud enough to shake everything within hearing distance:

"My brethren! This is the true nature of our foe! Kill every last one of your feeble traitors…and every filthy Japanese, too!!"

He spoke in Korean, but somehow Asuna was able to accurately recognize the meaning of his every word.

PoH's Mate-Chopper shot its dark-red aura from its raised position to the ends of the wasteland.

Ohhhh…

Ohhhhhhhhh!!

Half of the combined Chinese and Korean army raised their swords in similar fashion and roared with ferocious gusto. There was nothing Asuna could do now to stop them from attacking the more peaceful faction…or from attacking the few Japanese survivors and the remaining Underworld soldiers.

Suddenly something pushed her, and she fell to the ground. The damaged rapier came loose from her grip and tumbled onto the dry soil.

Far, far ahead, a black-haired young man reached his one arm toward her, struggling with every fiber of his being.

"……Kirito," she whispered.

Asuna reached out to her beloved in return and awaited the end.

7

It was just a brief nap in the middle of the classroom, but when I woke up, it felt like the longest dream I'd ever had.

A dream that was fun and painful and sad. As I walked down the empty hallway, I tried to remember what had happened in it, but nothing was coming to me. Eventually, I gave up on it and changed into my regular shoes at the shoe lockers inside the school entrance. Outside of the gate, the dry, chilly autumn breeze rustled my shaggy bangs.

I shifted my book bag to my left shoulder, stuck my hands into the pockets of my school trousers, and began to walk, head downcast. Up ahead, students from the same school were chatting and laughing. I stuck the earbuds from my audio player in to shut out the sound of their hopes, dreams, love, and friendship; hunched my back; and headed home.

At the convenience store on the way home, I stopped to check out this week's gaming magazines and bought the one that had the longest special preview of *Sword Art Online*, the game that was about to launch in a month. I also added some funds to the digital-currency account I used to play online games.

That was an intermediate step I could remove by just getting a credit card, but after I brought it up with my mom, she said that I couldn't have one until I was in college. I couldn't complain about that, though; I was fortunate enough just to get an allowance each month. I wasn't even her real son, after all.

I walked out the automatic doors of the store, imagining a blissful post-cash world where everything could happen electronically. Then I noticed that there was a group of five people squatting in a corner of the parking lot who hadn't been there when I walked into the store—they must have shown up while I was distracted by the magazines. They laughed and yelled and scattered empty bags of junk food around them.

Their uniforms marked them as belonging to my middle school, but I ignored them and made to leave, of course. Before I could get away, one of them saw me and stared with interest.

He was so small that if not for the uniform, he might look like he belonged to an elementary school. We were in different classes, but I recognized him. In fact, he had even been my friend for a time.

He and I had both played in the closed beta test for *Sword Art Online* over summer vacation.

It was practically a miracle that out of a thousand lucky testers, two were chosen from the same year at the same middle school. Enough of a miracle that a totally antisocial loner like me heard the rumor and reached out to make contact.

Our interaction started just before vacation, and it lasted until the end of vacation—technically speaking, to the end of the beta. Once every three days or so, we formed a party together in that virtual world, and we got along well enough, but once the new school term started and I saw him at school for the first time in a month, I had a sudden flare-up of my odd personal tic: I began to wonder *Who really is this person anyway?* when I supposedly knew them well already.

It was a sensation that inside the flesh-and-blood person across from me was a total stranger. Once that happened, I couldn't actually get any closer to them. At times, it even happened with my own family.

He seemed to want to keep being friends with me, both in the full release of *SAO* in October and around school in the real world.

Eventually, he caught on to the way I was acting around him, though, and he drifted away. We hadn't spoken once since then.

Why was he here now, loitering in a convenience store parking lot with students of a type we'd normally never be associated with? The reason became clear from the penetrating gaze he was giving me and from the words the boy with the bowl cut the color of flan next to him said to me.

"The fuck you lookin' at, huh?"

Instantly, the other three glared at me, mouths puckered, uttering threatening comments like "Aaah?" and "Huuuh?"

It seemed clear that the more boisterous members of his class had singled him out, choosing him to be the weakest link of their group and an easy mark to run errands for them and lend them money. He was looking to me for help.

All I had to do was say, *Hey, let's walk home together.* But I couldn't do it. My mouth wouldn't move to make the sounds.

Instead, the only thing I could squeeze through my throat, which felt as if it were sealed with glue, was "…Nothing."

Then I abandoned the boy I'd called friend just a month ago, and I started walking on my way. He didn't say anything, but out of the corner of my eye, I thought I saw his childish face screw up like he was about to burst into tears.

I quickly left the lot and headed down the road, away from the evening sun, my back hunched with shame. I walked and walked, saying nothing, staring at the asphalt below my feet. The sun set behind me with alarming speed, shrouding me and the town in purple darkness. The familiar route home began to feel like a totally unfamiliar place. No people or cars came down the road. The only sound was my footsteps.

Step, step, step.........shuk, shuk, shuk.

"Huh…?"

I came to a halt. Somehow, I had walked off the asphalt and onto short grass. I wondered whether there had been any unpaved ground on the way home from school and looked up in confusion.

What I saw was not a residential street of Kawagoe City, Saitama

Prefecture, but a small path leading through a deep, unfamiliar forest.

After looking at my surroundings, I examined myself. The black school uniform I'd been wearing was gone, replaced by a navy-blue tunic and leather armor. I was wearing fingerless gloves and short boots with metal rivets. Over my shoulder was no longer the bag I took to school, but a short and rather heavy sword.

"Where am I…?" I wondered, but no one was around to answer. I shrugged and began to walk down the forest path.

In less than a minute, my memory began to prickle. The shape of the ancient trees with the twisted branches. The sensation of the growth underfoot. This was the forest to the northwest of the Town of Beginnings on the first floor of Aincrad, the floating castle. That meant I would arrive at Horunka if I followed this path.

I needed to get to town so I could rent an inn room. I just wanted to get into bed. I wanted to sleep again and not have to think.

The only light on the forest floor as I walked and walked was the hazy moonlight. But suddenly, I heard a faint cry up ahead—or at least, I thought I did?

I paused, then resumed walking. The trees opened up ahead on the right, allowing the blue moonlight to illuminate a side path. Again, I heard a cry—and the creaking growl of a monster.

I picked up the pace as I approached the break in the trees, then peered around a thick trunk. There was a spacious hollow up ahead, almost like a rounded stage. Creepy silhouettes writhed in the unbroken moonlight of the clearing.

There were five or six plant-type monsters that looked like giant pitcher plants whipping their sharp tentacles around. A young man dressed in an outfit similar to mine was surrounded by them. He swung his sword around desperately, but no matter how many of the tentacles he sliced through, they simply grew back with no end.

I recognized his profile.

He had formed a party with me for the purpose of efficiently collecting the items these plant monsters dropped. His name was… was…Kopel. But why was he surrounded by so many of them?

Whatever the case, he was a companion of mine, so I had to save him.

But once again, my feet would not move. For all the success I had in trying to get them to act, they might as well have been rooted to the ground.

A tentacle swept Kopel's feet out from behind, and he toppled onto the grass. The monsters' sinister grins revealed rows of human teeth, and they opened and closed their jaws loudly as they descended upon him.

Kopel looked to me with despair in his eyes and reached out a hand.

But just as quickly, he was overrun by the swarm of monsters, and a moment later, I heard the faint burst of his avatar and saw a blue light peek through.

"Ahhhh…," I groaned, letting my face fall, the same way I had when I had abandoned my friend outside the convenience store.

In time, I slowly stood back up, looking at nothing but the grass around my feet. I turned and walked down the narrow path again. My footsteps were the only sound in the moonlit forest.

Shuk, shuk, shuk………tok, tok, tok.

I came to a stop. Somehow, the short grass underfoot had changed to bluish stone blocks. I looked up and saw that I was no longer in a forest on the first floor of Aincrad but in some unfamiliar dim hallway. Probably somewhere in a labyrinth…but from the appearance, I couldn't tell what floor. All I could do was keep walking.

Barely even cognizant that my equipment and sword had changed, I walked silently down the corridor. And walked and walked, as though chasing my own shadow cast by the lanterns set into the walls. The labyrinths of Aincrad were about a thousand feet across at the largest, so there couldn't have been a hallway this straight and long. But I never stopped or turned back. I just kept walking.

Eventually, I heard a faint voice coming from up ahead. It wasn't a scream; it was a shout of happiness. Multiple cheers followed in its wake.

The voices seemed familiar, nostalgic. My pace picked up a little as I rushed for the source of the cheering.

In time, I reached an opening in the left wall, through which warm-yellow light shone. I kept my legs moving all the way to the entrance, though they felt heavy and tired now, for some reason.

I peered around the side and saw a surprisingly spacious room. Along the far wall, four players stood with their backs to me.

Even without seeing their faces, I instantly knew who they were.

The one with the wild hair and the odd hat who used a spear was Sasamaru.

The tall mace-user with the shield was Tetsuo.

The smaller dagger-user with the beanie was Ducker.

And lastly, the short-haired girl with the short spear…Sachi.

They were members of the guild I belonged to. Keita, our leader, was off negotiating to buy us a guild home, so we were spending time in the labyrinth to earn some money for furniture and such.

Thank goodness…They're all right, I thought for some strange reason. I tried to call out to them, but once again, my mouth would not move. My feet were stuck to the ground and couldn't come loose.

As I watched, helpless, the four of them leaned over. They were peering at something—a large treasure chest placed next to the wall. As soon as my mind registered that fact, I felt a chill run down my back.

Ducker the thief excitedly examined the chest, looking for traps to disarm.

No. Stop. Don't, I screamed, over and over, but the words never left my mind. I couldn't move my legs to rush into the room to stop them.

Ducker threw the lid of the chest open.

Instantly, there was an ear-piercing alarm, and hidden doors on both sidewalls of the room opened up. Bloodthirsty monsters poured into the room in ghastly numbers.

"Ah...ah......!"

At last, a sound came from my throat: a faint, cracked shriek.

That was all I could do. Not a finger would move. I could only watch as my friends and companions were surrounded by monsters.

Sasamaru was the first to die. Ducker was next, and after him, Tetsuo burst into blue particles, leaving only Sachi. She spun around and looked at me.

Her lips formed a hint of a sad smile and opened and closed.

The next moment, monster weapons and claws rained down on her without mercy, and her fragile body was enveloped in blue light.

".........!!"

I screamed in total silence as Sachi, too, was reduced to a plethora of glass shards that soon vanished.

Dozens of monsters simply melted into the air, and the room was full of darkness. My body was able to move again, and I fell to my knees.

I'm sick of this. I don't want to keep walking. I don't want to see anything else.

I curled up on the cold floor, covered my ears, and squeezed my eyes shut. But the memories just kept flooding back, like frigid water pooling up around me, enveloping me.

Two years of battle in a floating castle of iron and stone.

Endless sky in a land of fairies.

Crimson bullets flying left and right in an evening wasteland.

I don't want to remember. I don't want to know what comes next.

But despite my prayers, the current of memories pushed me onward.

Suddenly cut off from the real world.

Waking up in an empty space in a deep forest.

Guided by the sound of an ax chopping wood, until I arrived at the root of a massive tree and met him.

A battle with goblins. The giant tree toppling down.

A long, long journey to the center of the world. Two years training at an academy.

With every step, he was beside me, smiling peacefully.

With him, I knew I could do anything.

We raced up a chalk-white tower together and defeated powerful opponents.

And then we reached the top

and crossed swords with the ruler of the world,

and at the end of a long, agonizing battle,

he lost

his life…

"Aaaaaaaaaaaaah!!" I screamed, holding my head in my hands.

It was me. My powerlessness, my foolishness, my weakness: It killed him. Blood was spilled that did not need to be spilled. Life was lost that was not meant to end.

I should have been the one to die. My life there was temporary in the first place. Our roles could have been reversed, and everything would have continued as it was meant to.

"Aaaah…*Aaaaaaaah!!*" I screamed and writhed and rolled and reached for the sword that should have been on my back. I was going to press it against my heart or slit my own throat.

But my fingers found nothing over my shoulder. I groped around, thinking I had dropped it, but the only thing I felt was sticky, clinging black liquid extending forever.

I grabbed the collar of my black shirt and ripped it with my hands.

Curled fingers like claws touched the center of my emaciated chest.

The skin split, and my flesh tore apart, but I felt no pain. With both hands, I ripped into my own chest.

So that I could expose my heart, pull it out, and crush it.

This was all I could do for him…The last act of atonement for those I had betrayed and abandoned…

"Kirito…"

Someone called my name.

I stopped moving, looked around with empty eyes.

Beyond the darkness, there was now a girl with chestnut-brown hair standing alone.

Her hazel eyes were wet and staring right at me.

"Kirito…"

A new voice arrived. To the right, a girl with glasses. Behind the glass lenses, her eyes were glowing with tears, too.

"Big Brother…"

Then another:

Her black bangs were cut straight across. Tears fell from her large eyes.

The will and emotions of the three girls became light that surged and flowed into me.

A warmth like a pillar of sunlight healed my wounds and melted away my sadness.

……*But.*

But…oh, but.

I could not possibly be worthy of receiving their absolution.

"I'm sorry," I heard myself say. "I'm sorry, Asuna. Sorry, Sinon. Sorry, Sugu. I can't stand anymore. I can't fight. I'm sorry……"

And with the heart I'd pulled from my chest in my grasp, I prepared to crush it in one swift, decisive movement.

———

"Why…? What's the matter, Kirito?!"

Despite the way his consciousness seemed to be slipping away like the blood flowing from the bullet wound in his shoulder, Takeru Higa focused on the screen.

The three Soul Translators housing Asuna Yuuki, Shino Asada, and Suguha Kirigaya were sending a tremendous amount of mnemonic data in an attempt to complement Kazuto Kirigaya's damaged fluctlight. Even Higa, who'd run as many tests and experiments as anyone, was astonished at the miraculous volume of data that was being provided.

But the 3-D graph on the remote monitor of Kazuto's fluctlight activity remained in stasis just below the recovery line.

"Even this…still isn't enough……?" Higa groaned.

Kazuto's recovering self-image wasn't on pace to bring him back to reality. It was linking only to painful memories that tormented him, preventing him from breaking free. All that awaited him in that case was an eternal nightmare refrain. Even being shut down entirely would be preferable to that hell.

Just one more person.

If only there was one more person with deep ties to Kazuto who had an accumulation of powerful memories!

But according to Lieutenant Colonel Seijirou Kikuoka, the three girls currently connected were the three people in the world who loved him the most and knew him the best. And there were no more Soul Translators available to use either in the Roppongi office or on the *Ocean Turtle*.

"Dammit…it's not fair…"

Higa gritted his teeth and clenched his fist to slam it against the side of the duct. But as soon as the thought entered his mind, he let his hand uncurl.

"……What's…this…? Where is this connection from…?" he muttered, leaning closer to peer at the monitor through blood- and sweat-stained lenses.

He had previously failed to notice, on Kazuto's fluctlight-status window, that in addition to the three connected lines indicating the girls in the STLs, there was one more—a very thin, faint gray line coming from the bottom of the screen.

Fascinated, he lifted his finger to the touch-panel screen and flicked it upward. The display scrolled in that direction, revealing the source of the gray line.

"From the…Main Visualizer?! But why…?!" he shouted, momentarily forgetting his gravely injured state.

The Main Visualizer was a massive piece of data storage at the core of the Lightcube Cluster, where the souls of all the Underworlders were kept. The Main Visualizer was where the information about the Underworld's terrain, buildings, and objects was stored—but not any human souls.

"Objects…objects from memories…," Higa repeated to himself, thinking on overdrive. "Fluctlight memories and Underworld objects are treated the same when it comes to data formatting…So if someone was able to burn their mind, their will, into an object…would it then function as a kind of…simulated…fluctlight……?"

He could only half believe the idea he was suggesting. If it was possible, then every nonliving thing in the Underworld could be controlled solely by its owner's will.

But at this point, even this faint little connection seemed like the only hope remaining.

Higa couldn't begin to guess whether this would help the situation or only make it worse, but regardless, he opened a connection from the Main Visualizer access to Kazuto's STL.

——◆——

"Kirito."

Right before I crushed my own heart, a new voice called my name. A voice that was powerful, warm, and enveloping.

"Kirito."

Ever so slowly, I raised my head to see.

Where endless darkness had been just a moment ago, *he* now stood on two solid legs.

Spotless blue clothes. A flaxen cowlick that shone even in the darkness. A gentle, subtle smile on his lips.

And in those dark-green eyes was a kind but powerful light, just as there had always been.

I lifted my hands away from my chest, which was now perfectly whole again, extended them toward him, and stood up.

I heard myself whisper his name through trembling lips.

"...Eugeo."

Once more.

"You're alive, Eugeo."

My best friend, and the greatest partner I could ever have, just tinged his gentle smile with sadness and shook his head.

"This is the memory of me that lives inside you," he said. "And the fragment of memory I left behind."

"Mem...ory..."

"That's right. Have you forgotten already? We were so sure of what we declared. Memories," Eugeo said, opening his right palm and pressing it to his chest, "live here."

Like looking in a mirror, I made the exact same action. "Forever in here."

As Eugeo grinned happily again, Asuna strode forward to join him. "We are always connected to you through our hearts."

Sinon walked forward on Eugeo's other side and nodded, causing the hair tied at the sides of her head to wave. "No matter how far apart we might be...no matter when the time comes for us to part."

Then Suguha hopped forward next to her and said happily, "Memories and feelings are connections that last for eternity. Isn't that right?"

Hot, clear liquid burst from my eyes at last. I took a step forward and gazed desperately into the eyes of my eternal friend.

"Are you sure, Eugeo...? Can I really...move forward again?"

His answer was swift and unwavering.

"Yes, you can, Kirito. Many, many people are waiting for you. Come...Let's go. Together. To wherever this takes us."

Two hands reached out from opposite directions and made contact. Then Asuna, Sinon, and Suguha added their own.

Instantly, the four people turned into waves of pure-white light, flowing into me.

And then...

8

Asuna reached and reached for Kirito—until a red armored boot stomped down on her hand.

She looked up to see a red knight, whose eyes were burning with hatred through the slit in his helmet, raise a sword up high with both hands in a backhand stabbing position. He issued some fierce insult and started to thrust downward.

Asuna didn't have the strength to fight back, but she was determined to at least keep from shutting her eyes. She focused on the steel tip.

Ting.

There was a sharp, metallic noise and a resulting shower of orange sparks.

The knight's sword jolted back up into the air, as though it had been deflected by some other, invisible sword.

"Uh…?" the knight grunted in confusion and swung the sword down again. That created more sparks and did not get him any closer to killing Asuna. A third and fourth attempt achieved the same result.

There was no fifth try. Sortiliena raced over to Asuna and used the knock-back skill Torrent to push the red knight backward with the pommel of her greatsword.

As she helped Asuna up, Sortiliena asked her, with undisguised shock, "Was that...*your* Incarnate Sword, Asuna?!"

"Incar...?" Asuna repeated, unfamiliar with this word. She shook her head. "No, it wasn't me."

"Then...perhaps Renly...," Sortiliena suggested, turning to look. Asuna followed her gaze, but the young wounded knight was giving directions to his squad to fight back the approaching horde of red warriors and wasn't in any state to be paying attention to Asuna.

This wasn't the time to be searching for the source of the phenomenon, however; they had to save every last Underworld life they could. Asuna got to her feet with Sortiliena's help, willing whatever shreds of concentration she had left to help her take in the state of the scene around her.

Promptly, she felt fresh despair steal over her heart like cold black water.

Over 80 percent of the twenty thousand remaining Chinese and Koreans were launching into battle with their own kind. But the difference in morale was stark—the players seeking to continue the fight overwhelmed those who didn't. Little blue pillars of avatar destruction dotted the battlefield, accompanied by fierce war cries.

Also, a small percentage of the knights—but still over two thousand in number—were moving in on the Japanese players and the Underworlders, who were clumped in one place. The Japanese players barely had any strength left, and Renly and the rest of the Underworlders were gravely wounded. Despite the advantages of sacred arts and sword skills, there was very little they could do to vanquish their enemy.

Asuna couldn't even think of what to say. All she did was cling to Sortiliena's arm.

Elsewhere, PoH's echoing laughter rang out long and loud. The Grim Reaper, who still had a huge hole in his chest, stood over the prone form of Kirito. His hands were spread wide, massive Mate-Chopper in one hand and his fingers spread out on the other, and he leaned backward with majestic laughter. Dark clouds above swirled into an enormous vortex as the life resources spilled on the battlefield hung down in a whirlpool that ended directly in PoH's body.

Technically, it was the cursed blade in his hand that was absorbing the resources. If they could destroy that, the energy flow to its owner would stop, and the heartless reaper would die instantly.

But the situation was so bad that even the defeat of the enemy commander would not bring it under control. PoH's inflammatory words and evil aura were pushing the war hawks onward. If they lost their commander now, that would only give them more fuel to slaughter all the Japanese and Underworlders in a blind rage.

What can we do? What can I do...?

Asuna hung her head, racked with panic and desperation—but then she noticed a strange phenomenon around them.

Where the ground was visible, the blackened gravel was now covered by a trail of faint-white mist. It drifted past her feet, rippling like a length of ribbon made of finest silk, and spread out as it continued past. A sweet, gentle scent tickled her nostrils.

Is that...the smell of roses...?

Asuna and Sortiliena followed the ribbon of mist back to its source with their eyes. And when they saw where it was coming from, they both let out little gasps.

"Oh......"

And again.

"Ohhh."

The source of the mist was a skinny young man lying on the ground many yards away.

Technically, it was the bluish-white longsword in his left hand. The blade was snapped off halfway up, but it looked like the mist was surrounding the entire weapon and even glowing a little bit.

"Kirito...," called out Asuna, her quavering lips forming the name of the person she loved more than any other.

"Then that Incarnation…was Kirito's…" Sortiliena gasped, voice thick with emotion.

The white mist reached the position of the allied Chinese and Korean soldiers who were standing all around, and it continued to expand beyond them. They were too occupied with the battle to notice that everything from their knees downward was enveloped by a layer of white ribbon.

Only at this point did PoH notice what was happening and stop laughing. He stared at his feet, then sprang around to look at Kirito. His tall, lanky frame jolted once, then he flipped the Mate-Chopper around for a better grip and strode forward.

One step. Two steps.

But he did not finish the third step.

Someone whispered…chanted…in a quiet but sure voice that seemed to carry across the entire battlefield.

Enhance Armament.

Asuna heard it inside her head, too. It was Kirito's voice, but it sounded like there was some other, unfamiliar voice speaking in chorus with him.

The next moment, the entire battlefield was enveloped in a vast, stunning phenomenon on the scale of Stacia's terrain-altering powers.

From the mist emerged vines of crystal clear ice, binding the bodies of the twenty-thousand-plus Chinese and Korean players, as well as PoH. They looked extremely fragile, likely to shatter the moment you touched them, but the furiously battling soldiers were immobilized so completely that time might as well have stopped by magic.

After a brief silence, shouts of surprise and anger arose, but they too died down in time. Every avatar wrapped in the icy vines was soon covered in a shroud of frost and frozen solid in moments.

Asuna briefly glanced over her shoulder toward the red knight who had tried to save Klein. He, too, was an ice sculpture now.

But he didn't seem to be in any pain; his eyes were peacefully closed, as far as she could see through his helm visor. The technique wasn't meant to destroy or inflict pain, just to stop those it touched.

She faced forward again to see that PoH was frozen white as well. She looked at Sortiliena and nodded to indicate her state. "Thank you, Liena...I'm fine now."

The chief guard let go of her, and she rushed toward Kirito, crunching the frost on the ground underfoot. Behind her followed Sortiliena and Ronie, who came running up from the Human Guardian Army's forces.

Kirito was still facedown on the ground, clutching the broken sword in his left hand. But Asuna could tell that at this very moment, his mind was coming back to him. If she could touch his hand, cradle him, call out to him, he would respond. He would surely respond.

The span of a few dozen yards felt like it continued to the ends of the earth. Less than twenty seconds felt longer than eternity. But with each stride of her aching legs, the form of her beloved grew larger and larger in her view. Almost there. Almost within reach...

In the instant that her outstretched hand was going to touch that familiar black hair, she heard a tremendous, earsplitting crash.

The women looked up and saw, very close by, the figure of PoH breaking through the ice vines and frost to take one violent step forward.

"I've been waiting my whole life for this!! C'mon, Kirito...Let's dance!!"

As far as Asuna knew, this was the first time, going all the way back to their *SAO* days, that PoH had actually spoken that name. He readied the Mate-Chopper and leaped like some monstrous bird.

The frighteningly thick blade descended, exuding an evil red-black aura. And it was aimed not at Kirito but at Asuna and the other two women.

"No—!"

Sortiliena rushed forward, raising her damaged longsword over her head to block the reaper's blow. But the enlarged dagger, nearly three times its original size now, didn't even need to touch her blade directly; its wicked aura alone split Sortiliena's sword in two.

The shock knocked the chief guard backward. Asuna and Ronie stood behind her in an attempt to keep her upright. The three of them ended up clumped together, with the wicked blade coming down in a lethal swing...

Claaaaang!

There was a tremendous ringing just above them, knocking them onto their behinds.

But the knife hadn't touched them. It was vibrating, like it had struck some invisible barrier hanging in the air. The exact same thing that had prevented the red knight from hitting Asuna earlier.

This time, she definitely felt it. She was being protected by warm, strong, familiar arms. Just before the invisible barrier, she could see something faintly glowing. Painted in the air in little golden motes of light was a hand with fingers outstretched—a *right* hand.

Then she heard a scraping sound.

Asuna's head turned automatically to the left.

Though Kirito's face was still against the ground, his left hand had the broken white sword pointed into the soil. And with that as a base, his frail, emaciated body was slowly, slowly rising up off the ground.

The empty right sleeve of his black shirt swayed in the breeze. No—not quite. It was gradually filling out, moving closer to the place where the illusionary hand supported the barrier.

When the sleeve made contact with the hand, it created a golden brilliance, dispersing the evil miasma that lurked on the other side of the wall. The barrier slammed PoH's body, knocking him far backward.

When the brilliance faded, Asuna was looking at a perfectly

whole—if still slightly emaciated—hand and arm. Her eyes followed his arm upward, past his shoulder.

And then she saw long bangs waving in the breeze. Lips forming a gentle smile. And two black pupils gazing back at her from the same level.

His lips moved, and his voice emerged:

"I'm back, Asuna."

Tears burst from her eyes, never-ending, and she couldn't stop a high-pitched peal from leaving her throat. She clenched her hands before her chest and channeled her wave of emotion into words.

"......Welcome home, Kirito."

Next, Sortiliena and Ronie called out his name in unison. Kirito nodded to them with a smile and faced forward again. There was a stern quality to his expression.

Over thirty feet away, PoH got back to his feet with a smoothness that seemed to ignore the power of gravity.

The Chinese and Korean players that had been about to kill one another were still entirely frozen by the ice vines, which should have stopped the generation of fresh spatial resources, but the swirling black clouds were still on the move overhead, and PoH's knife was still absorbing power. The Grim Reaper wasn't going to stop unless his weapon was destroyed.

Kirito stood up a second later. He faltered but kept his balance. Asuna had to stifle the urge to rush to his side and keep him stable. She barely had the strength to stand herself, so throwing herself into the situation would only make her a liability. Now was the time to believe in Kirito. Just believing would be a source of strength in itself.

Kirito lifted his regenerated arm and drew the black sword from its sheath, right from where it lay on the ground. Then he rose again and felt its weight in his palm.

It was a different shape from his old sword, Elucidator, and the other sword was broken in half—but the image of him dual-wielding black and white blades belonged to none other than the Black Swordsman, who had protected, guided, and granted strength to Asuna from the day they had met.

The white longsword in his left hand sparkled like diamond dust, exuding its frosty aura. The superpower that was immobilizing over twenty thousand soldiers at once was still being maintained, but there was no hint of effort or concentration on Kirito's face. It was as though someone *else* was standing at his side, sharing his burden.

Kirito trudged forward, holding two swords at once, staring directly into the two red eyes shining from PoH's hood. The man spread his arms in a welcoming gesture, exposing the giant hole in his chest.

"...So, you're awake at last. How long has it been since we stared each other in the face and had a conversation in person?"

The reaper's voice was harsh, like rusted metal scraping together. Kirito channeled his Aincrad days; his voice was aloof but with a sharp edge at its core. "You know, I've lost track. But I know this time will be the last."

PoH whistled in admiration. "How nice...You're the best, Kirito. C'mon...Let's pick up where we left off. We haven't really cut loose since Aincrad."

He lifted the Mate-Chopper—which was more of a machete now that it was three times its usual size—as though it were as light as a feather. The black clouds overhead swirled even harder, and dark-red sparks danced around the thick slab of metal.

Kirito, meanwhile, lifted his black sword straight back.

But the moment the sword reached a vertical angle, his weakened body faltered, unable to support the full weight of the weapon.

Asuna already knew that the Underworld wasn't the same as any other VRMMO world built under The Seed's specifications. Every object that existed here was a mnemonic visual created solely through memory and was subject to the influence of the brain's power to envision and imagine.

According to Alice, Kirito had been in an unresponsive state for nearly half a year in this time-accelerated world. He might not have any memory of that span of time, but he would know that his body had been inactive for all of it. So the weakened image of himself in his mind was actually physically crippling him.

But as a matter of fact, that might not have been all of it.

Takeru Higa of Rath had given her an explanation of why Kirito's self-image had been damaged like that.

It turned out that he had a number of helpers—artificial fluctlights, of course...He had friends. Most of them died in the battle against the Church, but when he finally succeeded in opening the circuit to the outside, he was strongly blaming himself. In other words, he was attacking his own fluctlight. Just then, our shady attackers cut the power line, and the momentary power surge caused an instant spike in the STL's output. The result was that Kirito's self-destructive impulse was actualized...and his ego was deactivated.

She'd found it difficult to absorb at the time, but in summary, Kirito had lost someone important to him here, and his sadness had been so great that it had destroyed him. Asuna knew this person's name, because it had come up over and over again during the night she'd spent trading stories in the tent with Alice, Ronie, and Sortiliena: Eugeo the sword disciple.

Through some miracle, Kirito had recovered, but he still was not accepting of Eugeo's death. An unending sadness was casting its pall over his mind...and even his physical body.

Kirito, Asuna thought, watching him hold the black sword aloft, *I can't imagine what kind of horrible, heartbreaking things you went through. But I can tell you this: Your friend still lives on inside you. The same way that Yuuki still lives inside me. And that memory will bring you strength. Strength to pick up your sword and fight again.*

And, as if her thoughts had become words in his ears, Kirito held the broken sword to his chest, even as the black sword was on high.

Sensing this was a chance to strike, PoH moved. His slender form tilted forward, then burst across the wreckage-strewn ground, closing thirty feet in a blink. His thick machete slid forward, seemingly weightless.

Rather than sidestepping it, Kirito struck with his right sword to deflect the blow. But Asuna could see that his attack had lost its usual bite.

When the longsword made contact with the machete, it fortunately avoided being knocked aside, but Kirito could not bring enough momentum for an even stalemate; the power of the knife pushed his sword straight down. His knee bent, and his back arched like a bow. His boots slid a foot along the dirt.

"...Come on—don't disappoint me. I've been waiting almost two years for this moment...," growled the reaper in the black poncho. Like its blade, the Mate-Chopper's handle was enlarged, too, and he added his other hand for leverage.

The point of contact creaked, and Kirito's knee sank even lower. If only he could switch to a two-handed grip, like PoH... but he had the white sword clutched in his left hand. It was split in two, so it could not be used to attack.

Within Death's hood, thick lips curved sadistically. Slowly but surely, the blade of the machete approached Kirito's neck.

"Kirito...!" gasped Sortiliena. She made to stand, holding her broken sword. But Asuna grabbed her shoulder to hold her back.

"It's all right, Liena," she whispered, suppressing her own fear. This woman had apparently been his instructor at the sword-fighting academy he'd attended. "Kirito will be all right. He won't lose to that awful man...He'd never."

And Ronie, whom Kirito had instructed in turn, tearfully agreed. "That's right. Kirito won't lose this fight."

"......Of course," said Sortiliena. She reached up to squeeze Asuna's hand where it rested on her shoulder.

But then, as if mocking their assurances, PoH's Mate-Chopper dug down farther. Kirito's left knee hit the ground. The arm holding up the black sword was trembling with effort. He seemed to be nearly out of strength.

PoH leaned in closer to Kirito's strained features. "Drop that piece-of-shit sword and use your other hand already," he mocked. "Those Chinese and Koreans you're keeping frozen were killing all your friends, you know that? Why should you care if they kill one another this time?"

Despite the force pressing down on him, Kirito mustered an icy reply to the devil's temptations. "I know exactly how you do things. You make people fight, you sow the seeds of hatred, and you set up the next conflict. You caused plenty of chaos that way in *SAO*, but you're not going to get away with that in the Underworld…I'll make sure of that."

"Oh yeah? How so? Once they're unfrozen, they're going to slaughter the surviving Japanese and all your precious Underworlders. The only way to stop that is to kill them. Just smash them all to pieces while they're frozen. Your friends can handle that. Just give the orders…Tell them to kill all the Chinese and Koreans."

"……"

Kirito did not respond to the venomous suggestion. But Asuna could tell exactly what PoH's plot was about.

The Chinese and Korean players wrapped in icy vines didn't seem to be in any pain at the moment, but if they were broken apart, it would cause tremendous agony. The pain would lead to anger and make whatever rage they felt toward the Japanese players permanent.

The deaths of the invading soldiers would also spill a great amount of resources that his Mate-Chopper could absorb. He would have enough power to win the fight against Kirito and slaughter every remaining person.

Kirito had to know that, and he wasn't going to fall for it. But in order to prevent that disaster, he had to use the sword in his left hand to maintain the freezing spell, making his chances in the fight against his archenemy dire.

With each tremble of the hand holding off the huge machete, more sparks flew off where they intersected. The heavy blade got closer, slowly but surely. There was only a fist's worth of space between it and Kirito's left shoulder.

"…But if you wanna be stubborn and die, that's fine by me," PoH said, a venomous smile on his lips. "Don't worry. After I kill you, I'll murder the Flash and everyone else, too."

The reaper's eyes glowed like will-o'-the-wisps in the darkness of the hood. His mouth opened all the way to his cheekbones, revealing sharp fangs.

"Come on…Let me taste your lifeblood, Kirito."

PoH licked his lips with a pointed, reptilian tongue and put even more strength into the Mate-Chopper. The black sword screamed in protest. The fatal edge was closing the gap, a fraction of an inch per second…

Suddenly, from just over Asuna's shoulder, she heard a voice praying, *"Please, Eugeo, save Kirito."*

Asuna, Sortiliena, and Ronie turned around to see Tiese, the red-haired girl, with her hands clasped before her chest. A moment later, Asuna sensed Tiese's hair billowing outward nearly imperceptibly and a ripple like a breeze in the air.

She turned to face forward again.

The enlarged Mate-Chopper had just made contact with Kirito's shoulder. That was enough for the fabric of his black shirt to split. Asuna held her breath, anticipating the sight of her lover's blood flowing.

But…instead, the Mate-Chopper stopped there.

In fact, it was inching back upward, bit by bit. But where was Kirito's exhausted arm finding the strength…?

"Ah……," murmured someone, either Ronie or Sortiliena.

Asuna saw it, too: another arm, golden and translucent, gripping the handle of the black sword.

A moment later, Kirito noticed it as well. His eyes widened, then his face scrunched up. Tears welled in his eyes and fell, glistening in the light.

His lips budged, too, but she couldn't make out his voice.

Then, a moment later, a fierce scream erupted from his throat.

"Raaaaaaaaah!!"

He jolted the Mate-Chopper backward. PoH's arms were thrown back, and he toppled over, swearing. Kirito promptly stood up from his kneeling position and thrust his broken white sword upward into the air.

"Release Recollection!!"

An impossibly bright burst of light covered everything, turning the world white. PoH put up a hand to block his face.

Through squinting eyes, Asuna saw the ugly, broken blade of the sword collecting the concentrated and crystallized light as it regenerated itself. In just a few seconds, the sword was whole again.

Schwing!! It flashed even brighter, a pulse that spread outward. After a moment of silence, a pure, grand wave of sound came into being, like hundreds, thousands of bells ringing at once. The four women looked around, wide-eyed.

The frozen-white VRMMO players from China and Korea sprouted millions of flowers—brilliant-blue roses, as delicate as if carved from lapis lazuli.

The great bloom of roses began to exude silver particles from the blossoms' cores. It was pure life resources—Asuna understood on instinct that this was the HP of the players.

Players who had been surging with fury just minutes ago, ready to kill one another, now turned to pillars of light with their eyes peacefully closed. They vanished without pain or suffering of any kind. It was the most serene possible way to achieve a forced log-out.

Now the seeds of hatred PoH had tried to plant in the other players would not bloom into flowers of their own.

"What the hell...do you think you're doing?!" snarled the reaper, his plot undone. But just as quickly, he regained his wild smirk and lifted his machete.

Asuna knew what he was planning to do. Now there were life

resources—what the Underworlders would call "sacred power"—floating all over the battlefield from the millions of blue roses. He was going to use his weapon's suction power to absorb all of it.

"Kirito...!" she cried, feeling a jolt of panic.

Absorbing the lives of two thousand murdered Japanese players earlier had caused the Mate-Chopper to swell to three times its size and given it power at least equal to Stacia's GM equipment. If it absorbed ten times that number, PoH would turn into a demon...a true devil. If Kirito was immobilized from executing the wide-scale art, then Asuna would have to help...

But before she could will a last burst of strength into her wilted legs, she heard Yuuki's voice again, whispering into her ear like a gentle breeze.

It's all right...Look.

That was when Asuna realized that the silver lights gathering in midair and forming several rippling ribbon strips were completely ignoring PoH's Mate-Chopper. No matter how hard he thrust it into the sky and focused, they made no motion toward the blade.

The voice sounded in her head again.

You said it, remember? *Life is a tool that transports and relates the heart.*

All these people from different countries who gathered in this place? They don't really want to kill one another.

Everyone has the same wish. To go to a world of excitement and fun...A great, beautiful, thrilling world like the land of fairies where you and I met, Asuna...That's all there is to it.

"...Yeah. You're right, Yuuki," Asuna whispered, inaudible to anyone else.

Right on that cue, Kirito lifted the black sword in his other hand so that both his swords were pointing to the sky. The swirling black clouds that PoH had summoned began to reverse direction and dissipate. A little hole of blue sky peeked through the center, allowing a ray of golden sun to hit the black blade and make it shine like crystal.

"Release Recollection," Kirito said, for the second sword this time, savoring the sound of the words.

Instantly, the softly rippling sheets of silver began to knit themselves together and flow into the black sword.

"Suck!" screamed PoH in English, and he swung the Mate-Chopper to compete with the flow. But the ribbons had a mind of their own and avoided his evil dagger, fusing with Kirito's sword instead.

"...Eugeo told me that Kirito's black sword was once a gigantic cedar tree at the very far north of the human realm," explained Tiese in a trembling voice.

Sortiliena nodded in recognition. "Of course...that's why it has the ability to suck in sacred power..."

Their words fused with what she'd just heard Yuuki say, and Asuna finally understood the nature of what was happening.

If Kirito's black sword had the ability to absorb resources, then why was it able to pull in what the blue roses were exuding, even though PoH's Mate-Chopper couldn't, despite the fact that it, too, had absorbing powers? That was because the evil dagger sucked in not *life* resources but *death* resources.

PoH himself had said it: The Mate-Chopper got stronger the more people it killed. If it was the owner's power of imagination that granted the wicked knife the ability to absorb resources, then it could devour death resources spilled by bloody murder, but it could not suck up the life resources that the white sword coaxed out through nonlethal means.

But Kirito's black sword was different. If it was originally created from a tree that grew on the strength of the earth and the sun, then both the sword and the mental association in the mind of its owner would allow it to absorb that life.

The white sword in his left hand froze targets across a wide stretch of land, releasing their life into the air.

The black sword in his right hand then sucked up that life power from all over, converting it to energy.

It was a very simple but thus incredibly powerful bit of synergy. The perfect pairing. Ideal partners.

As it drew in the vast length of silvery ribbon, the center of the black sword began to shine a dazzling golden color. The resources were traveling through the hilt into Kirito's arm, as well.

His shriveled body, as skinny as a stick, rapidly began to regain its original strength. The recovery phenomenon wasn't isolated to just his body; the shirt that had been ripped here and there during the fighting was instantly repaired. Fingerless gloves appeared on his hands, and riveted boots on his feet.

The line of light traveled from his shoulders down his arms, then down his back. A moment later, a shining black leather texture appeared there. It was his trademark long coat from the *SAO* days. When the ends of the coat settled down and lay still, the two sheaths lying discarded on the ground flew up and affixed themselves to his back in a crossed configuration.

"……Kiri…to……"

Asuna, overwhelmed by emotion, stared at the figure of Kirito the Black Swordsman, back in his dual-wielding form, through eyes blurred with tears. Sortiliena and Ronie had shining streaks down their cheeks on either side of her, too. Behind them, Tiese was sobbing.

A few seconds later, Kirito had finished absorbing all the ribbons of life, and he easily lowered his swords. The majority of the Chinese and Korean players on the battlefield had logged out already. Asuna turned around and indicated her gratitude with a look to the red knight who'd tried to save Klein. Then he, too, vanished, and the wasteland where so much horrible slaughter had taken place was as quiet as though it had never happened.

All she could hear was the sound of dry wind howling and the high-pitched squeaking of metal. It was coming from the black sword that glowed with a golden aura, engorged with so much energy.

PoH gave up on seizing resources at last and lowered the Mate-Chopper in silence. There was still a giant hole in his chest from Asuna's Mother's Rosario skill. When the resource power left in his wicked knife was depleted, his life would end.

That must have been clear to him, but he just stood there in silence now. No insults or taunts. He didn't seem to be giving up, either. There was a freezing-cold aura exuding from his skin, and Asuna could feel it prickling her just from looking at him from a distance.

One side of his mouth curled into a sneer, and his lips parted.

"You really are the best, Kirito. Then and now, no one else has made me *want* to kill them as much as you do. I hate to bring this all to an end, but I'm not going to get a better stage to do it on than this one..."

PoH lifted the machete and thrust out his free hand. He beckoned with his long fingers, curling them to show off the tattoo of the laughing face in the coffin on the back of his hand.

"...Let's enjoy this, Black Swordsman," he said, an invitation of pure, concentrated malice.

"Yes," Kirito agreed, "let's end this."

He spread his feet apart and dropped his hips, holding the white sword forward and the black sword behind him. The hostility and concentration between the two combatants intensified, sparks flying in the space between them.

As they'd both claimed, the next trading of blows would be the last, Asuna could sense. Her eyes were wide open, and her breath caught in her throat.

Another dry gust of wind blew past, and when it stopped, the Black Swordsman and the black reaper moved together.

PoH's Mate-Chopper emitted a dark-red light, sticky and viscous in quality. As he shot forward with terrifying speed, his body split into three.

Asuna didn't know this sword skill, but for his part, Kirito left his right sword down, activating his white sword with a crimson glow instead. That would be the One-Handed Sword skill Deadly Sins.

PoH slashed at him, forward, left, and right, but Kirito's combination attack deflected each of them. The giant bloodred dagger and the ruby longsword caused the earth and the atmosphere to quake with each impact.

Once the three PoHs had attacked twice each, six times in total, the left and right afterimages vanished. The real one then pulled back and swung down ferociously. Kirito swiped at a left angle to block the attack. A shock wave and an explosion of sparks resulted.

Deadly Sins was a seven-part skill; it would cause Kirito to suffer a movement delay. If PoH had another attack ready, Kirito couldn't defend against it.

The reaper's hood blew back from the impact of his overhead swing being blocked, exposing his full appearance for the first time since the *SAO* days.

There was a ghastly smile on his face, which was fiercely sculpted and not quite Japanese looking. PoH swung his gloomy, glowing knife toward Kirito's shoulder yet again: an eighth attack.

But in that moment, Kirito's black sword flashed red. It was a shade deeper and hotter than that of Deadly Sins—the color of flame.

Canceling out the delay that should have lasted at least a full second, the black sword was thrust with impossible speed. He was executing a technique that only he could do: Skill Connect, a seamless transition between sword skills with separate weapons.

With a roar like a combustion engine firing, the heavy thrust Vorpal Strike met in midair with what was probably the last of an eight-part combination attack from PoH.

This caused the greatest shock wave of all, which rippled outward, creating cracks in the ground. It whipped up ferocious winds of dust and heat, but Asuna narrowed her eyes only the minimum amount necessary; she was determined to see the end of this duel.

When the gust of wind had dissipated, she saw the two of them

motionless, tips of the black sword and red machete intersecting before them. The fight wasn't over yet. They were focusing the maximum amount of energy into the minimum point of intersection, each pushing with all his strength to overpower the other.

In terms of the accumulated resources in each weapon, Kirito's black sword ought to be utterly overwhelming PoH's Mate-Chopper, but it wasn't turning out that way. In this world, the power of imagination, the power to envision—what the knights called "Incarnation"—had the potential to overturn any numerical value.

The simplicity of PoH's Incarnation was what made it so powerful. He fought to kill…to fill the world with discord, mistrust, hostility, and malice.

Then why did Kirito fight?

Here in this world, he had lost a treasured friend. And while there might have been external circumstances involved, he had experienced enough despair to be in a vacant state for half of an entire year. But now he was standing again, wielding his swords. What kind of Incarnation was giving him strength…?

Asuna couldn't put the answer into words—but she didn't think she needed to. Kirito had fought with so many things on his shoulders to this point. He'd done it in *SAO*, in *ALO*, and in *GGO*. He was doing it right now.

Hesitation, suffering, and sadness could be strength, too. Tears could be turned into light. And that light would never be defeated by PoH's darkness.

Isn't that right…Kirito?

Asuna didn't know whether her prayer reached his ears. But just then, there was a faint but definite sound in response.

Crack.

PoH's weapon of evil, the Mate-Chopper, created so that man could kill man, now had a glowing red crack running from tip to base like a bolt of lightning.

Then the huge machete burst into countless tiny shards—and Kirito's Vorpal Strike extended onward for another twenty feet, obliterating PoH's right arm.

Another gust of wind interfered with Asuna's field of view. She could no longer sit; she had to rise. So did Tiese, Sortiliena, and Ronie, and behind them, Klein, Silica, and Lisbeth.

In time, the dust settled, revealing the two former *SAO* players locked in tight formation.

PoH's remaining arm dangled at his side without a weapon, Kirito's black sword penetrating deep through his chest. But that was the place where Asuna had burst the hole in the first place, so he didn't appear to have suffered any new physical damage.

He smiled confidently, blood dripping from the hole and his mouth, probably because the Mate-Chopper was no longer providing him with the resources to keep him alive.

"…Yeah…that's more like it. But…this isn't the end. I might log out of this world, but I'll always come back to threaten you," he vowed. "Over and over, until I've slit your and Flash's throats and carved out your hearts…"

Kirito betrayed no hint of emotion. He quietly replied, "No, this is the end. You won't be logging out of the Underworld."

The black sword flashed for a brief instant.

When the light subsided, Kirito slowly pulled the blade out of the hole in PoH's chest and took a few steps back. Despite the lack of support, PoH did not collapse. The same awful grin was slapped across his face, and he tried to say something else.

But when his mouth opened, it made a creaking noise and froze in place. So did his limbs. They paused in an unnatural pose, cracking and changing texture. The shining black leather turned to a kind of fabric, covered in hairline cracks. The metal rivets became protruding lumps. The Grim Reaper was undergoing an abnormal transformation of sorts.

Kirito went on: "This sword was originally a huge tree that the people of Rulid called the Gigas Cedar. For two hundred years, they chopped at it with their axes, to no avail. I sent the memory of this sword into your body."

Indeed, over half of the surface of PoH's body was turning into a kind of charcoal-black tree bark. His legs fused into one limb, growing roots into the earth. His arms turned into eerily gnarled, twisted branches, and his hair sharpened into needles. Lastly, his eyes and mouth became a trio of small knotholes.

"When they see that the Chinese and Korean players are logging out, your friends will resume the time acceleration. I don't know if it'll be years or decades until you're let out of the STL, but you'd better pray it's on the shorter side. If some enterprising frontiersmen start a village here, you might have children coming to chop you down with an ax."

It was impossible to say whether PoH actually perceived the words at this point. There was no longer a human being standing there across from Kirito, but an ugly cedar tree only six feet tall.

Kirito stared at the tree for a moment before turning to Asuna's group. He smiled and nodded to them, then looked at the wounded Japanese players and Underworlders. He raised the black sword again, which still harbored a golden glow at its center.

"System Call. Transfer Durability to Local Area."

Shaaaa...

A sound filled the battlefield, faint in volume but stretching from end to end.

It was raining.

The resources released by the sword took form in the sky overhead and descended to earth as little droplets of delicate light. The wounded and exhausted Japanese players and the members of the Human Guardian Army who were utterly spent from consecutive battles all felt their bodies being healed. And perhaps their hearts and minds, too...

Having expelled all of the black sword's resources, Kirito put it and the white sword he was holding in his other hand back into their scabbards over his shoulders.

Asuna watched the black-clad swordsman take step after deliberate step through the all-healing rain of light. She couldn't move or even speak. It felt like all of it would vanish if she spoke, returning to illusion. So she just kept her eyes open, smiled, and waited.

Instead, it was Klein who stepped forward.

His severed left arm and skewered torso were back to pristine condition. But the samurai still clutched his chest like he was in great pain, tottering forward.

"Kirito…Kirito, man…," he said, his usual cheery self, though his voice cracked a bit. "You gotta stop it with takin' all the juiciest, most heroic scenes…"

He was practically crying. The tall, lanky samurai grabbed the dual-swordsman in black by the shoulders and pressed his bandana-less forehead against the shorter man's neck. His back trembled, and huge sobs left his throat.

"Aaah…aaaaaaaah…"

Kirito put his arms around his weeping friend's back. He shut his eyes and clenched his jaws; there were shining tracks down his cheeks, too.

"…Kirito," Ronie said. She got up and began to run for him. Teardrops flew off her face as she plowed straight into his shoulder. Sortiliena followed close behind her.

Even Agil's eyes were wet. Lisbeth and Silica were hugging each other and crying. The Japanese players in the area—the *ALO* leaders like Sakuya, Alicia, and Eugene; Siune and Jun from the Sleeping Knights; and many others—had faces wet and shining, from both the rain of light and the tears that adorned their cheeks.

Even the soldiers and priests of the more distant Human Guardian Army were uniformly red-eyed. They knelt as a group, each pressing a fist to their chest and hanging their head in salute.

"……From the moment I first met him, I knew. I knew that he would save us all with his two swords," said a gentle voice behind Asuna.

She turned around to see the young Integrity Knight Renly and his dragon mount behind him. Both had been gravely wounded, but the signs of their damage were now limited only to the armor they wore.

Asuna was so full of emotion that all she could do was nod

once or twice. Renly's head bobbed in return, then he walked to Tiese, who was still kneeling on the ground, and crouched next to her.

An examination of the battlefield showed that not a single one of the twenty thousand Chinese and Korean VRMMO players was left. Every last one was gone.

Once the attackers discovered that the players had logged out, they would surely cancel their strategy of bringing in real-world help and raise the acceleration rate to maximum again. Once that happened, Klein and all the others using AmuSpheres would automatically get kicked out.

Kirito must have been aware of that, too. He clapped Klein on the shoulder, pulled away, and looked out on the rest of the Japanese players.

Then he bowed his head deeply and said, "Thank you, everyone... Your feelings for me, and the blood and tears you shed, will not go to waste. Truly, thank you all."

Yes...the battle was not over yet.

The deadly PoH and his army of American, Chinese, and Korean players were gone, but there was still the head honcho of the enemy left, Emperor Vecta. He had kidnapped Alice the Integrity Knight, the core of Project Alicization, and was flying south at this very moment to the distant World's End Altar.

Asuna sucked in a deep breath and stood up at last. She made her way through the other players, all standing stock-still and reeling with their own emotions, and walked steadily toward Kirito.

He lifted his face and looked straight at her.

For an instant, she was seized by a powerful urge, and she held her breath.

She wanted to leap into the arms of her beloved. She wanted to cry with the abandon of a child, to unleash all her pent-up emotions.

But she kept them in check for now—barely—and reported the present concern.

"Kirito...Emperor Vecta took Alice."

"Yeah. I do remember the situation, if fuzzily," Kirito said, his expression sharp. He held out his hand. "Let's go save her. I'll need your help, Asuna."

"......!......"

It was all she could take.

Asuna rushed over to seize his hand and pressed it to her cheek.

His other arm went around her back and pulled her in close.

The embrace was only momentary, but Asuna felt that, within that moment, an incredible amount of information that couldn't be expressed in words was traded between them.

He gazed into her eyes again, right up close, nodded, and looked to the sky to the south. He raised his right hand in that direction, his fingers waving around as if searching for something.

"......Found them."

"Huh...?" Asuna murmured, but Kirito only grinned and did not elaborate.

He looked around at the rest of the group again, clapped Klein on the shoulder, rubbed Ronie's head, and said, "Well, we're off."

And then...

―――∿―――

Lisbeth watched as Kirito and Asuna burst off into the sky, glowing brilliant green and heading south at a phenomenal speed. She blinked a few times in surprise, then exhaled long and slow.

"Well, I guess he hasn't lost his edge or his sense of abandon..."

Nearby, Silica giggled.

Klein clapped his hands together. "Damn, who does he think he is...?" he shouted, then name-dropped the hero of an action comic from generations ago. "He's freakin' invincible. He always gets all the best scenes, I tell ya..."

Fresh tears glistened on his cheeks. Ever since they'd first met in Aincrad and he'd been smitten by Kirito, the youth had always been that to Klein: an invincible, unstoppable, eternal hero.

He is to me, too.

Lisbeth looked to the south, her vision clouded by endless tears. She wanted to commit this world to her memory before she logged out in a few moments, never to return to it.

All so she could relate the image to the many players who'd been logged out in agony and humiliation, to let them know that their painful efforts were not in vain.

CHAPTER TWENTY-TWO

1

"Dammit!!"

Critter, the information-warfare specialist on the *Ocean Turtle* assault team, slammed his hand on the console as he stared at the results coming through on the monitor.

The amalgamation of red dots, nearly thirty thousand at its peak, was rapidly disappearing, starting in the middle and trickling outward. In other words, the Chinese and Korean VRMMO players brought into the Underworld through Vassago's scheme were being wiped out somehow and automatically logging off the system.

In the center of the red circle, the human army in blue and Japanese troops in white still remained at around a thousand. It was too large of a number to ignore entirely—and if those thousand had the strength to wipe out a combined army of thirty thousand, they had to be even more dangerous.

"...What the hell is that moron doing...?" swore Critter, clicking his tongue and staring at a point on the monitor.

There was just one bright-red dot remaining very close to the Japanese squad. That would be Vassago, who had used his own personal converted account to dive from the STL room next door. He was directly adjacent to the enemy, but he wasn't even moving, much less fighting them.

Perhaps he was being held prisoner or immobilized. Or maybe he still had a secret trick up his sleeve that would allow him to take care of this army of a thousand...

Critter wanted to rush into the STL room right now, slap Vassago awake, and yank him around by the collar, but he held that urge in. With the admin controls to the Underworld currently locked, they couldn't reset any accounts. So if he forcefully logged Vassago out, the account he was using would not be usable again. About the only thing Critter *could* do was operate the time-acceleration feature, since it was isolated from the Seed program core. But that required some careful timing.

He took a deep breath and zoomed out on the map. At the far south end of the Underworld, another red dot was still rapidly on the move. That was the captain of the assault team, Gabriel Miller.

If Captain Miller either had captured Alice or was in close pursuit, the question now was: How likely was it for the human army to catch up to him?

The insertion of the American, Chinese, and Korean players had severely impeded the human army's southward advance. In terms of internal distance, Captain Miller had to be several hundred miles ahead of them. A jet fighter could close that gap in a blink, but that technology wasn't likely to exist in the Underworld. At best, they might have some kind of winged mount to ride on.

They're not going to catch him, Critter decided after three seconds of consideration.

He glanced at the watch on his left wrist. It was 9:40 AM, July 7th.

The SDF commandos were supposed to be sent in by the defense ship at six in the evening, giving them eight hours and twenty minutes. Captain Miller had left instructions to resume acceleration when the time remaining hit eight hours—meaning ten AM. But now that essentially all the external players had been wiped out, there was no reason to maintain real-time speed.

Which meant that it would be better to accelerate Underworld time by a thousand again, giving Captain Miller time to secure Alice.

"Here goes nothing…Best of luck in there, Vassago," Critter said to the stationary red dot on the battlefield and reached for the lever that operated the Fluctlight Acceleration (FLA) rate. When he glanced up at the slider on the main monitor that corresponded to the lever's placement, his eyes stopped on the scale markings next to the gauge.

The slider needle was at the bottom, next to the ×1 indicator. The scale was marked in ×100 increments, and a red line cut across at ×1,000. But as a matter of fact, the scale continued upward until another partition at ×1,200. That, apparently, was the safety line for a biological human diving with an STL.

Yet, the rate slider continued even farther, until it ultimately reached ×5,000. If no human being was in a dive—meaning only artificial fluctlights were present in the world simulation—the internal time could be accelerated that fast.

Changing the FLA involved using the physical lever on the console board, then pressing a nearby button with a plastic cap that opened and closed over it. Being careful not to press the button, Critter slowly pushed the lever, which looked like the throttle on a ship or an airplane.

The slider graphic on the monitor smoothly rose, and the digital number readout rotated rapidly. When he got to ×1,000, there was a strong resistance on the lever. He pushed it again, harder, and it moved farther before stopping at ×1,200 again. It didn't seem as though it was going to budge beyond that, no matter how hard he pushed.

"Hmm…"

His curiosity piqued, Critter examined the large metal lever. He quickly noticed that, next to the activation button, there was a shining silver keyhole.

"Gotcha." He grinned, scratching his bald head with a finger.

The safety limit being twelve hundred times regular speed

meant that the real danger area was a bit beyond that. It couldn't be a bad idea to test unlocking the safety mechanism, just in case internal time was in a major crunch.

Critter spun his chair around and snapped his fingers to draw the attention of the team members who had just returned to the control room.

"Anyone here good at lock picking?"

———ᴡᴠᴠ———

What a soft...and wonderful scent...

It was the best sleep he'd had in months. So when Takeru Higa heard a voice in his ear desperately trying to wake him up, he resisted to the best of his ability.

"...I said, Higa! Hello?! Open your eyes! Come on!!"

This person sounds really frantic, though. It's not like I got stabbed or shot or anyth...ing......

"...Aaugh!!"

As his mind regained consciousness, his memory flooded back in a rush, and Higa bolted awake.

Right before him was a thirty-something man with black-framed glasses.

"Whoa—?!" he screamed.

He tried to lurch backward to get away, but his body wouldn't listen. Instead, a terrible pain seared his right shoulder, and Higa screamed a third time.

That's right. I got shot by that man in the cable duct. I knew I was bleeding bad, but I focused on controlling the STLs instead. I connected the output of the three girls' fluctlights to Kirigaya's STL, but it didn't wake him up...and then...something else happened...

"...Wh-what about Kirito?" he said, trying to wriggle away from the face of the man in glasses, who was peering at him very closely.

Instead, his answer came from a smooth female voice. "Kirigaya's fluctlight activity has returned to full status. In fact, if anything, it might be *too* active right now."

"Oh…th-that's…good…," Higa said, exhaling.

It was nothing short of a miracle that his self-image had recovered from the state it had been in. And speaking of miracles, the fact that Higa was still alive after how much blood he'd lost…

These realizations gave him reason to examine his surroundings and condition.

He was resting on the floor of the sub-control room. His upper body was uncovered, and his right shoulder was bandaged. There was a catheter in his left arm, supplying him with blood.

On his left side, in the glasses, was Lieutenant Colonel Seijirou Kikuoka. Sitting directly on the floor to his left was Dr. Rinko Koujiro, her white coat removed. On the other end of the catheter tube was Sergeant First Class Natsuki Aki, a registered nurse, who was exchanging blood packs. She must have been the one who had seen to his wound.

Higa looked back to Kikuoka, who exhaled deeply and finally spoke.

"Good grief…After all my warnings not to do anything too reckless…But then again, I guess this is my fault for failing to catch the fact that we had a mole on the engineering team…"

His bangs were bedraggled, and there were sweat marks on his lenses. Rinko appeared to be drenched in sweat, too. They must have been hard at work saving Higa's life. Then that wonderfully pleasant feeling while he dreamed must have been…

Hmm?

Who tried to pump my heart, and who gave me mouth-to-mouth?

He nearly asked the question of them, but he caught himself in time. Some truths were better off unknown.

Instead, he asked a much more important question: "What's the state of the Underworld…and of Alice?"

Kikuoka brushed Higa's left shoulder and said, "All the players connecting from America, China, and Korea have been logged out. In fact, there were nearly thirty thousand from China and Korea alone, but…"

"What…? From China and Korea, too?! Not as reinforcements…but as enemies?!" Higa blurted out. He tried to get up again, but the shock of the pain from his right shoulder stabbed him in the brain.

"Don't get up *now!*" Sergeant First Class Aki scolded. "The bullet went all the way through, but I only just got the bleeding to stop."

"Y-yes, ma'am…" Higa relaxed and let Rinko fill him in on the situation.

"Apparently, they recruited the Chinese and Koreans on social media, riling them up by playing on their natural rivalry as online gamers."

"Oh…I see…," Higa lamented. His participation in Project Alicization was partially spurred on by the death of a Korean friend who'd been blown up in a terrorist attack while serving his military years in Iraq. It was galling to think that the project had now led to further inflammation of the hostilities between Japan itself and Korean gamers—even if it was the attackers who were doing it.

He found himself shaking his head, then grimaced at the pain. "How many from China and Korea, again?" he asked.

"It seems they hit nearly thirty thousand. The two thousand players who came to our side from Japan were essentially wiped out," Kikuoka said. He closed his eyes for a moment before continuing, "At that point, there were still over twenty thousand hostile troops present. Fortunately, that's when Kirito awoke and took care of them in one blow…"

"W-wait, what?" Higa stammered, cutting off his superior. "Kirito neutralized an army of twenty thousand, all alone…in a single instant?! That's impossible! The Underworld doesn't have a weapon or command capable of attacking on a physical scale or intensity of that sort. Or at least…it shouldn't…"

Only then did Higa recall the conversation he'd had with Yanai right around the time the man had shot him in the cable duct.

Nobuyuki Sugou's former employee Yanai not only was a spy for the attackers invading the ship but was obsessed with the artificial fluctlight known as Administrator, the pontifex of the Axiom Church. How had it come to that?

And then there was the question of the "fourth": the irregular fluctlight connected to Kazuto Kirigaya's fluctlight from the Main Visualizer itself. That—he or she—had become the key to Kazuto's recovery. But Higa had never even imagined that an inanimate object without a mind of its own could function as a human consciousness, even a simulated one.

"...Hey...Kiku...," he said, feeling a chill that had nothing to do with his blood loss. "Do you think...we've been creating... something much, much bigger—?"

Right at that moment, the speaker in the command console issued a piercing alarm.

It was the sound that Higa had programmed to alert him to a change in the time-acceleration rate of the simulation.

—⁓—

Ashen clouds rushed past Asuna and me with blinding speed. A bloodred sky hung above us, and blackened wasteland stretched out forever below.

In all the vast human-owned lands, only the pontifex herself had mastered the art of flying, according to Alice the Integrity Knight. Now Administrator was gone from the Underworld, as was her counterpart Cardinal, so there was no way to know exactly what the command to perform the flying art was. In other words, my flight through the Dark Territory was not a function of any sacred art, but direct control of events through the power of imagination...what the Integrity Knights would call Incarnation.

I could hear the words of Charlotte the giant spider, the familiar sent by Cardinal to observe me on my trip all the way from the remote village of Rulid.

The formal arts are nothing but a tool to harness and refine Incarnation—what you call a mental image. At this point, you need neither chants nor catalysts.

Now wipe your tears and get to your feet. Feel the prayer of the flowers.

Feel the ways of the world…

From the moment I fell into a closed-off state immediately after fighting Administrator on the top floor of Central Cathedral of the Axiom Church, to the moment I recovered just minutes ago, I had been deeply connected to those "ways of the world."

I could clearly sense the sacred power floating in the air around me and easily convert its elements without requiring any elaborate commands. I had spoken the spell's words earlier when healing Klein, Lisbeth, and the others, but I probably could have produced the same effect with my imagination alone.

At the moment, I had wind elements forming a protective barrier around Asuna and me, and I was also popping those wind elements in succession from behind to propel us like a jet engine. It was many times faster than a dragon, I was sure, but it was still going to take at least five minutes to catch up to Alice on Amayori to the south of us.

There were so many things I wanted to say to Asuna, so many things to apologize and thank her for, while we had this time. But as we flew together, hands clasped, I found I could not look at her.

The reason was that just after I reawakened and the omnipotent sensation of my body's blood turning into light finally faded, the memories of what had happened to me recently started coming back to me, clarifying and ordering themselves.

The big problem was what had happened late last night.

As I lay in the center of the tent, Asuna and Alice and Ronie and Sortiliena sat around me, each of them telling stories about me…Specifically, revealing stories of my many bad behaviors and incidents over the years. Recalling it was a living hell.

Kirito snuck right out of the academy to buy honey pies from the

Jumping Deer and nut cookies from the Sunflower and brought them back for Tiese and me, Ronie had said.

And when I graduated, he gave me a whole bunch of zephilia flowers that only bloom in the western empire. He said it took an entire year to make them bloom here, Liena had bragged.

When we were climbing the outer wall of the cathedral, Kirito pulled a steamed bun out of his pocket and gave me half. He tried to warm it up with heat elements and nearly burned it to a crisp, Alice had added.

The very first time I met him, he gave me cream to spread on black bread. And there were the blueberry tarts and huge roll cakes and all the other things we ate together..., Asuna had finished wistfully.

For some reason, they'd kept competing to one-up the others with food-based stories. After that came all the things I'd done and the things I'd said, one after the other, without end...

"Ah..."

I put my head in my hands, despite the fact that we were flying at high speed, and screamed.

"Aaaaaah!"

Instantly, my concentration was lost, and the generation and activation of wind elements stopped. My body was blasted with sudden, ferocious wind resistance, and I started to go into a tailspin.

I muttered a panicked curse and spread out my wide, long coat into the form of black wings that gave me aerial stability again. But my relief was highly temporary, because—

"Eyaaaaaa!!"

—Asuna came plummeting from above, screaming. I reached out to catch her. The attempt was successful—but not by much— and she looked back at me with big hazel-brown eyes, face-to-face. If I was going to apologize, now was the time.

"Asuna, it's not what you think!!"

That was an excuse, not an apology, but it was too late to stop now.

"Liena and Alice and Ronie, there was nothing between us! I swear to Stacia, nothing at all happened!!" I pleaded.

Asuna stared at me...and her face crinkled into a smile. She placed her slender hands on my cheeks and said, with both exasperation and fondness, "You haven't changed, Kirito. They say you were fighting and fighting in here for two years, so I wondered if maybe that would have made you...more mature...but..."

Clear liquid suddenly sprang from Asuna's eyes. Her lips trembled, and her voice grew hoarse. "I'm so glad...It's really you, Kirito...You haven't changed at all...You're still my Kirito..."

Her words penetrated deep into my chest. I felt something hot begin to rise within me, but I caught it before it could reach my throat.

"...I'm just me. Of course that won't change."

"But...but you're like a god now. You froze that entire huge army all at once...then fully healed two hundred people in a single moment...and now you can fly..."

I couldn't help but chuckle at that. "No, I've just figured out how this world works better than most. Once you get used to the concept, you'll be able to fly very quickly, too, Asuna."

"...I don't need to."

"What?"

"I'd rather have you fly and carry me in your arms like this," she said, smiling and sniffling, and took her hands off my cheeks to circle my back instead, where she squeezed me tight. I returned her embrace.

"Thank you...thank you, Asuna. You suffered all those terrible wounds to help protect the people of the Underworld...I'm sure it must have been agony..."

It was two years ago, when a goblin captain slashed me in a cave under the mountains, that I had learned just how real the pain was in this world. The blade had only carved a little bit of the flesh of my shoulder, but it had hurt so bad I couldn't even stand up for a while.

Asuna, however, had faced an army summoned by PoH and

never stopped fighting, even as she suffered gruesome wounds all over her body. Without Asuna's hard effort, Tiese and Ronie and the rest of the Human Guardian Army would have been eliminated long ago.

"No...it wasn't just me," she said, her cheek moving against mine. "Shino-non and Leafa and Liz and Silica and Klein and Agil...and the Sleeping Knights and everyone from *ALO*—they all did incredibly. And Renly the Integrity Knight, the guards of the human army, Sortiliena, Ronie, Tiese..."

Suddenly, Asuna gasped, and her body went tense. I had a feeling I knew why, even before she said it.

"Oh...Kirito! The commander...Bercouli went chasing after the enemy emperor, all on his own, and..."

"......"

I nodded to her without a word, then shook my head.

I was already aware that the massive strength of Bercouli Synthesis One, the oldest of the Integrity Knights, whom I'd never had the chance to speak to in person, was already gone from this earth.

Just before this war started, we'd shared a brief clash of imaginary swords—Incarnate Swords. As the memory came back to me, I realized that Bercouli had already sensed his coming death at the time.

For the conclusion of his life of three hundred years, he'd chosen to fight to protect Alice.

Asuna understood the meaning of my gesture, clutched me even harder, and wept. It did not last long, however; she stifled her sobs to ask, "Is Alice...all right...?"

"Yeah, he hasn't caught her yet. She's going to reach the southern end of the Dark Territory very soon...and get to the third system console. But there's a massive presence chasing after her..."

"I see...In that case, we have to protect her. For Bercouli."

When Asuna pulled away, her face was wet with tears but firmly resolved. I gave her a slow nod. Her eyes wavered a tiny bit.

"But for now...just for this brief moment, be my Kirito alone," she whispered. Her lips approached and met mine.

Beneath the red sky of another world, flanked by black wings that flapped slowly, Asuna and I shared a long, passionate kiss.

In that moment, at last, I recalled why I had awakened in this world two and a half years ago.

It was the last Monday of June in the real world.

As I walked Asuna back home, we were attacked by the third perpetrator of the Death Gun incident, the principal member of the red guild, Laughing Coffin: Johnny Black. My memory of the scene ended when I was injected with a muscle relaxant by his high-pressure injection gun. I probably went into respiratory arrest, suffered some kind of brain damage, and was put into the Underworld with the STL for restorative purposes.

Through whatever twist of fate, Laughing Coffin's leader, PoH, was among the group that attacked the *Ocean Turtle*, and he was now stuck in the ground of the Dark Territory, transformed into a miniature version of the Gigas Cedar. When the time acceleration started again, he would be stuck without vision or hearing for days, possibly weeks, before he was pulled out of the system. However long it would be, he would suffer some kind of mental damage—possibly as bad as mine had been the last six months. It was cruel, I believed—but not unnecessarily so.

He had tried to murder Asuna…and other people I truly cared about.

After many seconds where our existences felt like they were melting together into one, our lips came apart.

"Doesn't it remind you of back then…?" Asuna said, her look pensive. I knew why.

She was remembering the moment right after *SAO*, the game of death, had been beaten, when we'd shared a kiss under a sunset sky, against the backdrop of the collapsing castle. But that had been a kiss of parting.

To sweep away any hint of foreboding, I grinned and said, "C'mon—let's go. Let's beat Emperor Vecta, save Alice, and get everyone back to the real wo—"

Before I could finish that last word, a panicked voice spoke directly inside my head.

Kirito!! Kirigaya!! Can you hear me, Kirito?!

That gravelly voice...

"Uh...is that Mr. Kikuoka? How are you talking to me without a system console around...?"

I don't have to explain that to you! We've got major trouble!! It's the time acceleration...They've tampered with the safety limiter on the FLA!!

———⌇———

Critter watched, slightly uneasily, as Brigg's bearded face turned red and sweaty as he tweaked the two wires around in the keyhole.

Brigg had eagerly nominated himself for the lock-picking job, but given the importance of the time accelerator's safety function, it wasn't just some simple old-school cylinder lock. With time, his finger movements got more and more violent, and the volume of his curses rose.

Right behind Brigg, Hans checked his digital wristwatch and gleefully announced, "That's three minutes. Two more, and you owe me fifty bucks."

"Shut the hell up! Two minutes is nothing...Once I get this open, I'll be able to spend a night in Hawaii on the way...home..."

The sound of the wires rotating the lock was sounding less like unlocking and more like destruction. Critter wanted to interject and tell him to stop there, but now that the other two had put a bet on the result, there was no stopping them.

"And *one* minute left! Get ready to pay up."

"For fuck's sake!!" Brigg finally shouted. He got to his feet and threw the wires to the floor.

Critter was relieved that he had finally given up on picking the lock—until the red-faced soldier drew his massive handgun from its holster and pressed the muzzle to the lock.

"Hey, hey, whoa......"

One blast. Then another.

Brigg put the pistol back in his holster, then looked at the stunned Hans and Critter and shrugged.

"Lock's picked."

Critter stared at the two-inch hole left in the console panel with his mouth hanging open. Two or three little bursts of sparks lit up the darkness of the hole, and then the operating lever, which was still in its tilted position, began to move again. After about five inches, it came to a stop with a little thunk. On the monitor, the readout was not just above ×1,200, where Critter had wanted to test it. The number on the screen glowed ×5,000, the maximum value.

"...F-five......"

He tried to calculate on the spot how many minutes one second of real time would take at that speed—when there was another dull metallic sound.

"N...no way......"

Critter gaped as he saw the number on the monitor go *past* five thousand, then past ten thousand...

No way, we're still fine. As long as nobody touches the activation button, it won't actually change the acceleration rate. I can still pull the lever back, and it'll be like nothing ever happened.

"Don't...don't touch it!! Nobody touch it!!" he shrieked, waving Hans and Brigg away from the console.

Then he snuck closer and carefully reached out.

And just before his hand could touch the lever—*boom.*

There was a soft little bursting sound.

The red activation button and its plastic cover blew off.

Then the huge monitor on the wall of the main control room turned red, and an unpleasant alarm blared out of the speakers. A countdown appeared, starting at fifteen minutes and spinning downward with alarming speed.

—∿∿—

When he heard the alarm that indicated the acceleration rate was being altered again, Higa tried to jump up once more and grimaced in pain.

"Higa! We just told you to calm down," Dr. Koujiro said, rushing over and putting a hand to Higa's back.

At that very moment, the main monitor of the sub-control room turned red.

"Wh-what's that?!" shouted Kikuoka. With Rinko's support, Higa could see past the commander's shoulder to the screen.

Displayed in a bold font were a fifteen-minute countdown and a warning message that all three safety-limit stages on the FLA system were unlocked and that the entire Underworld was heading into a maximum-acceleration phase.

"Wha.........?"

Higa was speechless. Instead, Dr. Koujiro took it upon herself to ask, "What does that mean, maximum acceleration?! Wasn't the limit of the FLA twelve hundred times the normal speed?!"

"...That's the limit when a flesh-and-blood human is in a dive... but artificial fluctlights can go up to five thousand...," Higa said mechanically, pulling the number from memory.

The scientist's chilly eyes tightened dangerously. "Five thousand?! Then that means...one second here is about eighty minutes...Just eighteen seconds will correspond to an entire day!!"

Her mental arithmetic was impressive. But Higa and Kikuoka shared a look and shook their heads awkwardly.

"Huh...? What do I have wrong?"

"Twelve hundred is a safety limit taking the life span of the human soul into account...and five thousand is just the limit of what we can observe as it's happening in the Underworld. But neither of them is the actual limit of the hardware..."

Higa's throat was burning, bone-dry. Dr. Koujiro's arm twitched as it held him around his back.

"Th-then," she asked tremulously, "what is...the hardware limit...?"

"As you know, the Underworld is constructed by and calculated with light quantums. Its transmission speed within the Main Visualizer is theoretically limitless...meaning that the actual limit is placed on it by the architecture of the lower server..."

"Get to the point! What's the number?!"

He pulled his gaze away from the screen to look at Rinko. "In the maximum-acceleration phase...the FLA rate is just a bit over *five million* to one. The two STLs in Roppongi can't manage that sort of speed over the satellite connection, so they'll get cut off automatically...but Kirigaya and Asuna in the STLs onboard the *Ocean Turtle*..."

A minute of real-world time would be equal to ten years in the Underworld. Rinko calculated the number instantly, and her eyes went so wide they twitched with shock.

"My...my God...We have to...we have to get Asuna and Kirigaya out of those STLs right away!!" she gasped, attempting to stand, but this time Higa held her arm back.

"No, Rinko! It's already in an early acceleration phase—if you try to pull them out of the machine now, they'll suffer fluctlight damage!!"

"Then perform the operation to disengage them!!"

"Why do you think I went down the cable duct?! You can only perform STL operations from the main control room!!" shrieked Higa, his voice rising.

He looked at the commander, who stood before the console. Kikuoka already seemed to understand where Higa was going with this.

"...Kiku, I'm going down there again."

Sergeant First Class Aki looked horrified by this notion and opened her mouth to say something, then stopped herself. Instead, she approached and murmured, "I'll take out the catheter now."

The commander scowled bitterly but nodded. "All right. I'll go, too. I'm strong enough to carry you down that ladder, I think."

"N...no, Lieutenant Colonel!!" shouted Lieutenant Nakanishi, the leader of the security team. He strode forward crisply, his face pale. "It's too dangerous. I'll—"

"We need you to defend the stairs. This will require opening the pressure barrier again...and we don't have Ichiemon this time, plus Niemon's not operational."

Everyone in the sub-control room looked to the left back corner.

The human silhouette hanging from a coat-hanger-like support frame did not belong to an actual human. It was a humanoid machine body that Higa had researched and developed as a part of Project Alicization called the Electroactive Muscled Operative Machine #2, nicknamed Niemon. Compared to Ichiemon, which had been used as a decoy in the previous barrier-opening mission and destroyed, Niemon had been given a greatly improved appearance, as it was developed to hold a lightcube on board.

Naturally, the socket on its head was currently empty, so even if turned on, it would not move. It couldn't be an autonomous shield the way that Ichiemon was.

Kikuoka looked away from the soulless robot and back to Nakanishi. With a tremendously stern look, he gave the officer orders.

"You will be engaging directly with the enemy, so your danger is clearly higher. But I need you to go."

Nakanishi clenched his jaw and snapped off a salute. "Sir, yes, sir!"

While the military officers were talking, Higa timidly lifted his hand. It hurt, but at least his fingers were capable of moving.

The countdown to the maximum-acceleration phase on the monitor was down to ten minutes and change. But to reopen the pressure-resistant barrier wall, climb down that endless ladder, and perform the STL disengagement from the monitoring port there would take at least thirty minutes.

And in the extra twenty minutes, two hundred years was going to pass inside the Underworld. That would easily surpass the 150 years that were the life span of the human soul. And even before that point, it would still be an unbearable, seemingly infinite length of time for real-world people to suffer inside the Underworld...

Inside the Underworld.........

"Yes...that's it!!" cried Higa. He swung his left arm, from which the blood-transfusion catheter had just been removed, toward Kikuoka. "K-Kiku!! When I operated the STL earlier, I set up a communication channel to Kirito! Talk to him on line C-12!!"

"B-but...what should I say...?"

"Tell him to escape from inside!! If he either reaches a system console or loses all his HP in the next ten minutes, the STL will automatically begin disengagement protocol!! But once the maximum-acceleration phase begins, the console won't function, and dying would be even worse!! You'd have to live out two hundred years with all your sensory organs blocked...Just warn him all about that!!"

—∿∿—

"Two..."

Two hundred years?!

I barely caught the words before they flew out of my mouth. Inches away from my face, Asuna looked befuddled; she couldn't hear Kikuoka's voice the way I could.

"Listen to me, Kirito—you have ten minutes! You need to get to the console and log out in that time!! And if that's impossible, you can also reduce your HP to zero...but that's not as certain, and it's more dangerous. That's because..."

We might be forced to live out two centuries in a simulated state of death, I already knew. So I cut Kikuoka off and said, "Got it. I'll try to find a way to escape through the console! With Alice, of course—so be ready for that outcome!"

"...I'm sorry. In fact, I want you to prioritize your own escape over Alice's status. Listen, even if we could erase your memory after you log out, two hundred years is far beyond the life span of

the human soul! The likelihood we could bring you back to consciousness is...almost zero...," Kikuoka said, the bitterness clear in his voice.

"Don't worry—I'll come back," I stated softly. "And, Mr. Kikuoka, I apologize for what I said to you half a year ago...I mean, last night."

"Don't. We deserve every last bit of criticism. I'll make sure we've got bandages for all the punches you owe us...All right, looks like Higa's ready. I've got to go."

"Okay. I'll see you in ten minutes, Mr. Kikuoka."

The signal ended there.

I was still hovering in midair, coat hem flapping to keep us aloft, Asuna held tight in my arms.

"...Kirito, did you get some kind of message from Mr. Kikuoka? Was it...something bad?" she asked.

I shook my head from side to side. "No...he just said that the time rate's going to accelerate again in ten minutes, so he wants us to hurry it up."

Asuna blinked, then gave me a little smile. "Of course. It wouldn't be fair to Alice if we're just floating around doing *this*. Let's go save her!"

"Yeah. I'm going to start flying again."

I clutched Asuna and generated another huge mass of wind elements. A gust of glowing-green wind arose to envelop us.

And so I flew to the south, sensing Alice's distant presence—and the massive abnormality that pursued her.

2

He's going to catch me.

Alice, atop Amayori's saddle, looked over her shoulder and bit her lip.

The eerie black dot in the red sky was clearly larger than it had been five minutes ago. It wasn't that the enemy's speed had picked up; Amayori and Takiguri were simply running out of strength.

That only made sense, because they'd been flying consecutively without any breaks. If anything, it was a miracle that they'd brought her this far. They'd traveled a distance many times greater than the length of the human territory—from Centoria to the End Mountains—in just half a day. Both dragons were clearly expending great amounts of life to continue flying at this point.

But why wasn't her pursuer losing stamina, then?

From what she could tell upon performing a farseeing art with crystal elements, he was riding an odd creature that was not at all like the dragons. It would best be described as a disc with wings. She'd never seen such a thing in the human realm or the Dark Territory.

According to the archer named Sinon—another visitor from Kirito's "real world"—her pursuer was indeed the emperor of the Dark Territory, the God of Darkness, Vecta, but at the same time, he was a real-world person in an antagonistic position to Kirito and Sinon.

Emperor Vecta had lost earlier to Commander Bercouli's sacrificial attack—the Memory Release art of the Time-Splitting Sword, most likely. But he had come back to this place in a new form to continue his pursuit of Alice.

That horrifying resurrection, which seemed to mock Bercouli's death, filled her with a rage that would never be quelled. But as she flew alone, Alice found the time to discover what she truly ought to do.

If the enemy was immortal in this world, then he would need to be killed in the real world. And to do that, she would need to reach the World's End Altar.

Ahead, far across the red sky, she could see the faint outline of a cliff face on an impossible scale. It was the Wall at the End of the World, as spoken of in the founding myth. Unlike the mountains around the human realm, which a dragon could fly over, the cliff that surrounded the Dark Territory was said to have an immeasurable height.

Just before the sheer wall, at about the same height at which Alice was flying, hovered a small island in the air, all alone.

It looked like a little cup with a pointed bottom. She couldn't guess what force was keeping it floating in the air like that. Upon closer examination, there appeared to be some kind of artificial construction in the center of its flat top. That was probably none other than the World's End Altar. The exit of this world, and the entrance to the real world.

Fewer than ten kilors remained between her and the altar, but Emperor Vecta was likely to catch up to her just a bit before she reached the floating island, sadly.

Alice took a deep breath and exhaled. Then she brushed the neck of her dragon. "Thank you, Amayori and Takiguri. This is far enough. Take me down to the ground," she commanded.

The beasts crooned weakly and began a parallel spiral descent. The ground below had turned into a chilly-looking dark-gray desert not long ago. It was just an empty sea of sand, as though the gods had gotten bored of creation and stopped there. The dragons came to a lengthy landing and practically collapsed.

Alice immediately jumped off the back of Amayori, who trilled, *frululululu*, from deep in its throat. She rummaged in the leather saddlebag and pulled out the one little bottled elixir still left. Then she poured half of the blue liquid into Amayori's slack mouth and the rest of it into the mouth of the older brother nearby. Even the Axiom Church's spiritual elixir wasn't nearly enough to recover the massive life total of the majestic dragons, but it should at least give them the strength to take off again.

She reached out with both hands to scratch the soft hair beneath the chins of both dragons at once.

"Amayori. Takiguri."

Just saying their names brought tears to her eyes. She fought the urge to cry and continued, "This is good-bye. My final order to you…Fly back to the human world and return to your dragon nests in the west. Amayori, find yourself a husband—Takiguri, find yourself a wife. Bear many children and raise them to be strong. Strong enough that they can carry knights, too."

Amayori suddenly raised its head and licked Alice's cheek. Takiguri nuzzled her waist and sniffed at the Frostscale Whip hanging there, which had belonged to Eldrie.

Once they pulled away from her, Alice commanded, "Go!! Fly straight and do not turn back!!"

Krululululu!! the dragons trilled, lifting their necks. They stood up and began to run to the west without looking back. Their wings spread wide, grabbing the desert air and lifting their massive bodies. Brother and sister beat their wings, which were so close that their ends nearly touched, lifting off at the same time.

Amayori *did* crane its long neck around, though. The dragon's beautiful crystalline eye stared straight at Alice. A large droplet of liquid filled its lid, then sparkled as it fell free.

"Ama…yori…?" Alice murmured.

But before she could even finish speaking the dragon's name, it and its brother dragon tilted to their right, making a hard turn. With fierce bellows, they rose in a straight line not to the west, but dead north. Toward the pursuer in black, who was now close enough to be visible.

"No…no, you can't!! Amayori, nooooo!!" she screamed, breaking into a run.

But the fine sand of the desert clung to her boots. Alice fell to the ground, hands outstretched, and could only watch as Amayori and Takiguri shot higher into the sky toward the invincible enemy.

Silver scales caught the red sunlight and blazed like flame.

Jaws full of glittering sharp teeth opened wide.

The sibling dragons unleashed their greatest weapon as soon as the pursuer was within range: their heat beams. White light shot across the sky, like a manifestation of their very life force burning.

The enemy, atop his strange mount, did not bother to change his flight path in the face of the oncoming superheated flame. He simply held out his left hand and spread his fingers.

There was no way to defend against it. The dragons' beams were the highest-priority attack in the world, with the exception of the Integrity Knights' Perfect Weapon Control arts, and certain multilayered spells cast by groups of elite arts-users. And this was *two* beams. There was not enough time to execute a defensive art strong enough to counteract them.

Or so Alice estimated.

And prayed.

But the two screaming, resonating beams of pure heat did not envelop the enemy's body in their all-consuming power. Instead, something that beggared Alice's understanding occurred.

A swirl of absolute darkness grew from the pursuer's palm.

It looked as though the space around it simply warped and stretched to fall *into* the darkness. Even the all-powerful fire from the dragons was no exception. The direct path of the beams curved, sucked toward the man's palm.

And with nothing more than a brief little illumination, and no flashing or explosions, the two lines of heat were devoured by the darkness.

Alice did not miss the sight of a faint smile stretching across the enemy's mouth, despite the fact that he was only a black dot flying high enough that no art or sword strike could reach him.

Then, with a horrible noise like scraping sand, the blackness surrounding the man's left hand shot out several bolts of black lightning.

It was as if he had swallowed the dragons' fire breath and made that power his own. The lightning burst mercilessly through their wings and limbs. The two dragons lurched, and blood even redder than the sky behind it sprayed into the void.

"Ah…ah……," Alice gasped. She hurled her hands upward. "Amayoriiii!! Get away!! You don't have to do this!! Just fly awaaaay!!"

She knew that the dragons could hear her scream. But the mounts seemed to be only spurred on further by the sound of her voice. They beat their wings and charged again.

Their mouths opened wide. From between their fangs, the air wavered with heat haze, and light flickered unsteadily.

Zwamp!! The heat beams scorched the sky a second time.

Once again, the man deployed a shield of darkness and let the flames hit it. This was clearly leading to another counterattack, like the last one, but the dragons boldly continued their charge. They beat their wings furiously, even while the beams lasted, trying to get as close as possible to the enemy.

The blood spray from their wounds turned to flame. Their silver scales fell loose, disintegrating into motes of light in the air.

The dragons' very existence was converting into light elements.

Those beams of light, representing their very life force burning away, began to fill the dark vortex, saturating it. White smoke began to rise from the man's palm, which was seemingly unable to withstand the raging heat.

But just after that, a veil of smoky, black darkness covered his entire form. The hungering void in his hand grew in power, and soon its black lightning began to push back the white heat beams.

For just one second, there was parity between the dueling strength of white and black, and then it was all the other way.

Countless bolts of crackling black lightning seized upon Amayori and Takiguri, whose wings were finally slowing from lack of strength.

"Amayori!! Amayoriiiiii!!" screamed Alice, but all her words landed upon was endless desert sand, like her tears.

In that moment, the stars fell.

Two gleaming stars, dropping out of the red sky at tremendous speed.

One headed straight for the ground.

The other came to a complete stop right in the median point between the dragons and the pursuer. The light itself disintegrated, revealing what it was hiding within.

A person.

A swordsman.

Slightly shaggy black hair and a long black coat trailed in the wind. White and black swords crossed each other behind his back. His arms were folded over his chest, and he stared calmly at the approaching storm of darkness.

Bam!! Bzzsh!!

Lightning blasted the swordsman. But not quite—it only deflected off him without making contact. It was as though an invisible wall stood before the still figure with arms folded, blocking the lightning and forcing it to discharge harmlessly into empty air.

Alice held her breath and watched through wide eyes.

Then the black-clad swordsman turned and looked down at her.

His youthful face crinkled into a smile, and his dark eyes were strong with purpose. Alice felt sparks shooting deep in her chest. The heat instantly spread, burning her insides, filling her heart with drive.

She could feel more tears were flooding into her eyes now. "Kiri...to……"

The swordsman, awake again after a half-year slumber, gave her a nod with a smile that was powerful but somehow shy, then turned away and raised his right hand in front of him. He pointed toward the dying dragons, who were flapping their wings with the last bit of strength remaining. The tips of their wings and the ends of their tails were already melting into light.

Amayori looked at Kirito, with whom it had lived for half a year at the cottage outside of Rulid, and trilled softly.

Kirito nodded back to it and closed his eyes.

Without warning, iridescent film surrounded the two dragons. It was like a giant soap bubble had formed around them. But the dragons were not alarmed; they folded their wings, tucked in their heads, and rolled into balls.

The rainbow orb slowly descended directly over Alice. She was so stunned that she nearly forgot to breathe.

And then something very strange happened. The enormous rainbow-tinted bodies of Amayori and Takiguri began to shrink. No, not shrink—they were getting youthful, growing in reverse.

Sharp talons rounded. Thick, hard scales reverted into soft, downy growths. Their tails and necks shrank, and smaller wings sprouted fine hair.

By the time they came down to Alice's outstretched arms, the dragons were less than fifty cens in size. Takiguri was covered in a white pelt with a bluish tint, its eyes closed in peaceful sleep.

And Amayori was like a green ball of fluff, the same way as when she'd first met it at Central Cathedral. The little dragon looked right at Alice, opened its jaws to expose teeth like little pearls, and trilled, "*Kyuru!!*"

"Ama…yori…," Alice gasped. Tears trickled down her cheeks and sparkled as they bounced off the dragon's soft, feathery hide.

The rainbow film surrounding the two infant dragons grew brighter, all at once. The sensation of soft feathers on Alice's arms turned to smooth hardness. After a few blinks, she realized that she was cradling two large eggs.

The silvery eggs shrank smaller and smaller, until they were capable of resting side by side in the palm of her hand, and the rainbow glow around them faded at last.

As she nestled the eggs against her cheek, Alice tried to interpret what had just happened. Kirito must have determined that the maximum value of Amayori's and Takiguri's lives was so great that sacred arts alone could not restore it. So instead, he shrank that maximum value as small as it could go—effectively returning them to their embryonic egg form and preventing them from reaching death.

Alice was currently the most powerful user of sacred arts in the entire world, and even she couldn't imagine what combination could produce such an effect. But she was not worried. The only thought she kept was warm certainty that she would one day meet the dragons again.

She wrapped the two eggs between her hands gently and looked up to the sky again.

"Thank you…and welcome back, Kirito," she whispered tearily.

There was no way her voice could reach the figure floating in the distant sky, but the man in the black coat nodded firmly back to her and smiled again. She heard a familiar voice in her mind.

No. I'm sorry for having put you through so much. Thank you, Alice. We'll meet again in the real world.

Then Kirito slowly turned and faced the darkness-shrouded pursuer.

Sparks crackled here and there in empty space, as if the world itself was unable to withstand the pressure of two massive sources of competing Incarnation.

"…Kirito…"

That enemy will not be defeated by any typical attack, even from you, Alice thought, biting her lip in concern.

From very close by, a voice said, "It'll be all right, Alice."

She spun around to see a real-worlder standing near her in pearly-white armor.

"Asuna…"

The girl with long brown hair swaying in the wind just smiled

at her and reached out to touch her back. "Let's put our trust in Kirito. The two of us need to rush to the World's End Altar."

"R-right," she replied, but she knew it would not be as easy as that.

Alice looked to the south, where the Wall at the End of the World rose high above the horizon—and a small white island floated before it.

"The altar is probably atop that island," she said after a moment. "But we can't ride on the dragons anymore, so I don't know how to get up that high…"

"Don't worry. Let me handle that," assured Asuna, drawing a thin sword from her waist. She pointed it at the distant island and let her long lashes droop low.

Suddenly, there was a booming angelic chorus—*Laaaaaaaa!*— just like the one Asuna had heard during the Dark Army's ambush last night. A rainbow of light fell directly downward onto the gray desert from the sky.

The ground rumbled beneath their feet, and a white stone slab rose out of the sand just before them.

Grunk, gru-gru-grunk! Another slab appeared behind it, slightly higher, and then another. Alice watched in awe as a white staircase formed itself in the air, building up to the distant floating island in just a dozen or so seconds.

When the altering of the geography was complete, Asuna lowered her sword and fell to a knee in the sand.

"A-Asuna…!!"

"I'm…fine. Let's hurry…We've only got about eight minutes until the altar closes…"

Closes?

Alice didn't understand the meaning of that in the moment, but Asuna grabbed her by the hand before she could ask. She got to her feet, pulled by Asuna, and began to run up the white stone staircase. As she ran, she glanced over her shoulder to look once more at her pursuer and the swordsman in black facing off in the sky.

*There are many, many things I want to say to you and ask of you.
So you'd better win. Win and then come back to me.*

———

The sight of the two swordfighters practically flying up the white stairs to the island floating over the gray desert was so beautiful, so poetic, so symbolic that I could only marvel at it. I had to sear the image into my mind.

Alice. Asuna.

This is good-bye.

There was a reason I hadn't told Asuna that the acceleration rate was going to reach five million times real speed and that if we didn't escape before then, we'd be trapped in here for two hundred years of perceived time.

If they knew that, both Asuna and Alice would stand with me to fight. Even if it meant they'd fail to escape before the time limit.

As soon as I'd become conscious of the presence of the foe pursuing Alice, I'd shivered at the alienness of his nature. But in fact, *presence* wasn't even the right word. The only *thing* there was nothing. He was a void, a black hole that devoured all information, even light.

The chances of defeating an enemy like this before the time limit, then escaping with all three of us present, was extremely low.

So that made it clear to me what my priority should be: I had to log Asuna and Alice out of the Underworld. Nothing could come before that—nothing.

So I fixed the painting-like image of beauty below me into my mind, then turned away to face the enemy hovering nearby.

It was utterly unfathomable, now that I was finally facing off with it.

It was male. I was pretty sure of that.

But that was all I was sure of.

The form of his face, if it was an avatar of his choosing, seemed to be intentionally designed to match the "average white male" appearance. His features weren't bad; it was just that there was nothing *notable* about them. He could only be described as having white skin, blue eyes, and blond hair.

His physical figure was utterly average for a white male. A body, neither fat nor skinny, wrapped in a military jacket. It wasn't clear whether that meant he was a soldier—because the jacket's black-and-gray camouflage pattern was constantly shifting and moving like some kind of slime mold. He also had a sword on his left side that appeared to be a Divine Object.

Asuna had warned me on the trip here that this man was a member of the special-ops team that had invaded the *Ocean Turtle*. That would make him a mercenary hired by some group or company looking to steal tech related to artificial fluctlights. But the man floating there and staring at me with lifeless marble-like eyes did not feel like the type of human being who was motivated by crass concerns like money. He didn't feel like a human being at all.

When one second had passed, I spoke.

"…Who are you?"

His answer was immediate. The man's voice was smooth and yet somehow metallic in nature.

"One who seeks, steals, and snatches away."

Instantly, the aura of darkness surrounding his being writhed and amplified. I felt a slight breeze blowing from behind. The air—the very information that made up the world—was being sucked into the darkness.

"What do you seek?"

"Souls."

With each answer, the suction increased. It wasn't just the information of the world, either—I felt my own consciousness beginning to succumb to that empty gravity.

Then something resembling an expression floated past his lips. The faintest of smiles, but one utterly removed from anything you might call emotion.

"And who are you? Why are you here? What right do you have to stand before me?"

Who...am I?

The hero the Underworld always needed? Hardly.

A knight who protects the human realm? No.

Each suggestion that came to my mind was rejected, and each slipped right out of me, like it was being stolen. And yet, for some reason, I couldn't stop the thoughts from coming.

The hero who defeated the deadly game of SAO? No.

The greatest VRMMO player alive? No.

The Black Swordsman? The Dual-Wielder? No, no.

None of those things were what I wanted.

So what was I...?

I could feel my mind starting to fade, to slip away—when I thought I heard a familiar voice call my name.

My head rose—I hadn't realized it had dipped—and I named myself as I had been called.

"I'm Kirito. Kirito the Swordsman."

Bzak!! Sparks flew, and the tendrils of darkness clinging to me were cut loose. Immediately, my mind felt sharp and focused again.

What just happened to me?

Was this man using the STL to interfere directly with my mind? I hastily strengthened the defensive wall of imagination around me and focused on the man's eyes. They were truly empty—bottomless darkness that absorbed the minds of others.

"...And your name is?" I asked, barely realizing what I was doing.

The man thought briefly. "Gabriel. My name is Gabriel Miller."

I could sense that this was not a character name or an online alias but the man's actual identity. For just a few seconds, his appearance had changed. His gaze had become sharper, icy, dangerous. His lips pulled back, and his cheekbones sharpened.

As his features returned to that earlier fake look, the aura of darkness he exuded instantly thickened. At this stage, I finally realized that the man's right arm was entirely missing from the shoulder down. The unsteady mass of darkness that was acting as his right arm slid down to his left side and grabbed the sword.

He drew it with a squelch, but the sword did not have a physical blade to it. There was just an empty darkness there, extending about three feet from the hilt like black fire. It was a truly unreal thing.

With his shadow arm holding a blade of malignant darkness, the man swung it forth, the blade issuing an eerie vibration. I distanced myself a bit and pulled out the two swords over my shoulders—Blue Rose in my left hand, Night Sky in my right.

In terms of blackness, the sword carved from the Gigas Cedar's branch was no slouch itself. But while my sword reflected the light like some black crystal substance, the man's sword was as dark as if the space itself had been removed from existence. This was a level beyond PoH's Mate-Chopper and its ability to absorb resources.

But there was no retreat, not even against the most unfathomable of opponents. I had to hold off this enemy until Asuna and Alice could finish climbing that staircase hundreds of yards tall.

"Let's go, Gabriel!!" I said, choosing to speak his name. The wing-shaped ends of my coat flapped powerfully, pushing me upward. I crossed the swords before my body.

"Generate All Elements!"

Using the air around me itself as a terminal, I generated dozens of each and every type of element, then activated all of them at once as I fell.

"Discharge!!"

Flaming arrows, spears of ice, blades of wind, and many other elements raced through the air. My swords swung downward, following the spells.

Gabriel Miller did not move a muscle to evade any of it. He just grinned thinly and spread his hands.

Omnicolored light stabbed through the blue-tinged darkness covering his body.

I didn't miss the way he faltered briefly above the waist. I slashed his torso with my right sword and thrust through his chest with my left. The sticky darkness burst aside, leaving a chill on my skin where it brushed me.

My momentum took me past him a good distance before I turned back toward him.

I caught sight of the darkness pulling back in from its undefined shape—and Gabriel turning to face me as though nothing had happened. There wasn't a single scratch on his jacket.

I knew it.

He had the ability to absorb and drain slashes, thrusts, flames, ice, wind, water projectiles, steel arrows, crystal edges, light beams, and dark curses.

And my right shoulder, which his sword of nothingness had brushed when we passed each other, sprayed blood from the place where both coat and flesh had simply vanished.

Gabriel Miller glanced down at the Priestess of Light, Alice, and the other girl with her as they ran up the white staircase hanging in the air. He gauged their time of arrival at the system console to be five minutes from now.

That meant he couldn't be wasting time with this bothersome interloper. The logical choice would be to neutralize the young man and proceed to the floating island quickly. But Gabriel found himself just the tiniest bit interested in his opponent and chose to hover here.

At first glance, he was nothing but a child. Compared to the aged swordsman he'd fought to mutual death earlier, there was nothing imposing about this boy. Like Sinon, he was probably some Japanese VRMMO player cooperating with Rath somehow, but even that girl had more presence than he did.

For one thing, the boy was exuding barely anything you might call fighting spirit.

There had been a brief moment when Gabriel was able to glean his will, when he asked who he was, but that circuit had closed instantly. Since then, he'd deflected all of Gabriel's mental feelers as completely as though he was covered in a transparent shell. There was no joy in fighting an enemy whose mind he couldn't taste.

Better to eliminate him at once and go after Alice, Gabriel thought briefly.

But when the young man transformed the ends of his coat into wings, then wielded all kinds of magic at once, Gabriel changed his mind a bit. He sensed that the boy was accustomed to this world.

Once Gabriel acquired Alice and the Soul Translation tech and fled to a third country, he still had to do the work of building a virtual world just for himself and to his exact liking. Stealing this young man's level of control wouldn't be a bad idea, to ensure that he could perform the task efficiently.

So the first step would be to crack the shell of his imagination.

Gabriel smiled almost imperceptibly, then spoke in Japanese to the boy in black.

"I'll give you three minutes. Entertain me."

———∞———

"How very generous of you," I muttered, sealing the wound on my shoulder with a single trace of a finger.

There was plenty backing up Gabriel Miller's confidence, however. For one thing, the fact that he was immune to basically any kind of attack.

No, there must be at least one kind of attack that works on him. I'm sure that it was Sinon who blew his arm off—she was fighting him first. She must have imagined her Hecate II rifle and shot him with it. That would mean that even Gabriel can't absorb a bullet attack.

It couldn't be a coincidence that he was also wearing a military jacket. He would know the power of an antimateriel sniper rifle from real-life experience, and perhaps that meant he couldn't completely negate the thought of the damage he would suffer with willpower alone.

But Sinon would be able to materialize a gun in the Underworld only because it was as familiar to her as her own arms and legs. I couldn't repeat an accomplishment like that, and even if I could somehow make a pistol, it wasn't going to have the power to stop him.

In other words, I had to find something aside from a gun that this eerie man would recognize as a source of damage. And that would mean knowing Gabriel as a person. I had to figure out how he lived, what he wanted, and why he was here.

I held my swords perfectly still before me and let a smile curl the corners of my mouth.

"All right. I'll give you some entertainment."

Where was his confidence coming from?

Clearly he had spent a long time logged in to the Underworld and was very familiar with the systems that underpinned this world, but he was still just a child. A gamer. He'd just been shown that his flashy swordsmanship and fanciful magic attacks were completely meaningless. How could he still wear that impertinent smile?

Gabriel found the fearless attitude to be mildly unpleasant and came to the conclusion that it must be a bluff to buy time.

The boy knew that dying in this world would have no ill effects on his real-life body, and he was relying upon that knowledge. All he wanted to do was draw out their fight until his companion could escort Alice away safely.

He was just a stupid child, after all. Three minutes was more time than he deserved.

Gabriel raised the empty blade he held in the hand built of

willpower—and stuck it into the back of the winged creature that he rode upon.

The monster was, like his sword and stonebow, simply the repurposed form of the jetpack that his converted character had brought over. While he could control it at will, it was slightly unstable with him being able to touch it with only his feet. A more logical choice would be to turn it into wings only, like the boy was doing.

The monster screeched briefly at the skewer in its back before it was sucked into the void. Gabriel moved the data that came through the blade from his arm to his back and focused his mind.

With a great flapping, black wings just like the boy's sprouted from his shoulder blades. These were not the membraned wings of a bat, but those belonging to a bird of prey, covered in sharp feathers. They were much more suitable for a man bearing the name of an archangel.

"...I've already stolen one thing from you," Gabriel whispered, pointing his empty blade at the young man.

I'd been planning to get rid of the man's flying disc–shaped mount with my next attack, so I was briefly taken aback when got rid of it himself.

He didn't miss his chance. He slid into sword range with a flap of his black eagle wings. The speed of his thrust without any windup was astonishing. I'd taken him for an amateur when it came to swordplay, but that couldn't be further from the truth. I swept my swords upward, aiming their intersection at the point of attack.

Gzyrk!

The sword of inky darkness came to a halt just before my nose with an eerie sound.

The Blue Rose Sword and the Night-Sky Blade rattled violently. While my weapons weren't being corroded, it did feel like I was trying to cut emptiness itself. It wasn't hard to imagine that the actual swords were being put under terrible strain.

But the choice of a Cross Block rather than a backstep was intentional on my part. Rather than pushing back against Gabriel's downward swing, I pushed it to the right and gave him a tremendous high kick.

"Raaah!!" I screamed. The toe of my boot glowed orange as it shot upward and caught his pointed chin. The darkness burst outward, and Gabriel's upper half rocked backward.

How about that?!

I beat the air with my wings, darting backward to add distance between us and give me time to watch him. Maybe it wasn't a gunshot, but if he really was a special-ops commando, he would have taken some combatives training and should recognize the damage of a good blow.

Gabriel's head rocked back into position, but on the surface at least, he was totally unharmed. The darkness that splattered from his chin reformed at once into smooth skin. He rubbed it with his hand and grinned.

"Ah, I see. Unfortunately, that kind of showy action only looks good on TV. Real martial arts are more—"

Fwip!!

The air cracked, and in midsentence, Gabriel rushed at me so fast he was nothing but a blur of black. His sword came down from the left, and I used the Blue Rose Sword to block it on instinct, swinging back with the Night-Sky Blade. The edge caught the top of the enemy's shoulder and, with a sensation like being surrounded by dense liquid, came to a stop.

My right arm was stuck in full extension. Something slithered around it: Gabriel's left arm. It wrapped around me like a thick snake until it had full control of the joint—and with a horrible *gurnch*, I felt agony assault my brain like lightning.

"Aaagh…," I gasped.

Right up close, Gabriel whispered, "—*Like this.*"

That was just the start of a ferocious rush.

The sword of emptiness lashed out with a blinding combo of what felt like infinite strikes. I tried to defend against them with just my left sword, but they slipped past my block here and there, carving out little pieces of me. I had no time to focus on recovering from my broken right arm.

"Hrg...oahg...," I grunted, beating my wings in an attempt to put distance between myself and Gabriel. As I bolted backward, I ran the fingers of my left hand across my other arm, which was just barely able to hold on to its sword.

Right when the light began to gather there, Gabriel raised his hand, curved the fingers like claws, then opened them wide.

Over ten bolts of black lightning spread outward, then bent at sharp angles and bore down on me. I gritted my teeth and put up an imaginary wall for defense. I'd had total confidence when I'd used the same technique to protect Alice's dragons from the lightning, but half of my concentration was going to healing my arm now—and it was that very understanding that weakened the strength of the shield.

Dull vibrations rattled my body in several places. Three bolts of darkness penetrated my shield and drove into my torso and legs. Before the pain, I felt only a ferocious chill running through my senses. There was blue-black nothingness clinging to the places where I was zapped, eating away at my very existence.

"Rrrgh!!" I grunted again, then sucked in a breath and screamed for energy. It dispersed the emptiness, but fresh blood gushed from the new wounds that remained.

"Ha-ha-ha."

I looked up to see Gabriel's empty features twisting with mirth.

"Ha-ha-ha, ha-ha-ha-ha-ha."

It wasn't laughter. His lips were upturned, but the muscles around his eyes were still, and those marble-like eyes swirled only with hunger. Gabriel crossed his arms and made a gesture of gathering power.

The dark aura around him shuddered heavily. It flickered like a violent flame, growing thicker.

"Haaaaaah!!" he roared, throwing his arms wide.

Two new black wings grew above the ones he already had, and they spread themselves outward. Another pair grew from below, too.

Gabriel beat his six wings in order, top to bottom, and gradually gained altitude. A black ring appeared over his head, and his camo jacket lost its shape, transforming into a thin cloth of wriggling darkness.

Somehow, his eyes were no longer human, either. The sockets were filled with nothing but dark light.

He had become an Angel of Death.

A transcendental being that hunted the souls of humans and stole them. What attack could possibly work against a self-image like this?

I tore my eyes from this personification of horror and checked on Asuna and Alice, who were racing up the midair staircase, hand in hand. They had just crossed the halfway point. It would take another two or three minutes for them to get to the floating island.

At this point, I was already losing confidence in my ability to buy that much time.

—◦◦◦—

Sheer omnipotence.

Gabriel laughed a third time at the fabulous power that rippled through his very being.

So this was what imagination—or what the elder swordsman had called Incarnation—could accomplish in this place.

Now he had the same level of power as the swordsman who cut backward in time or the dark general who transformed into a whirlwind giant—even more power, in fact. Gabriel had assumed their abilities were the effect of some system command he didn't know about, but that wasn't true. They simply knew exactly how strong they were. And it was because this black-haired boy had exhibited all his little tricks that Gabriel understood how it really worked.

I shall give you one more minute as a sign of my appreciation.

Gabriel spread his six wings and raised his sword of darkness.

Within the next minute, he would carve up this boy's flesh, extract his soul, and devour it—to gain even greater power.

With dark-purple sparks shrouding his form, Gabriel went into a charge.

—◦◦◦—

I looked up at an enemy that was no longer even human.

There was nothing I could imagine now that he would fear and consider a threat. Even the right arm that Sinon had blown off was perfectly regenerated, a sure sign that even bullets would no longer harm him.

In the end, I just didn't have the willpower.

I hadn't underestimated Gabriel Miller. His eerie, alien nature deserved the highest level of caution. But in a sense, perhaps I had given up on winning this fight before it even started for that very reason. I was thinking only of buying time, extending the fight until Alice and Asuna could escape, so that both he and I would be trapped in Hell for two hundred years, never to return to reality.

Oh...that's it.

Maybe...I wanted this to happen?

A true other reality, something greater than even Aincrad. The utopia that Akihiko Kayaba wanted and tried to create. Wasn't that what the Underworld really was?

In the two years I'd spent trapped in *SAO*, I'd constantly asked myself whether I really wanted to escape. The reason that I was a hesitant member of the frontier group that pushed to clear the game was because I felt a vague premonition that there was a hard time limit on how long I could live there. With my body stuck in a hospital bed and living off only fluids, it was just a matter of time before I wasted away physically.

But in the accelerated time flow of the Underworld, that wasn't a concern. With five million seconds passing here for each one second in reality, there was no need to think about my physical body. I would remain in this world until the life span of my soul reached its end. Could I really claim that I wasn't entertaining that thought, even if only in my subconscious?

And for what result? I wasn't thinking about *them*.

Suguha, Mom, Dad.

Yui, Klein, Agil, Liz, Silica...all the many other people who'd saved me.

And Alice.

Asuna.

All those people who would mourn my loss and shed tears of grief.

In the end, I was a person who was incapable of truly knowing another person's mind.

Nothing about me had changed from the time I'd abandoned that friend in need during middle school...

You're wrong, Kirito.

A familiar voice.

A faint warmth in my frozen left hand.

*   *   *

If you don't want to leave this world, then it's not for your own sake. It's because you love the people you met here.

Selka, Tiese, Ronie, Miss Liena, the people in Rulid, the people you met in Centoria and at the academy, the Integrity Knights and men-at-arms...and Cardinal, and maybe even Administrator... and probably me.

Your love is huge and wide and deep. Enough to bear the weight of the entire world.

But the same can't be said of your opponent.

That man is the one who doesn't know others. He cannot understand them. That's why he seeks. And tries to steal. And tries to destroy. It's because...

He fears us.

—⁓⁓⁓—

Gabriel Miller saw the delicate tears trickle down the boy's cheeks. His sword-bearing hands curled inward toward his chest in fright.

He had succumbed to fear at last.

The fear and despair of death was the one emotion that Gabriel actually shared with other people.

From the day that he'd taken Alicia Clingerman into the woods behind his house to kill her, Gabriel had ended the lives of many people, seeking the shining brilliance of the soul. But he never again saw the cloud of light that he'd witnessed emerging from Alicia's forehead. Instead, he slaked his thirst by tasting the fear of his victims.

What flavor would he taste in the fear of this boy, who was so endlessly confident in himself? The old hunger and thirst roared up from the foundation of his being. Gabriel licked his lips and held his outstretched fingers high.

Little black orbs appeared and buzzed like flies. He lowered his fingers, and the orbs surged with very fine lasers that jabbed into the boy's body from all angles. Moments later, blood sprayed from him in a red mist.

"Ha-ha-ha-ha-ha!!" bellowed Gabriel, rushing downward with his empty sword at the ready.

He easily thrust it through the boy's stomach.

The torso covered in a black shirt and coat was ripped apart by the howling, hungering void and split effortlessly in two.

Blood and flesh, bone and organ, all went flying.

Gabriel thrust his left hand into the midst of that precious ruby-red splatter. He grabbed the largest pulsating jewel of all—the heart hanging from the boy's chest—and tore it free.

In his palm, the bloody mass continued beating in resistance. Gabriel lifted it to his mouth and, with no expression whatsoever on his face, whispered to the dying boy.

—∿—

"I will now devour your feelings, your memories, your mind and soul...your everything," said the Angel of Death. I could barely keep my eyelids open to see.

Gabriel Miller's colorless lips opened wide, and as if biting into a ripe apple, his sharp teeth touched the heart he'd stolen from me.

...*Creshk.*

It made a horrible, bloodcurdling sound.

His mouth gaped and gushed with blood. It wasn't my blood, however.

And there could be no faulting him for his reaction. He'd bitten down on countless tiny razors that I'd generated with steel elements inside my heart.

"Urgh," Gabriel grunted, bringing a hand to his mouth and backing away.

Ragged, I said, "As if you would find...the mind or memory... in there. The body is just...a vessel. Memories...are always..."

...in here. Blended together with my consciousness, fused into one, never to be separated.

The pain of having my heart torn out was so great that I couldn't even call it pain anymore. But this one moment was going to be my last and greatest chance. I would not get another one.

Even Eugeo had continued fighting with his body split in two. I spread my swords to either side, my blood spraying everywhere, and shouted, "Release Recollection!!"

Pure white and pitch-black exploded together.

The Blue Rose Sword, pointed straight ahead, emitted many vines of ice, which wrapped themselves dozens of times around Gabriel's body.

And the Night-Sky Blade, pointed straight up, formed a great pillar of darkness that stretched to the heavens.

The beam of black light extended with a tremendous roar, splitting the bloodred sky to go even beyond it, as if colliding with the sun itself, and spread in every direction.

The sky was covered.

That bloodred color was painted over with stunning speed, and the light of day was drowned out.

The darkness soon reached the horizon, then spread even farther beyond it.

But this was not the darkness of emptiness. It had a smooth texture and a faint warmth to it.

Infinite night.

—⁓⁓—

At the base of the eerie, looming rocks that dotted the empty wasteland, Sinon lay alone, quietly waiting for the last of her HP to run out.

The wounds where her legs had been blown off itched and stung endlessly, clouding her thoughts. She clutched the chain around her neck as though it were her lifeline, but she could tell that her arm was going steadily more numb.

As her thoughts faded, she began to wonder whether this was a sign of her log-out approaching or whether she was approaching actual unconsciousness—and that was when the color of the sky changed.

At noon, the eerie bloodred sky began to turn totally black with astonishing speed, starting in the south. The light of the sun was blotted out, the gray clouds vanished—and in a blink, the darkness enveloped Sinon.

But in fact, this was not total blackness.

There was a faint, ever-present source of light trickling onto the rocks overhead, the barren tree trunks, and even the chain around her neck. A gentle breeze blew past, rustling her bangs.

It was night. The curtain of night, gently embracing the world to heal it.

Suddenly, Sinon found herself recalling a scene from her distant past.

It was a desert night in a different world. Racked with the pain of an incident that had happened to her as a child, Sinon had hurled her agony at Kirito and bawled. The strength and tenderness he'd shown her by hugging and accepting her seemed to fill the starry sky above them.

That's it. This night...it's Kirito's heart.

He wasn't the blazing sun. He wasn't the sort to stand above everyone else and lead them with his radiance. But he *would* support you from behind when times were tough. He would ease your sadness and dry your tears. Like the stars that shone delicately but constantly. Like the night.

Kirito was engaging in combat with Subtilizer—Emperor Vecta—to protect this world and all the lives within it. He would be fighting back against a vast enemy, fighting and fighting and wringing every last ounce of strength he possessed.

Then please—let my heart reach him, too, Sinon prayed, gazing up at the night sky with teary eyes.

Directly overhead, a single pale-blue star flickered.

—⁂—

Leafa lay amid the throng of orcs and pugilists, also awaiting the end.

She no longer had the strength to stomp her foot and make use of Terraria's healing power. Her body, lacerated and pierced by countless blades, was as cold as ice. She couldn't move a finger.

"Leafa...don't die! Yoh not supposed ta die!!" howled Lilpilin, the chief of the orcs, who knelt at her side. Tears filled his beady eyes.

She gazed at him with a little smile and whispered, "Don't... cry. I know...I will come...back."

When he responded to this by hunching over further, shoulders trembling, Leafa thought, *I couldn't save Big Brother directly, but this was still for the best. I fulfilled my role. Didn't I...?*

That very moment, as if in response to the voice of her heart, the color vanished from the sky.

The red atmosphere of the Dark Territory suddenly plunged into darkness. Cries of shock and alarm arose from the orcs and pugilists. Even Lilpilin lifted his soggy face to stare in disbelief.

But Leafa was neither shocked nor afraid. She could sense the scent of her brother in the gentle night breeze from the south that followed the darkness and caressed her cheek.

"Big Brother...," she murmured, taking a deep breath.

Kirito was the person Suguha was closest to in her life—and also the most distant.

Before he discovered the truth on his own, he must have subconsciously sensed that all was not as it seemed—that his mother and father weren't his real parents. From the moment Suguha was old enough to understand, Kirito was plagued by a shadow of loneliness and isolation. He didn't try to form close ties with anyone else, and the moment it seemed like friendship was about to bloom, he destroyed it himself.

That tendency led him into an online-game obsession, and the fact that his obsession gave him the role of "the hero who saved *SAO*" didn't seem like an ironic coincidence to Suguha. She didn't think it was preordained salvation for him, either.

It was a path that her brother chose for himself. One that he would not run away from, but strive to bear as best he could. That was the strength Kirito possessed.

This night sky was nothing less than proof that Kirito chose to shoulder the burden of the world and everyone who lived in it. And that was because…

Big Brother's far more of a swordsman than I could ever be.

With the last of her strength, Leafa reached out her unfeeling arms and made a kendo grip above her chest.

Then she prayed, *Let the strength of my heart reach his sword.*

High overhead, a single green star flickered to life.

———※———

Lisbeth clutched Silica's hand, staring at the sunless sky.

The stunning sight of the red color turning into blackberry darkness reminded her of another unforgettable day.

The afternoon in early winter when *SAO* had been running for two whole years.

Lisbeth had rushed out of her shop to see the message plastered across the bottom of the floor above announcing that the deadly game had been defeated. Instantly, she knew it had been Kirito. *Kirito beat the final boss with the sword I forged.*

After they got back to the real world, Kirito once told Lisbeth, *The truth is I actually lost. Heathcliff's sword went through my chest, and my HP went to zero. But for some reason, my avatar didn't vanish right away. For just a few seconds, I could still use my right hand, and I managed to score a dual kill. I think it was you and Asuna and Silica and Klein and Agil who helped give me that extra moment. So in a way, it wasn't I who beat SAO. All you guys are the real heroes.*

At the time, she had just laughed it off and slapped him on the back, asking why he was being modest. But that was probably exactly how he felt. What he really wanted to say was that true power was found in the connections between people.

"…Hey, Silica," she murmured to her friend nearby, taking her eyes off the stars. "I think…I really do love Kirito."

Silica grinned and said, "So do I."

They returned to gazing up at the softly shining night sky.

Before she closed her eyes, she could see Klein in the distance, raising a fist, and Agil muttering to himself with his hands on his hips.

Lisbeth listened to the voices of all the Japanese players, who were praying and hoping in their own way.

We're diving into this world through our AmuSpheres...but I know you can hear us anyway, Kirito. Our hearts are connected.

Up above stretched a carpet of hundreds of stars.

—⁓—

Renly the Integrity Knight placed one hand on the neck of his dragon, Kazenui, as he held Tiese's hand with his other. He gazed up at the abrupt night overhead, nearly forgetting to breathe.

Changing the day into night was a frightful feat not found in any of the Church's records. But Renly was not afraid.

When he had been run through with two spears and had accepted his imminent death, light had rained down from the sky and healed his fatal wounds without a trace. This night contained the same nurturing warmth that the healing rain had.

As the weakest of the Integrity Knights, Renly found it very curious, and also unforgivable, that he had survived all the way to the end. He believed that dying bravely in battle, like Dakira and Eldrie had, was the only way to bring redemption to the late friend whose name he could no longer remember.

But as the rain of light had healed him, Renly had been able to feel something different. The black-haired swordsman who couldn't get up from his wheelchair had lost his only friend, too. He had closed off his heart in the pain and anguish of blaming himself for that death.

However, that swordsman had risen to his feet again. And like Renly's Double-Winged Blades, the weapon he used was a memento of his lost friend, and he sent the thousands of enemy soldiers back to their outside world with incredible skill. The sight of his back taught Renly something.

To live. To live, fight, and connect hearts and lives. That, and only that...

"...Only that is the proof of strength," Renly muttered, squeezing Tiese's hand a bit harder. The redheaded girl's other hand held Ronie's, and Sortiliena was on Ronie's other side. Tiese looked up at Renly. Even in the darkness, the deep red-brown of her eyes was visible. Those eyes softened, and she bobbed her head.

The four of them gazed at the black sky overhead and offered up their prayers.

Four powerful lights formed a constellation in the midst of hundreds of other stars.

—⁓—

Iskahn the champion pugilist watched from a short distance as the girl in green armor was caught in the throes of death, surrounded by kneeling orcs and pugilists. He was filled with an indescribable emotion.

There was a ferocity in the way she fought that went beyond even words like *demonic*. Iskahn felt like he understood now why the orcs had disobeyed the emperor's orders and rushed to the pugilists' aid. Chief Lilpilin and his three thousand troops had judged *her* to be more powerful.

But that wasn't true.

There was only one reason the orcs obeyed her—gave her their allegiance—and that was because she had told them they were human, according to what Lilpilin had said. When he'd proudly revealed that to Iskahn, his one eye had shone with a stunning purity, completely devoid of the hatred of humanity that had twisted it so much.

"Hey, woman...I mean, Sheyta," said Iskahn to the gray knight standing beside him. "What is power...? What does it mean to be strong...?"

Sheyta, now a knight without a sword, tilted her head with curiosity, causing her long ponytail to sway. Her cool eyes looked at the dragon behind them, then at Dampa, the stout warrior with both shoulders bandaged, and then to Iskahn. Her lips curled into a little smile.

"You already know the answer. You know there is a power greater than anger and hatred."

In that instant, the familiar bloodred sky of the Dark Territory was plunged into darkness.

Iskahn gasped and looked upward, where he saw a single green star twinkling silently.

Sheyta reached up and pointed at it. "That...that is true strength. True light."

"...Yeah...yeah...that's it," Iskahn murmured. Something entered his good eye, causing the green light to blur.

For the first time in his life, he squeezed his wounded fist not to punch, and he prayed for something other than victory.

In the green star's proximity, a deep-red one appeared, burning like a flame. Right beside it was a gray light.

Within moments, the surviving pugilists began to chant one of their war songs as a chorus, and a carpet of hundreds of stars came into view.

Three thousand orcs gazed into the night in the same way and added their own prayers. So did the dark knights in their close-knit group in the back. Some of them had joined the orcs in protecting the pugilists from the mystery army.

Soon the number of stars was over a thousand, and then ten thousand.

—◊◊◊—

The members of the main force of the Human Guardian Army at the Eastern Gate—the Integrity Knights Fanatio and Deusolbert, the apprentice knights Linel and Fizel, and a number of the lower knights—were all speechless, looking up at the untimely night sky.

The thoughts each cradled to his or her breast were different, but the strength in their prayers and wishes was equal.

Fanatio prayed for the world that the late Commander Bercouli had loved and the world in which the new life within her would live.

Deusolbert clenched the tiny ring that matched the one he wore on his left hand, and he prayed for the world in which he'd lived with the person whose finger he'd placed it on.

Linel and Fizel prayed that they would once again meet the swordsman who'd shown them what true strength was.

The other knights and men-at-arms prayed that peace would return to their beloved home and last forevermore.

In the mountainous region of the northeastern Dark Territory, the mountain goblins prayed, and in the wasteland to the west, the flatland goblins prayed.

In the central wetlands, the orcs waiting for the return of their husbands and fathers prayed, and in the highlands to the southwest, the giants prayed.

The dark-skinned humans in the city outside the Imperial Palace of Obsidia closed their eyes to pray, as did the ogres in the southeastern grasslands.

The blanket of night crossed the End Mountains, too, and instantly covered the Human Empire.

At the church in Rulid, a remote village at the northern end of the Norlangarth Empire, Selka the apprentice nun paused in the act of drawing water at the well for clothes washing and was stunned to see the pure-blue sky transitioning to blackness, starting in the southeast and heading in the opposite direction. The rope slipped from her palms, and the wooden bucket slapped back down into the water, but she didn't hear it.

Her voice escaped in a tremulous whisper.

"Sister…! Kirito……!"

On the night breeze, Selka could sense that, at this very moment, the two people she loved more than anyone else in the world were fighting for their lives.

That meant Kirito had opened his eyes again. He had recovered from his despair over the loss of Eugeo and stood on his own two feet once more.

Selka knelt in the short grass, crossed her hands over her chest, closed her eyes, and murmured, "Eugeo. Please...please protect my sister and Kirito."

When she looked up again, a little blue star flickered to life above her head. A number of colored stars sparked up around it within moments. She realized that all the children who had been playing in the church courtyard were now kneeling on the ground in silence, clutching their hands together in prayer.

So were the traders and housewives in the clearing in front of the church.

And the farmers in the pastures and barley fields.

Alice's father, Gasfut, prayed in his office. Old Man Garitta prayed at the edge of the forest. Not a single soul quaked in fear at this phenomenon.

The sky over Rulid was blanketed in sparkling stars.

In the same way, stardust covered the sky over the larger town of Zakkaria to the south. At Walde Farm on the outskirts of town, the farmer and his wife and their twin daughters, Teline and Telure, prayed at the windows.

All the people in the villages and towns across the four empires offered silent prayers.

So did the residents of the massive city of Centoria in the middle of the human realm. Including the students at Swordcraft Academy and the teachers.

The many monks and bishops of the Axiom Church were no exception.

The girl who operated the levitating platform that connected the fiftieth to eightieth floors of Central Cathedral did something for the first time in her long, long life. While on duty, she removed her hands from the tube for generating wind elements and clasped them together as she gazed up at the endless starry sky beyond the windows.

She knew nothing of the world outside the cathedral. The death of the pontifex and the invasion of the Dark Army had effected no change in her life.

So she prayed for just one thing.

I pray that I might see those two young swordsmen again.

The midday night that covered the entirety of the vast Underworld glittered with well over ten thousand stars of every color.

With a chorus of sound like bells ringing, they began to shoot across the sky toward a single point, starting from the most remote location and moving inward.

That point was at the southern tip of the world…

…at the end of the pitch-black sword raised on high near a little floating island called the World's End Altar.

—⁂—

Alice was finally seeing the end of the staircase up ahead as she ran—but then she noticed that her own shadow on the white stone underfoot suddenly melted into a much larger shadow.

She looked up on the run and witnessed a sight that beggared belief.

An enemy with six black wings, wielding a sword of emptiness without clear form.

Ice vines binding the man dozens of times over.

Clutching the shining white longsword that was the source of the ice, a swordsman in black with dragon wings.

The swordsman's body was missing below the chest. His life should have instantly been obliterated, but unfathomable willpower kept him fighting.

The real miracle, however, was in the sky above them.

From the black longsword held high in the swordsman's other hand, a surge of darkness shot straight upward into the sky and from there blanketed the entire world.

But it was not utter void.

Countless little lights sparkled in the sky to the north, swarms of stars twinkling in every color, painting the sky...the night.

And suddenly—they began to move.

With pure, delicate melodies like bells or harp strings, the stars gathered toward the very southern end of the world. They trailed lines of white, blue, red, green, and yellow, forming a vast rainbow across the night sky.

With a burst of intuition, Alice knew that these stars represented the hearts and minds of all the people living in this world.

The lightlanders.

The darklanders.

The humans.

The demi-humans.

All were joined as one in prayer.

"Kirito!!!" called out Alice, throwing her hand into the air.

Take my heart, too. I may have a heart of scant months and years, in this artificial life as a knight, but this feeling I have—the emotion that surges from my chest—must be real.

A brilliant golden star was hurled from her fingertips and flew straight for Kirito's sword.

—◇◇◇—

Asuna did not turn back.

The one way that she could live up to Kirito's battle to the death was to not waste a single second of the time she had and to head directly for the system console.

So Asuna pulled Alice by the hand and expended every ounce of her concentration on running up the staircase.

Still, she could not stop the burning feeling that filled her lungs. That emotion turned into two droplets that slid down her eyelashes and cheeks before dripping off. The drops were borne on the night breeze and melted into one, becoming a star that sparkled in every color.

For just an instant, Asuna looked up at the star, which left an aurora trail behind it, then she refocused on the ascent. She held on to faith.

—⁓—

Gabriel Miller was in disbelief that he could be bound by mere ice.

A moment earlier, he had rebuffed magic attacks of every kind, and he had even nullified a slash attack from a sword.

Yes, the dozens of razors that the boy had implanted in his own heart had damaged him. But that was only because his mental image of chewing had given him a solid, physical mouth. At this point, his entire being was covered in a thick layer of defensive darkness.

I am the one who reaps. The one who steals all heat, all life, all existence.

I am the abyss.

"NULLLLLLL!!" he growled, but it was not so much a word as it was an inhuman sound that tore through his suggestion of a throat.

The three pairs of black wings on his back all transformed into blades of emptiness, just like the one in his right hand. They beat violently, tearing the space around them. The pale vines of ice were severed, giving him freedom of movement again.

"LLLLLLL!!" he howled, an openmouthed discordance, arranging his seven empty swords—hand and wings—in every direction.

He thrust his one empty hand before him to release wires of darkness that would bind the boy instead so he could see how it felt.

It was only then that Gabriel noticed the red color was gone from the sky—and that thousands of shooting stars were soaring just over his head.

—⁓—

In the moment that I released the memory of the Night-Sky Blade, I was actually unable to summon a concrete image.

All that I held was the distant echo of what Eugeo had said when the sword that I'd referred to as "the black one" for so very long was finally given a name.

In fact, I think your black sword should be called the Night-Sky Blade. What do you say?
Envelop......this...little world...as gently...as the night......sky......

The darkness that surged from the sword turned day into night and created the very night sky it was named for.

When the thousands of stars came from the north and flowed into the sword in a rainbow cascade, I could sense what had happened.

The power of the Night-Sky Blade was to absorb resources from a vast range of space. And the greatest resource in this world was not the sacred spatial resource that the system itself designated, like the sun and the earth. It was the power of the human heart. The power of prayer, of wishes, of hope.

Finally, the last of the seemingly endless waterfall of stars shot into my sword.

When two additional lights came up from the surface, golden and iridescent, and melted into the weapon, too, the Night-Sky Blade shone multicolored with the wishes of all humanity.

The light flowed from the hilt into my arm, filling my body. The bottom half of my body, which Gabriel had destroyed, instantly regrew itself with the warming glow of the brilliance.

The starlight gathered in my left arm, too, causing the Blue Rose Sword there to shine as well.

"Yaaaaaah!!" I bellowed, pulling back the swords.

"NULLLLLLL!!" screeched Gabriel, who bore down on me, free from his icy prison.

There was nothing human about him now. His form shone and gleamed like some eerie liquid metal, coated in a black aura, while violet-blue light like the fires of Hell licked from his eye sockets.

The mammoth sword of pure void in his hand pulled back, and the similar blades coming from the ends of his wings stretched toward me from all directions. A second later, his other hand sent out a tangle of dense black wires that leaped at me.

"...Haaah!!" I shouted, deploying a wall of light to deflect them.

The wing-flap ends of my coat beat hard. With my left sword held before me and my right sword behind me, I leaped off the empty air.

There was hardly any distance between us, so a full-speed charge would take less than a second. But I felt a ripple in time, like the moment was being extended indefinitely.

On my right, a figure appeared.

It was a knight in black armor, with a mustache and an enormous sword. His arm hugged a tan-skinned female knight close to him. He said to me, "*Young man, cast aside your urge to kill. His empty soul cannot be cut with an Incarnation of murder.*"

To his left appeared a powerful man with short hair. A steel longsword hung from his casual blue clothes. A broad grin creased his hearty features: Integrity Knight Commander Bercouli.

"*Don't give in to fear, boy. The weight of the world itself rests upon your sword.*"

To Bercouli's side was a girl with perfect white skin and long silver hair. Administrator's mirror eyes and enigmatic smile were followed by a whispered message. "*Show me now. Exhibit all the holy power that you received from me.*"

Lastly, right in front of me appeared a young girl wearing a robe and a scholar's cap. On her shoulder, next to the hanging brown curls of her hair, was a small spider. It was the other pontifex, Cardinal.

"*Kirito, you must believe. Believe in the hearts of all the people you loved and who love you.*"

Behind her tiny spectacles, her dark-brown eyes glinted kindly.

Then all of them disappeared—and my last and greatest foe, Gabriel Miller, entered sword range.

With more power in my arms than I'd ever possessed before, I executed the Dual Blades sword skill that I had practiced more, and relied upon more, than any other in my repertoire.

Starburst Stream. A sixteen-part combination attack.

"Raaaaaaaah!!"

Swords brimming with starlight left behind stunning trails in the air.

Gabriel's six wings and one blade roared toward me from all directions.

With each clash of light and emptiness, giant flashes and explosions shook the world itself.

Faster.

No, *faster.*

"Raaaaaaaah!!" I howled, speeding up my body, fusing it with my consciousness, accelerating the swords.

"NULLLLL!!" screamed Gabriel, striking back with seven swords.

Ten strikes.

Eleven.

With each clash, the energy released dispersed outward into space, crackling off in search of equilibrium as bolts of lightning.

Twelve.

Thirteen.

There was no anger, no hatred, no murder in my heart anymore. Only the endless strength of countless prayers was fueling me now.

It's time for you...

Fourteen.

...to feel the brilliance...

Fifteen.

...of all the hearts in this world, Gabriel!!

The sixteenth and final swing was a full overhead slash from the left, delivered after climactic pause.

Gabriel narrowed his inhuman eyes, certain of his victory. An instant faster than my devastating final blow, the black wing from the enemy's right shoulder severed my left arm at the root.

The arm brimming with light burst, leaving behind only the Blue Rose Sword in the air.

"LLLLLLLLL!!" crowed Gabriel as the empty sword in his right hand came crackling downward, wreathed in black lightning.

Fwap.

With a reassuring sound, two hands that did not belong to me grabbed the hilt of the Blue Rose Sword.

Bursts of white and black flashed with a tremendous cracking sound.

The Blue Rose Sword stopped the empty blade firmly in place.

Eugeo turned to me, his flaxen hair swaying. *"Now's the moment, Kirito!!"*

"Thank you, Eugeo!!" I shouted back. *"Raaaaaaaaaaaaaah!!"*

I drove another slash from the right, the seventeenth in the sequence, directly onto the top of Gabriel's left shoulder with all my strength. That black liquid metal sprayed as the sword dug in deep and came to a stop right where his heart should be.

And then…

All the starlight that filled Eugeo and me, the Night-Sky Blade and Blue Rose Sword, flowed into Gabriel's heart as a rainbow surge.

—◦◦◦◦—

Gabriel Miller could feel a deluge of unlimited color and energy pouring into the empty abyss within himself. His vision was covered with every shade of color, and a chaotic chorus of voices passed through his hearing.

Dear God, please…

Let him be safe…

End the war…

I love you…

The world…

Please…

Please save the world!

"...Hah, hah, hah."

Despite the boy's sword through his heart, Gabriel spread his arms and wings wide and laughed.

"Ha-ha-ha, ha-ha-ha-ha-ha-ha!!"

It is pointless.

You cannot fulfill my hunger, my endless emptiness, with mere light.

It would be as pointless and arrogant as attempting to warm the universe itself with human hands.

"I will drink every last drop and devour every last morsel!!" shouted Gabriel, black lightning shooting from his eyes and mouth.

"You can't! Not when the only thing you feel about the strength of the heart is fear!!" the boy shouted back, a golden surge pouring from his being.

His sword blazed even brighter, sending infinite heat and light into the enemy's frozen heart.

Gabriel's vision turned sizzling white, and his ears were saturated with sound. But it did nothing to stop his gales of laughter.

"Ha-ha-ha-ha-ha, haaaaa-ha-ha-ha-ha-ha!!"

―――

I had no fear.

The void that filled my enemy was nothing short of a black hole, but I had swirling galaxies born of a multitude of prayers within me.

The hue of the dark-purple lightning shooting from Gabriel's eyes and mouth gradually began to shift.

From purple to red. To orange. To yellow—and then to white.

Crack, went a faint noise, and a tiny fissure ran through the liquid-metal body surrounding the Night-Sky Blade.

Then another. And another.

More white light poured from the cracks. The base of the six wings extending from his back began to glow with fire. Where his mouth opened wide with laughter, it began to crumble and lose definition. Holes appeared in his shoulders and chest.

Beams and curtains of light were shooting out of every crack running all over Gabriel's body, and still he did not stop laughing.

"Ha-ha-ha-ha-ha-ha-ha-ha-ha-haaaaaaaaaa*aaaaaaaaa*..."

His voice grew higher and higher pitched until it was nothing more than a metallic whirring vanishing from hearing range.

The great dark angel's form was entirely covered with white cracks—and in a single instant, it compressed, imploded...

And released.

An explosion of light on a gargantuan scale formed a spiral that shot upward to the heavens.

———✺———

"—Ha-ha-ha-ha-ha-ha-ha!!"

Gabriel Miller sprang upright, laughing uproariously. The first thing that he saw was a wall of gray metal panels. Warning labels written in Japanese corresponded to cables and ducts all over its surface.

"Ha-ha-ha, hah, hah......"

As his laughter subsided, replaced by heavy breathing, Gabriel blinked and blinked. When his breathing normalized, he looked to the sides. He was in STL Room One on the *Ocean Turtle*. Apparently, some unforeseen factor had booted him out of the simulation.

What...a disappointing conclusion! He was just about to gobble up the entirety of that vast flood of light and finish the job of devouring the boy's heart.

Perhaps there was still time to dive back in. Gabriel grimaced and turned around to check.

Resting on the seat of the STL was a tall white man with his eyes closed.

...*Who is that?* he thought momentarily. *Is there a member like this on the assault team? And what is he doing on my machine anyway?*

But then he realized something.

That's my face.

Chief technical officer of Glowgen Defense Systems, Gabriel Miller.

Then who am I, looking down at me?

Gabriel lifted his hands to examine them. All he saw was a hazy translucent light instead.

What is this? What happened?

And then he heard a quiet voice over his shoulder.

"...You've finally come to this side, Gabe."

He spun around. Standing there in a white blouse and a dark-blue pleated skirt was a young girl. Her face was downcast, so he couldn't see it past her airy golden hair. But Gabriel knew at once who this girl was.

"...Alicia," he said, for the first time in nearly twenty years. His face broke into a smile. "So this is where you've been, Allie."

Alicia Clingerman. The childhood friend of Gabriel Miller, and the very first person he'd killed on his noble quest in search of the human soul.

The fact that he had failed to capture Alicia's soul despite seeing it so clearly was an extremely sore spot for Gabriel for years. But apparently, he hadn't completely lost her. She had stayed with him after all.

Gabriel momentarily forgot the bizarre situation he was in and reached out to her. Alicia's hand snapped forward in a blur of movement and snatched his, hard.

She was cold. Cold as ice. A freezing sensation prickled his flesh through the skin like needles. Gabriel instinctually tried to pull away. But Alicia's tiny hand was as firm as a vise. His smile vanished.

"...It's cold. Let go of me, Allie," he murmured.

Her golden hair shook back and forth. "I won't, Gabe. We're going to be together forever. Come—let's go."

"Go…? Go where? I can't—I still have things to do," Gabriel protested, pulling back with all his might. But he did not move. In fact, he was slowly being pulled down toward her.

"Let go. Let go of me, Alicia," he said, more sternly this time.

Just then, she lifted her head. And the moment he saw her face below those neatly trimmed bangs, Gabriel felt his heart shrinking in his chest.

His guts surged upward. His breathing grew faster. Goose bumps rose on his skin.

What is this? What is this sensation, this feeling?

"A…a-a-ah…," he croaked, shaking his head in disbelief. "Let go. Stop. Let go."

He lifted his other hand to push Alicia away, but she grabbed that one just as fast. Fingers as cold and hard as metal dug into his skin.

Alicia giggled at him. "That's fear, Gabe. That's the real emotion you wanted to understand, right there. Isn't it lovely?"

Fear.

The source of the expressions he'd seen on all those people in their final moments when he'd killed them for his experiments, to satisfy his curiosity.

But now that he was experiencing it himself for the very first time, it was not a pleasant feeling. In fact, it was tremendously unpleasant. He didn't want to know this thing. He wanted it to be over.

But…

"You can't leave, Gabe. It's going to continue forever and ever. You are going to feel nothing but terror for the rest of eternity."

Her little shoes sank into the metal floor. So did Gabriel's feet.

"Ah…n…no. Let go…stop," he murmured absentmindedly, but the sinking sensation did not stop.

Suddenly, a white arm emerged from the floor and clung to Gabriel's leg. Then another. And another. And even more.

Gabriel could sense that these were the hands of people he had preyed upon. His fear escalated higher and higher. His heart was hammering at an incredible speed, and sweat beaded thick on his forehead.

"Stop…stop, stop-stop-stop-stop-stoppppp!!" screamed Gabriel. "Critter, get in here! Wake up, Vassago!! Hans!! Brigg!!"

But his subordinates did not burst in. The door to the main control room remained cold and silent. And Vassago, who was in the STL next to him, was not getting up.

By now, his translucent body had sunk into the floor to the waist. Alicia was visible only from the shoulders up as she dragged him down. Before her face disappeared entirely, it smiled with glee.

"Ah…aaah…Aaaaa*aaaaaah*!!" wailed Gabriel. Over and over. White hands grabbed his shoulders, his neck, his face.

"Aaaaa…aaaa……a………"

With a tiny splashing sound, he saw nothing but darkness.

Gabriel Miller understood the fate that awaited him, and he unleashed a scream that would last for eternity.

—∞—

The flow of time in the Underworld began to accelerate again.

The moment that time was no longer perfectly synchronized, the hundreds of Japanese players connected to the Underworld with AmuSpheres were kicked off, returned to their bedrooms or Internet-café booths, and left with nothing but whatever they'd been feeling moments before.

None of them spoke in the immediate aftermath. They all reflected on what they'd experienced in that strange world, committing it to their innermost memories. When any tears they'd shed had been wiped away, they went to their smartphones and AmuSpheres. They had to tell the friends who had logged out first exactly what had happened.

Just before the reacceleration began, Sinon and Leafa left the Underworld due to loss of life. The two woke up in Rath's Roppongi office, feeling the last traces of their pain fading away. They looked into each other's eyes and bobbed their heads.

Neither Shino nor Suguha had any doubt that Kirito had returned to life, had defeated the final enemy, had saved the world, and would return before long.

And the next time they saw him, they would express how they felt in words—whether he was capable of hearing them or not.

Each sensed this determination in the other girl, and they shared a secret little smile.

However…

With the safety limiter off on the Fluctlight Acceleration function, the pulse of time in the Underworld sped toward a level it had never before reached.

Over a thousand times as fast. Over five thousand.

Heading toward the far side of the chronometric wall, five million times as fast as time in the real world: the maximum-acceleration phase.

———

When the light of the stars vanished, so did the energy that was filling my being, and I floated in an exhausted state, face up to the sky.

The left arm that had been cut off and disintegrated was back on my shoulder. I squeezed the Blue Rose Sword in that hand with whatever strength I had left, and I fought back the tears that threatened to fall.

When Eugeo's soul had infused the Blue Rose Sword, saving me and pushing me onward yet one more time, I could sense intuitively that his act of stopping Gabriel's sword had consumed him at last.

In the real world and in the Underworld, the dead did not rise to life.

That's what made memories so precious and beautiful.

"…Isn't that right, Eugeo…?" I murmured.

There was no answer.

I lifted the two swords and slowly slid them into the sheaths affixed to my back. Within moments, the night sky overhead began to fade. The darkness melted away, returning the atmosphere to its normal color.

……Blue.

This time, for some reason, the sky over the Dark Territory was not its usual bloodred color. There was just pure crystal blue as far as the eye could see.

Was it the effect of the maximum-acceleration phase underway, or was a miracle caused by the prayers of tens of thousands of people at once?

There was no definite answer, but whatever the reason, the clear-azure color was so beautiful it made me want to cry. Longing and sentimentality threatened to tear me apart, so I simply let a lungful of the beautiful blue into my body.

Afterward, I closed my eyes, let out a long breath, and slowly turned.

When I opened my eyes again, I was looking at the white staircase far below, which was crumbling without a sound. I beat my wings and slowly descended along the collapsing staircase. My target was the little island in the sky.

The round floating island was covered with a wild bloom of flowers in all colors. A white stone path ran through the field and into a templelike building at the center of the island. I landed in the middle of that path, returned my coat from its current winged state to its usual hem, and looked around me.

A sweet, gentle scent like honey tickled my nose. A number of little lapis-blue butterflies fluttered about, and songbirds trilled from the branches of the few trees growing in the area. The clear-blue sky and soft sunlight made me feel as if I were in the midst of a pastoral painting.

The island was devoid of human presence.

I did not see anyone on the path or in the temple with its circular pillars, either.

"...Oh, good. They made it in time," I murmured.

After Gabriel had been sucked into the spiral of light and had vanished, I could feel the FLA function kicking in. The timing was such that I couldn't be sure whether Asuna and Alice had safely escaped to the real world through the console. Now I knew that they'd crossed the lengthy staircase and reached their goal in time.

Alice—the very reason this world was created, a soul like no other, the knight whose fluctlight broke through its boundaries—had traveled to the real world at last.

There would be many tribulations awaiting her after this. A world with completely different laws and common understanding, a limited mechanical body, and a fight against the forces who wanted to use true artificial intelligence for military purposes.

But Alice would be capable of handling it. She was the most powerful Integrity Knight in existence.

"......Hang in there......," I prayed, thinking of the golden knight I would never see again and looking up at the blue sky.

Yes, now that the maximum-acceleration phase had begun, I had completely lost the ability to voluntarily log out from within the Underworld. All three system consoles had stopped functioning, and even if I lost all my life now, I would have to wait in darkness without sensation for the phase to finish.

In the outside world, Kikuoka and the Rath team would be trying desperately to shut down my STL, but that would take at least twenty minutes. And in that time, two hundred years would pass in this world.

Would I lose consciousness with the end of my soul's life span first, or would the acceleration rate of five million times prove to be unbearable over a long period, causing me to disintegrate sooner?

All I knew for certain was that I could not return to the real world again.

My parents. Suguha. Sinon. Klein, Agil, Liz, Silica.

My friends at school and in *ALO*.

Alice.

And Asuna.

I would never again see the people I loved.

I fell to my knees on the white stones.

My hands flew forward to keep me from toppling face-first.

My vision blurred. Light sparkled and wavered, then fell and burst against the marble paving stone. Again and again. Over and over.

This time, at least, I knew I had the right to cry.

I cried for the precious things that I had lost and would never regain. Sobs leaked through my gritted teeth, and a stream of liquid dripped down my cheeks.

Drip, drip-drip.

The only sound was the droplets hitting the stone.

Drip.

Drip.

...*Tek.*

Tek, tek.

Suddenly, another sound overlaid it, a sound of a different density.

Tek, tek. It was coming closer. I could feel the vibrations through my fingertips.

The air rustled. There was something faint and familiar amid the rich scent of the flowers.

Tek.

...*Tek.*

The sound came to a stop just before me.

Then someone called my name.

CHAPTER TWENTY-THREE

1

Rinko Koujiro sat in the control seat at the console of Subcon, staring at the glass hatch placed just to the left of the board.

The LCD screen at the top of the hatch flashed a message in red letters: EJECTING...

There was the deep sound of pressurized air leaking. Eventually a small black quadrilateral shape appeared beyond the glass window. The LCD screen changed to COMPLETE.

Rinko reached out a trembling hand to open the little hatch and take out its contents.

It was a hard metal package, a cube a little over two inches to a side, and surprisingly heavy. A six-digit number was carved on its sheer face, and there was a very small connector port on it.

Trapped in this tiny cube was Alice's soul.

Following the commands of the system, the Lightcube Cluster installed in the center of the *Ocean Turtle*'s Main Shaft ejected a single specific cube, sealing it in a protective package and then shooting it through a pneumatic tube.

At the same time, it was a journey from the interior Underworld to the exterior real world.

Rinko was speechless for a moment, struck with an indescribable sensation, but recovered and picked up the cube carefully with both hands. She turned to the mic and shouted, "Asuna, Alice has been ejected! Only you and Kirigaya are left! Make it quick!!"

She glanced at the crimson countdown on the main monitor and added, "You've only got thirty seconds until the maximum acceleration starts!! Log out now!!"

There was a moment of silence.

Then words she never expected to hear came out of the speaker.

"I'm sorry, Rinko."

"Huh…? F-for what…?"

"I'm sorry. I'm…staying here. Thank you for everything. I will never forget what you did for us."

Asuna Yuuki's voice was calm and gentle and full of purpose, from what Rinko could hear through the speaker.

"Please take care of Alice. She's a very sweet person. She holds great love within her, and she is loved by many. For the sake of the souls who vanished for her sake…and for Kirito's sake, please don't let them turn her into a weapon."

Rinko was speechless again. All she could do was listen to Asuna's final words.

"And tell everyone else, too, that…I'm sorry…and thank you… and good-bye…"

The countdown hit zero.

—◈◈◈—

A long siren blared, and the heavy groan of machinery echoed throughout the cramped cable duct.

It was ten o'clock in the morning on July 7th. The fifteen-minute countdown was over, and the cooling system on the other side of the wall was running at full capacity. Huge fans desperately tried to suck out the incredible heat output of the machines supporting the Underworld simulation. If you looked at the *Ocean Turtle* from the sea, you would see heat haze rising from the top of its pyramid structure.

"......It's started...," grunted Takeru Higa.

"Yeah," replied Seijirou Kikuoka, who was carrying him down the narrow ladder.

When they'd determined that preventing the maximum-acceleration phase was impossible, they'd immediately prepped and headed into the maintenance cable duct again, but since Higa was injured, it had taken them eight minutes to get him strapped into a support harness.

Despite the fact that Kikuoka descended the rungs with such force that sweat poured off him, the maximum-acceleration phase started in the Underworld before they reached the pressure-resistant isolation barrier. Praying, Higa hit the intercom button to speak to Dr. Koujiro in the sub-control room.

"Rinko...how's it going?"

There was some static, followed by a connection sound, but all he received was heavy silence.

"...Rinko?"

"...*I'm sorry. We've safely retrieved Alice's lightcube. But...*," she said faintly and then delivered what came next.

Higa held his breath and closed his eyes tight.

"...All right. We'll do all we can. I'll get in touch to tell you when to open the connection hatch."

He released the button and expelled all the air in his lungs over a long, slow period.

Kikuoka didn't ask what he'd heard, sensing enough from Higa's reaction already. He continued to bound downward in silence.

"...Kiku..."

Several seconds later, Higa finally found the voice to tell the team commander what Dr. Koujiro had related to him.

Critter stared in silence at the new window on the main monitor and the message it contained.

It said, in very brief detail, that one lightcube had been ejected from the cluster and delivered to the sub-control room on the other side of the pressure-resistant barrier. Meaning that Rath had control of Alice now.

Or in other words, the entire ten-plus-hour operation to find Alice in the Underworld and abduct her had ended in total failure. Vassago and Captain Miller had dived in themselves, led the Dark Army in a military invasion of the human lands, fought in battle scenes that would make any Hollywood producer faint, even lured in tens of thousands of Americans, Chinese, and Koreans to fight with them—and all of it had been for nothing.

He scratched at his shaved head, exhaled through his nose, and thought about something else. If there were still over eight hours remaining until the defense ship arrived, could they physically steal Alice back now?

The barrier was extremely thick and made of a powerful composite metal, so they had no means of destroying it. But if Rath opened it up, like they had not long ago, that would be a different story.

In fact, why *had* they opened the barrier earlier? Did they really think they could overpower the team with one ugly, clumsy robot and a couple of smoke grenades?

Unless that had been a distraction…? If they had some other reason for opening the barrier, what in the world would that be?

Critter turned back to the team members who had resumed their card game and called out, "Hey, about that robot they sent in from above. It wasn't even loaded with any explosives or anything, right?"

Tall, lanky Hans twisted his mustache and said, "Oh, we looked it over, sweetie. No explosives, not even a single type of fixed weapon. I think they were using it as a ballistic shield, but we shot it to shit so bad it broke down, and the soldiers behind it had to retreat."

"Okay...By the way, their SDF members aren't called soldiers—they're technically 'personnel,'" Critter added, a pointless bit of trivia, as he turned the chair back around.

So it was possible that the robot maneuver was just a diversion. But even with smoke grenades, those stairs were tight, and there was no way anyone could have slipped by Hans and Brigg without them noticing.

Which would mean...

Critter picked up the tablet computer on the desk and brought up an interior map of the *Ocean Turtle*.

"Let's see...Here's the Main Shaft, and here's where the barrier splits it...and this is the staircase where they sent the robot through..."

Just then, the countdown on the monitor reached zero, and a high-pitched alarm began to sound. The Underworld's time acceleration was resuming. And because that muscle-bound idiot Brigg had broken the control lever, the acceleration rate was going crazy.

But whatever happened in the Underworld now didn't matter. The Alice retrieval plan was a failure, so Vassago and Captain Miller had probably "died" during their dives and would be logging out and coming out of the adjacent room soon.

In that case, it would be a good idea to think of the next tactical option to take before the captain got back. Critter zoomed in on the ship map and scrolled through it until he noticed something.

"Hey, there's a little hatch here, too. What is this...a cable duct...?"

—◈◈◈—

After she was done relaying the situation to Takeru Higa, Rinko leaned back in the mesh chair and let out a heavy breath.

Asuna Yuuki's decision to stay in the Underworld once it became clear that Kazuto Kirigaya would not be able to escape before the acceleration started was so youthful, so earnest—and so tragically beautiful.

She couldn't help but recall something from her own life: when the man she loved left her behind in the real world and vanished into cyberspace.

What would she have done if she'd been given the option to go with him? Would she have destroyed her brain with a prototype STL, too, and chosen to live on solely as an electronic copy of her consciousness?

"Akihiko...did you...?" she whispered, closing her eyes.

She'd thought that building the floating castle Aincrad and creating a true alternate world with ten thousand players trapped inside it was Akihiko Kayaba's only desire. But during that two-year period in the castle, he found something, learned something. And that thing changed his thinking.

There was more, something further beyond.

SAO was not the final destination, but only the beginning, he realized. And that led him to develop a higher-density version of the NerveGear in that villa in the forest of Nagano and to eventually kill himself within the prototype.

Using the data he'd left with her, Rinko designed the high-precision medical-user full-dive system, Medicuboid. With the vast data provided to the project by a girl's three-year test stay in the first Medicuboid prototype, Takeru Higa and Rath were able to put the finishing touches on their Soul Translator.

So depending on how you considered it, the Underworld—this ultimate example of an alternate reality—was born from the cornerstone of Akihiko Kayaba's grand vision. Did that mean that with the completion of the Underworld, Kayaba's desires had come to fruition?

No, that couldn't be the case...because that still didn't explain where the other element he left behind, The Seed Package, was supposed to fit into the puzzle.

VRMMOs based on The Seed's architecture had become the standard, which was how the Japanese players were able to convert their accounts and help fight back against the foreign assault. But there was no way that even Kayaba would have foreseen such an event years before it happened. The conversion function being used to save someone was only a secondary effect of its presence.

So what was the point of it? Why was it necessary for all those VR worlds to have a shared architecture that allowed them to be linked this way...?

On top of the console desk, Alice's lightcube package was held in a special aluminum-alloy case. The lightcube itself, a collection of light quantum gates, was nonvolatile in nature, but the gates' drive circuits in the package required power to run, so while it was in the case, Alice's soul was inactive.

Rinko brushed the silver case with her fingers and glanced into the left corner of the sub-control room to the humanoid silhouette there: the machine body Niemon.

In theory, if she put Alice's lightcube package into the robot's cranial socket, Niemon would become Alice's body and move and speak as she willed it to.

Rinko had to shake her head to dispel the momentary impulse to test it out and actually speak with Alice. Kazuto and Asuna were in a perilous situation at the moment, so this wasn't the time for indulging her curiosity. And though Niemon was more advanced than Ichiemon, Alice would likely be shocked to appear in a body that bore not a shred of femininity.

A few moments later, she took her hand off the aluminum-alloy case.

"Dr. Koujiro," said a voice behind her, and she spun around.

It was Lieutenant Nakanishi, who had returned to the sub-control room without drawing her attention.

"We're ready to reopen the barrier hatch. You can go ahead at any time."

"Oh...thank you," she said, checking the time on the monitor. One minute had passed since the activation of the maximum-acceleration phase. In internal time, that was...ten years.

It was unbelievable. The age of Kazuto Kirigaya's and Asuna Yuuki's souls was now greater than Rinko's. They had to be logged out as soon as humanly possible. If they could just be ejected before their soul life spans ended, it might be possible to erase all the memories that had accumulated since the start of the max-acceleration phase. But in theoretical terms, they had less than twelve minutes to actually execute such a thing.

Higa, Kikuoka…hurry!! Rinko prayed, biting her lip.

———◈———

Lieutenant Colonel Kikuoka wheezed with ragged breath. A cascade of sweat discolored his shirt and seeped into Higa's clothing.

Higa wanted to tell him he could get down on his own from here, but he kept stopping himself from doing so. Yanai's bullet had penetrated Higa's right shoulder, which still throbbed despite the maximal level of painkillers, and his body felt as heavy as lead after losing so much blood. He didn't feel capable of supporting his own weight.

And more importantly, Higa realized, it was a bit surprising that the lieutenant colonel would be so desperate in this situation.

The final goal of Project Alicization, acquiring the limit-surpassed fluctlight code-named A.L.I.C.E., had been met. All that was left was to analyze Alice's structure and compare it to that of other fluctlights, and they would be well on their way to mass-producing true bottom-up AI. The purpose of Rath's existence—to establish a foundation for Japanese defense in the coming age of drone warfare and to escape the control of America's military industry—would be fulfilled at last.

That was the dearest goal of Seijirou Kikuoka. He had gone to the Ministry of Internal Affairs, gotten involved in the *SAO* Incident, and maintained a connection to VRMMO players through his own avatar, Chrysheight, for that very reason.

So in terms of Kikuoka's priorities, keeping the pressure-resistant barrier sealed and protecting Alice's lightcube until the defense ship could arrive should be the obvious choice. Even if that meant the collapse of the fluctlights of Kazuto Kirigaya and

Asuna Yuuki. And if Dr. Koujiro protested against it, he could confine her if needed.

"Do…you find this to…be a…surprise?" Kikuoka asked out of the blue between heavy breaths. Higa actually gurgled in alarm.

"Er, I…uh…I guess I'll admit…that it seems a bit out of character for you…"

"No…kidding." Kikuoka groaned, rushing down the rungs—only a few dozen feet to go. "But…let me tell you…this. I've got a…good reason…for doing this."

"O-oh yeah…?"

"I make it…a point to always consider…the worst outcome. And for now…I want the enemy…to think…they have a chance at taking…Alice back."

"The worst outcome, huh?"

Could there be anything worse than the enemy finding out about the cable duct and attacking from below while the barrier was open?

Before Higa could extrapolate that idea any further, Kikuoka's soles finally landed on the titanium alloy of the hatch. While the commanding officer stopped and panted, Higa pressed on the intercom and said, "Rinko, we've made it! Open the barrier lock!!"

———

"Whoa…they really opened the damn thing!" shouted Critter, seeing the PRESSURE BARRIER OPEN warning on the main monitor.

But why? For what purpose?

It just didn't add up. Now that they had possession of Alice, what reason could Rath have for loosening their defenses?

There wasn't time to debate the question, though. Critter rotated his chair and instructed the other members, "Let's see, uh, Hans! You go to the stairs with everyone except for Brigg! Take your guns and seize control of the barrier!"

"You make it sound so simple," Hans complained, clicking his tongue and hoisting his assault rifle. A dozen or so men followed his lead.

"H-hey, what the hell am *I* supposed to do, then?" complained Brigg.

Critter snapped his fingers. "Don't worry—I've got a job for you, too. A very important one that will require your skills."

On the inside, Critter was thinking something else entirely: *I need this muscle-bound idiot where I can see him, so he doesn't screw anything else up.*

"Listen, pal, you and I are gonna check out this cable duct. I've got a feeling that this is what the enemy's *really* after, for some reason."

"Oh yeah? Well…that's more like it." Brigg grinned. He walked off, loudly checking the ammunition in his rifle, and Critter did his best not to sigh out loud.

Before he went running out of the main control room and down the hallway, in the opposite direction from Hans's group, Critter glanced at the door on the back wall—STL Room One.

Damn, why's Vassago taking so long to log out? He better not be relaxing in there, smoking a cigarette or something.

He considered going back just to check, but Brigg was already hustling into the hallway. Critter had no choice but to follow him now.

In a few minutes, they were at their destination. It looked just like a hallway that ran along the inner wall of the Main Shaft. But according to the ship map, there was a little hatch on the left side of the wall that led to a cable duct that connected to the upper half of the shaft. The shaft was split by that powerful barrier as well, of course, but if Critter's suspicions were correct…

He grabbed the rotating handle with sweaty hands and turned it left. After opening the heavy metal door, the first thing Critter saw was a tunnel about six feet deep and less than three feet tall, lit by dim orange lights. At the back, the tunnel went upward, and there were simple steps set into the wall.

And then he noticed, just below the steps, a mound of what looked like fabric...

"Whoa!!"

When he realized what it was, Critter pulled back abruptly, cracking the back of his head against the chin of Brigg, who was standing right behind him. But neither the pain in his skull nor the large man's swearing registered, he was so stunned.

The mysterious fabric was actually clothing. Clothes with someone inside them, a skinny body folded in on itself. Brigg pushed Critter aside and raised his rifle, but it took only a second or two for him to grunt, "He's dead."

The man's neck was twisted at an unnatural angle. Critter grimaced, then hesitantly leaned into the tunnel so that he could examine the dead man's face.

"Hey...isn't this that guy? The mole inside Rath...? Did they execute him when they found out he was a spy? It's a weird way to kill someone..."

He touched the man's skin, thoroughly grossed out, and felt how clammy it was. Based on the temperature, he had probably died the first time they opened the barrier. So did that mean the first time it opened was so this man could try to escape down to the lower part of the shaft? Had he missed a step and fallen to his death?

Then why had they opened the barrier again?

He wanted to check the state of the barrier hatch leading to the Upper Shaft, but to do that, he'd have to pull the body out, and he didn't want to do *that*.

He backed out of the tunnel and into the hallway, then told Brigg, "Go in there and see what's going on up in the duct."

The large bearded man snorted and crawled into the tunnel, then yanked the spy's body out of the way. That done, he went back into the tunnel again and peered up the vertical duct, twisting his upper half for the right angle.

Critter didn't know much about tactics, but he had to wonder whether it was safe to stick your head right into the vertical duct like that.

"Oh, shit!!" cried Brigg, then he lifted his assault rifle and fired.

Yellow flashes burned Critter's retinas, and two types of gunfire rattled his eardrums. He managed not to scream but watched as Brigg's massive body bounced off the floor of the tunnel as though it had been smashed by an invisible hammer.

"Aaaah! What the hell?!" shrieked Critter, falling onto his butt in the hallway. Brigg was collapsed and unmoving, in the same spot where the spy's body had just been. Critter didn't need to see the pooling blood on the floor to know that he'd suffered the same fate as the spy. One of Rath's combat members had been waiting up above and had shot him.

So what do I do now? Critter wondered, feeling a wave of sweat break over him. *Should I grab the assault rifle from Brigg's hand and win a shoot-out with the unseen enemy above to avenge his death? Hell no! I'm just a computer geek—my job is to think and hit keys.*

Critter practically crawled back to the main control room, thinking rapidly the whole time. At the very least, this indicated that Rath intended to be aggressive on the attack. But the assault team's side had the obvious advantage in strength. If they fought, the other side would suffer losses—and at worst, lose control of the Upper Shaft and possession of Alice.

Was Rath's commander envisioning a worst-case scenario beyond even that? Did he think that the assault team had enough firepower to blow up the entire *Ocean Turtle*? All the C4 they had couldn't even blow up one pressure-resistant hatch...

Firepower...

Then Critter inhaled sharply. The two bodies behind him in the hallway completely vanished from his mind.

They *did* have it.

There was one method they had to destroy the entire *Ocean Turtle* and sink Alice's lightcube and the Rath team to the bottom of the ocean.

The client had ordered them to destroy Alice if they determined that she was unrecoverable. But should they destroy this massive autonomous megafloat and the dozens of crew members aboard it just to fulfill that goal?

Critter couldn't make such an awful decision on his own. He'd have nightmares for the rest of his life.

He got to his feet and ran for the main control room, hoping to get his commanding officer's opinion.

—◇◆◇—

"K...Kiku! You all right, Kiku?!" hissed Higa as quietly as he could. The enemy had appeared at the bottom of the cable duct and fired off at least three rifle shots.

He got no response. Lieutenant Colonel Kikuoka had his shoulder pressed against the wall of the duct, Higa on his back, with one hand on the ladder step and the other holding a pistol.

No way, man. You can't be serious. We still need you!

"Ki..."

He was about to yell *Kikuokaaaaaa!!* when the lieutenant colonel coughed violently.

"*Koff...eurgh*...Oh, man. I am so glad I wore this bulletproof vest..."

"O-of course you did! Were you seriously thinking of wearing your aloha shirt down here...?" Higa asked, sighing with relief. He glanced down at Kikuoka's back again. "So you're not hurt, then?"

"Nope, but I did take one shot to the vest. Are you okay, though? There were a lot of ricochets."

"Y-yeah...Neither I nor the terminal got hit."

"Then let's hurry. We're almost to the maintenance port."

As Kikuoka rocked back and forth down the rungs again, Higa thought how surprising this was.

He'd always assumed that Lieutenant Colonel Kikuoka was not one for physical activities, but the muscles under his broad back were as hard as steel. And as for his marksmanship...he had been hanging by one hand from the ladder and had shot down the duct twice, one-handed, and double-tapped the enemy in the throat and chest.

I feel like I'll never run out of surprises from this guy for as long as I know him, Higa thought, shaking his head. He pulled the cable for the maintenance connector out of his pocket as the port came into view.

———ᴗᴠᴠᴔ———

As Critter raced back down the hallway and into the main control room, he heard rifle fire coming from the stairs.

Neither Captain Miller nor Vassago were in the room. They probably hadn't left the STLs yet. Even though it had been over five minutes since the acceleration had started.

Critter still wasn't sure whether he should really describe his idea to them, mostly because he could sense that if he did, they would tell him to carry it out immediately. They were not the kind of people who cared about the fate of innocent civilians who lay between them and their mission.

He yanked open the door to the STL room, still uncertain of what he should do.

"Captain Miller! Alice is under enemy..."

Any further words caught in his throat.

Right in front of him, lying on the gel bed of STL Unit One, with the machine covering his forehead and everything above it, was Gabriel Miller. His face wore an expression that Critter had never seen on him before.

In fact, Critter had never seen it on *any* human being.

His blue eyes were bulging so much they threatened to pop out of his skull. His mouth was open wide enough that the jaw joints almost had to be dislocated—and it was diagonal, not straight. His tongue extended far out of his mouth, as if it were an entirely separate living thing.

"C...Cap...tain...?" Critter gaped, his knees shaking. He knew that if he happened to see one of those protruding eyeballs move, he would scream.

It took him more than a few seconds to control his breathing and then reach out, slowly and hesitantly, to touch the man's left wrist where it hung from the side of the bed.

There was no pulse.

His skin was as cold as ice. Despite the lack of any external wounds, the assault team's commanding officer, Captain Gabriel Miller, was dead.

Critter clenched his stomach to keep its contents from rising and rasped, "Vassago...get up! The captain's d...dea..."

He made his way on trembling legs around the gel bed to the second unit, which was farther into the room.

This time, he did scream.

The second-in-command, Vassago Casals, was asleep peacefully, at first glance. His eyes were closed and his expression was placid. His hands were extended, resting at his sides.

The only difference was in that long, flowing black hair of his.

It was as white and shriveled as if he were over a hundred years old.

Critter backed away. He didn't even bother to check the pulse this time. Despite being a hacker who believed only in reason and source code, Critter truly thought in that moment that he was going to meet the same end that these two did if he stayed in the accursed room.

He tumbled backward through the open doorway and slammed the door shut with his foot.

Critter panted heavily and tried to put together what this meant. There was no way to know what had happened to Miller and Vassago, and he didn't *want* to know. All he could assume was that something had happened in the Underworld and that, most likely, it had totally destroyed their fluctlights.

In the end, the operation was a failure. Now that the team leader was dead, there was no way to get a decision on whether to destroy the whole ship with Alice in it. There was no reason to stay here any longer.

Critter picked the communication device up off the console and croaked, "Hans...come back. Brigg, Vassago, and the captain are dead."

Within a minute, the biggest dandy on the team came rushing back to the control room, his expression as sharp as a knife. "You said Brigg is dead?! How?!"

"H-he got shot from above...in the cable duct..."

Hans listened no further before rushing off with his rifle at the ready. Critter called out, "Stop! They've got Alice's lightcube. There's no reason to fight anymore..."

The soldier was silent for a while. Then he abruptly punched the wall with an incredible clatter and came stomping back to Critter. "No...there must still be orders. If we can't steal it, we destroy it. You've got an idea of what to do, don't you?"

Critter was overwhelmed by Hans's imposing presence and trembling mustache. He nodded nervously. "I...I do, kind of... but we can't. I can't make that kind of decision on my own."

"Say it. Tell me now!!" yelled Hans, pressing the muzzle of his assault rifle to Critter's throat. The mercenary and Brigg had been a duo for years, since long before Glowgen hired them. The ferocity of his gaze was too much for Critter.

"The...the engine..."

"Engine? Of the ship?"

"Yeah...this huge thing runs on a nuclear reactor..."

2

Ten minutes had passed.

Rinko Koujiro clenched her sweating palms, staring at the digital readout that continued to ascend without mercy.

A hundred years had passed within the Underworld since the initiation of the maximum-acceleration phase. It was impossible to imagine how Kazuto Kirigaya and Asuna Yuuki had experienced that length of time. All she knew was that the memory capacity of their fluctlights was running out, and soon.

According to Higa's assessment, the human soul stopped functioning properly once it had accumulated about 150 years of memories, and then it began to collapse. This hadn't been tested in an experiment, of course. The limit might actually be higher—or significantly lower.

All she could do now was pray that they finished the logging-out process before Kirito's and Asuna's souls imploded. If they could just avoid that, there was still hope that the two of them might return to their original selves.

Higa, Mr. Kikuoka...please.

So intent was she on her prayer that Rinko failed to notice that the frequent sounds of gunfire in the distance had stopped. She realized it only when Lieutenant Nakanishi rushed back to the sub-control room.

"Doctor! The enemy has begun to withdraw from the *Ocean Turtle*!"

"W...withdraw?!" she repeated, stunned.

Why now? With the barrier wall open, this would be the attackers' last chance to recover Alice. It was too early for them to give up. They still had eight hours until the Aegis warship *Nagato* arrived.

Rinko typed some commands on the keyboard to call up the status windows for various ship conditions and asked the lieutenant, "Did anyone get hurt in the fighting?"

"Yes, ma'am...We've got two light injuries, one more serious. He's being treated now, but I don't think it'll be fatal."

"I see..."

She let out the breath she'd been holding and glanced over at the man. There was a large medical patch stuck to Nakanishi's chiseled cheekbone, which had a small trace of blood blotting through. He was one of the two who were lightly injured.

They had to save those two kids so that this fighting wasn't all for nothing. At the very least, the news that the enemy was pulling out was good. On the status window, Rinko confirmed that the bay door to the submerged dock on the underside of the *Ocean Turtle* was open. That was how the attackers had gotten in the first time.

"Looks like they're going to escape with their submersible again. They're really in a rush, though...," she said, staring curiously. Then a vibration shook the entire Main Shaft.

A whining howl, like a dry breeze through branches, burst through the gigantic megafloat. Her pen rolled off the table and fell onto the floor.

"Wh...what is this?! What's happening?!"

"It sounds like...Ohhh...No, they couldn't—!!" Lieutenant Nakanishi groaned. "This vibration must be the main engine at full power, Doctor!!"

"Main engine...?"

"The pressurized water reactor at the base of the shaft."

When Rinko just sat there in muted horror, the lieutenant

leaped to the console and awkwardly interacted with the status screen, bringing up new windows until one of them showed a blurry image.

"Holy shit! All the control rods are raised!! What have they done?!" he demanded, slamming the console with a fist.

"But…there must be safety measures, right…?" Rinko asked.

"Of course. Before the reactor core reaches a critical state, the control rods automatically get inserted to stop fission from occurring. But…just look at this…"

He pointed at the spot on the monitor where it displayed real-time footage of the containment chamber. It was hard to tell through all the red light, but it looked like some small white object was stuck to one large yellow-painted piece of machinery.

"That looks like C4…plastic explosives. At that size, it's probably not enough to destroy *both* the containment structure and the pressurizer, but right below this spot is the CRD…That's the control-rod drive, which inserts the control-rod cluster into the core. If that gets destroyed, then the rods won't be able to drop on their own…"

"And…we won't be able to stop nuclear fission? What happens then…?"

"First, it'll heat up the primary cooling fluid until it results in a steam explosion, destroying the pressurizer…In the worst-case scenario, the core will melt down and break through the containment chamber and the ship's bilge into the seawater, thus evaporating lots more water and blowing up the entire shaft. Including Main Control, the Lightcube Cluster, and Sub Control."

"Wha…?"

Rinko looked down at the floor beneath her feet. Superheated steam, bursting up through this thick metal floor? It would mean that all the Rath employees, who'd done their best to avoid casualties; Kazuto and Asuna connected to The Soul Translators; and the thousands of artificial fluctlights in the Lightcube Cluster—all of them would be obliterated in an instant…

"I'll go and remove the C4," Lieutenant Nakanishi announced. His voice was low and determined. "They'll have set the timer for long enough that they can escape to a safe distance on their submersible. We should have five minutes...That's enough time for me."

"B-but, Lieutenant, the temperature in the engine room is already..."

"You think I've never been in a sauna before? It's not hard to run in there and pull off a detonator."

Assuming you have safety clothing on. But there's no time to arrange something like that, Rinko thought. She couldn't tell him that, though; there was steel resolve in his figure as he headed to the door.

But his high-laced black boots stopped just short of the sliding door.

There was a sound in the room that Rinko had never heard before. Nakanishi promptly reached for his holster, and they both looked to their left.

It was a high-pitched metal whirring coming from a right foot stepping out of its protective frame—belonging to the metal-and-plastic machine body of Niemon.

To the disbelief of Rinko and Nakanishi, the humanoid machine walked slowly toward them, its head sensors glowing red.

But it shouldn't be moving.

Higa had designed it, so he knew how it functioned better than anyone. Unlike Ichiemon, which was loaded with many ambulatory balancers, Niemon was designed to be an artificial fluctlight carrier, so without a lightcube inserted, it couldn't walk at all. Alice was the only fluctlight ejected from the cluster, and she was still held in the case on the desk. Niemon's head socket should be empty.

"Wh...why is Prototype Two moving...?" Nakanishi gasped, drawing his pistol. Niemon ignored him and walked straight toward Rinko, stopping about six feet away from her. A tinny electronic voice issued from a speaker somewhere in its head.

"I will go."

That voice.

The tang of the oil lubricating Niemon tickled her nostrils.

She had heard the same voice and smelled the same odor on the night that she landed on the *Ocean Turtle*, when she was dreaming in her cabin.

Rinko got to her feet, trembling slightly, and walked up to Niemon. In a tremulous voice, she asked, "Is that you…Akihiko…?"

The dim light of the sensors flickered, as though blinking, and the robot's head smoothly bobbed. She closed the space between them without thinking and touched its aluminum body with shaking hands. The robot's hands rose, whirring quietly, and touched her back.

"I'm sorry for leaving you alone for so long, Rinko."

Electronically generated or not, the voice undeniably belonged to the one man Rinko Koujiro had ever loved: Akihiko Kayaba.

"So this…is where you been," she whispered, not even realizing that she'd reverted to the hometown dialect she'd largely forgotten. Tears pooled in her eyes, blurring the lights of Niemon's sensors.

"There's no time. I'll only say what I need to say. You brought joy to my life, Rinko. You were the only thing keeping me connected to the real world. If possible…I want you to keep that connection going… Fulfill my dream…and connect these two worlds that are still apart…"

"Yes…of course. Of course…," she said, her head bobbing up and down. The machine seemed to smile. Then it let go of her body and smoothly changed its center of gravity, practically running out of the sub-control room.

Rinko started to follow it automatically, until the sliding door closed in her face. Then she inhaled deeply and clenched her jaw. She couldn't leave this room now. It was her job to monitor the situation around the ship.

Instead, she watched the feed of the engine room and clutched the locket around her neck. She heard Lieutenant Nakanishi murmur in a daze, "Why did he wait until now…?"

There had been many perils before this point. Yet Kayaba had waited until this moment to break his silent observation and act. Rinko thought she understood why.

"…It's not for the Underworld. He has no intention of interfering with the simulation. He made himself known so that he could protect Kirigaya and Asuna..."

———∿∿∿———

When Takeru Higa heard the groaning of the heavy turbines echoing up from the bottom of the duct, he finally understood the worst-case scenario Kikuoka was afraid of.

"K...Kiku, I think they're setting off the—," Higa groaned, but Kikuoka cut him off.

"I know that. Just put all your attention into shutting down the STLs," he ordered.

"O-okay...but..."

Higa felt a cold sweat break out all over his body when he inserted the cable into the maintenance panel at last. If the reactor went haywire, none of this would matter. The Underworld and Alice's lightcube would be utterly destroyed in a blast of superheated steam and radiation, and many human lives would be lost along with them.

But causing a reactor explosion wasn't actually that easy. You couldn't break the two thick metal containment layers surrounding the core with small arms, and there were multiple layers of safety systems on the controls. Even if it did continue to run at a reckless full output, the safety measures would kick in very soon, lowering the control rods to prevent fission from occurring.

Just then, in his usual laid-back manner, Kikuoka asked, "Hmm... Higa, do you think you can manage on your own from here?"

"Uh...yeah, if you attach my harness to the steps, I should be able to work...but, Kiku, you can't be considering going down..."

"Oh, I'm just going to check on things. I'm not going to make some heroic last stand. I'll be right back," Kikuoka reassured him, slipping out of the harness that connected the two of them and hanging the nylon belts over the ladder rungs, then snapping the buckles shut. When he was certain that Higa was firmly in place, he descended several steps.

"The rest is up to you, Higa," he said, his narrow eyes beaming through the black-framed glasses.

"B-be careful down there! They might still be around!" Higa shouted after him. Kikuoka gave him an uncharacteristic thumbs-up, then shot down the rungs with incredible speed. When he got to the bottom, where the hole led out to the hallway, he carefully checked the perimeter before sliding out.

It was only after Kikuoka had disappeared entirely that Higa noticed something was wrong.

While he typed away on the laptop's keyboard with his right hand, Higa tried to adjust the harness where it was biting into his stomach with his left hand, and he felt something slick and wet. He looked down at his palm in shock and saw, under the illumination of the orange emergency lights, a blackish liquid on his skin.

It was painfully obvious that the blood did not belong to him.

—◆◇◆—

In the Lower Shaft, which the attackers had controlled until a few minutes ago, most of the security cameras were destroyed, but they were still intact in the engine room that housed the reactor.

On the main monitor, Rinko had the feed zoomed in all the way. She clutched her locket in both hands and waited. On her left, Lieutenant Nakanishi had his hands clenched and resting on the console. Behind them, the security team that had come back from the defensive perimeter and the technicians were praying in their own individual ways.

Rinko asked them to evacuate to the bridge, but not a single one of them left the Main Shaft. Everyone present had given everything they had for Rath, the mysterious organization conducting top-secret R&D. They had their own hopes and dreams for the new age that true bottom-up artificial intelligence would bring.

Up to this point, Rinko had thought of herself as merely a guest temporarily visiting the ship. She'd had no intention of linking her goals to that of Seijirou Kikuoka, a man as impenetrable as any.

But she also realized now that she had come here to Rath because she was meant to. Artificial fluctlights weren't meant to be funneled into a narrow purpose like unmanned-weapons AI. And the Underworld was not just some highly advanced civilization simulator.

They were the beginning of a massive paradigm shift.

A new reality, a revolution from the closed-off nature of the real world. A world made incarnate by the invisible power of all those young people who had sought to break free from the existing system of reality.

That's what you really *wanted, isn't it, Akihiko? What you discovered in your two years in that castle was the endless possibility they represented. The blindingly bright power of the heart.*

The worst criminal act in history—locking up ten thousand people in a virtual prison and causing four thousand lives to be lost—was unforgivable in every way. Rinko's part in helping him carry out that crime would never be expunged from her history.

But just for now...just this once, let me wish.

Please, Akihiko. Save us...Save the world.

As if in answer to her prayer, there was movement at last in the remote feed on the screen. A silver mechanical body had appeared in the narrow hallway leading to the engine room containing the cutting-edge pressurized water reactor.

The machine's steps were duller now, perhaps because its battery output was already dimming. It clanked forward, step by heavy step, fighting its own weight.

Rinko couldn't imagine when and how Kayaba's thought-mimicking program had slipped into that body's memory. One thing was clear, however: The program contained within the robot had to be the one and only original copy. No intelligence could truly withstand the knowledge that there were identical copies of it in existence.

How long would the prototype's electronic circuits hold out? It surely hadn't been treated with special heat-resistant protection. All they needed to do was unplug the detonator to prevent an explosion, but if Niemon's memory should get destroyed some-how, Kayaba's consciousness would cease to exist.

Please, defuse the bomb safely and come back to me, Rinko prayed, biting her lip.

But Akihiko Kayaba probably intended for this to be his end. He'd fried his own brain in the act of writing a copy of his mind—and now he had found his purpose, his reason for dying.

The actuators of Niemon's mechanical joints whirred.

Its metal soles thudded against the floor.

With determined, careful strides, the machine body reached the door of the engine room at last. It reached out and awkwardly operated the control panel. The light turned green, and the thick metal door opened inward.

At that very moment, she heard high-speed rifle fire through the speakers. Niemon retreated awkwardly, lifting its arms to protect its body. A soldier dressed in black fatigues shouted something and leaped through the open doorway.

It was obviously one of the attackers. He wasn't covering his face with a helmet and goggles like before. The man had a soft-looking face with a narrow mustache, but even on the grainy security camera, the extreme expression on his face was clear.

"Wha...?! One of them stayed behind?!" Nakanishi exclaimed. "Why?! Does he *want* to die?!"

Niemon maintained a defensive posture as the man unloaded bullets on it. Sparks flew, and holes opened in the aluminum exterior. Nerve cables tore here and there, and lubricant spilled out of its polymer muscle cylinders.

"S-stop it!!" shrieked Rinko. But the enemy soldier on the screen screamed something in English and pulled the trigger a third time. The robot wobbled, taking step after step backward.

"Oh no! Number Two's exterior can't withstand this!" Nakani-shi said, reaching for his pistol, even though he knew he wouldn't make it in time.

Then a fresh series of gunshots rang out through the speakers.

A third figure came running down the hallway from the front, firing a pistol wildly. The enemy's body jolted left and right. Somehow this new person was hitting his target without mistakenly putting a single bullet into the robot body. But who...?

Rinko forgot to breathe. On-screen, blood burst from the enemy's chest, and he flew backward and stopped moving.

The mystery savior slowly descended to a knee in the middle of the hallway—and then sank to the floor on his side. With trembling fingers, Rinko rolled the mouse wheel to zoom in.

Bangs covered his forehead. Black-framed glasses slid off his ear. It looked like there was a slight smile on his lips.

"K...Kikuoka?!"

"Lieutenant Colonel!!" shouted Rinko and Nakanishi together.

This time, the SDF officer bolted out of the room for good. A number of the security staffers followed him. Rinko couldn't stop them now.

Instead, one of the technicians leaped to the console, typing a few keys and bringing up what appeared to be a status window for Prototype Number Two.

"Left arm, zero output. Right arm, sixty-five percent. Both legs at seventy percent. Battery remaining, thirty percent. We can do it. It can still move!!" the staffer shouted. Number Two seemed to hear him and resumed forward progress.

Zrr, chak. Zrr, chak. With each awkward step, its severed cables spit out sparks. When the ragged body passed through the doorway, Rinko switched the camera view to the angle from the engine room interior.

The second heat-resistant door was physically locked with a large lever. Niemon's right arm grabbed the lever and tried to push it down. Its elbow actuators spun, spraying more sparks.

"Please," Rinko murmured, just before cheers of encouragement burst out of the observers in the control room.

"You can do it, Niemon!!"

"That's it, just a bit more!!"

Ga-kunk. The lever shifted downward heavily.

The thick metal door burst open from the pressure on the other side. Even on the monitor, it was clear that a huge blast of heat was pouring through the doorway.

Number Two wobbled. The especially thick cable hanging from its back sparked worse than before.

"Oh...oh no!!" shouted one of the staffers suddenly.

"What...what's wrong?!"

"The battery cable's damaged!! If that gets cut off, it'll lose power to the body...and cease to move..."

Rinko and the other techs watched in silence. Even Kayaba, the brain controlling Niemon, seemed to realize how bad the damage was. The robot pinned the swinging cable down with its elbow and resumed walking, slowly and carefully.

The interior of the engine room was full of excess heat the reactor was putting off at maximum output, at a temperature that no human being could withstand in the flesh. Most likely the safety functions would kick in soon, automatically inserting the control rods back into their housing.

But if the plastic explosives went off first and destroyed the drive for the control rods? Then the neutrons coming off the nuclear fuel would destroy the uranium atoms in a chain reaction until it reached a critical point.

A core meltdown would then cause a steam-pressure explosion in the primary coolant, destroying the pressurizer, and the core would then break through the containment vessel from sheer gravity, then the bottom of the ship, and would leak into the water...

Rinko had a sudden vision of a pillar of smoke rising from the center of the *Ocean Turtle*.

She closed her eyes and prayed again. "Please...Akihiko...!!"

The cheers and chants resumed. Pushed onward by their encouragement, Number Two approached the nuclear reactor.

She switched to the final camera angle.

There was suddenly a terrible roar coming through the speakers. The footage on the screen was red with emergency lights. Number Two was practically dragging one foot as it proceeded through the searing heat. Only five or six yards until it reached the plastic explosives stuck to the upper part of the containment chamber.

The robot's right hand rose toward the detonator. Sparks were flying in streams from all over its body, and pieces of its exterior fell to the floor.

"You can do it…You can do it…You can do it!!"

One simple statement echoed around the control room. Rinko balled her hands into fists and screamed with them, nearly losing her voice.

Four more yards.

Three yards.

Two yards.

Then there was a veritable explosion of sparks from Number Two's back.

The black cable split and hung loose, like some exposed entrails.

All the sensors on the robot's head went out. The right arm slowly lowered.

Its knees shook and bent—and Number Two went silent.

On the monitor, the output graphs that had been bouncing up and down now sank to the bottom and turned black.

One of the techs whispered, "It's…lost all power…"

I don't believe in miracles, Akihiko Kayaba had said to Rinko on the day he'd woken in his bed in the mountain villa after *SAO* had been cleared earlier than expected and all its players had been released at last. His eyes were gentle and shining, and there was a faint smile playing around his scraggly, overgrown jaw.

But you know what? I saw a miracle today, for the first time in my life. My sword went through him and destroyed the last of his hit points, but it was like he refused to obey the system and go away…and he stuck his swords into me instead.

Maybe it was that moment I've been waiting for all this time…

"…Akihiko!!" shouted Rinko, not even noticing that blood was dripping from the hand that clenched her locket. "You're Heathcliff, the man with the Holy Sword!! You're the ultimate rival of Kirito the Black Swordsman!! You've got to have one miracle of your own in you!!"

Flick.

Flick-flick.

Red lights flickered. The lateral sensors on Number Two's head. Exposed muscle cylinders jittered.

A faint, purple light bobbed at the very bottom of the blacked-out status window. Then all the bars on the graph displaying limb and core output shot upward. Sparks flew as the robot's joint actuators spun into life.

"N...Number Two's active again!!" a staffer shrieked, right as the utterly ragged machine stood upright.

Tears poured from Rinko's eyes.

"Gooooo!!"

"Keep going!!"

Shouts filled the sub-control room.

One foot stepped forward, slick with oil that ran like blood.

The other foot dragged forward next, and it reached out its arm.

One step. Another step.

The battery compartment popped. Its body lurched—but it took another step.

The fingers of its fully extended arm made contact with the plastic explosives strapped to the containment vessel.

The thumb and index finger pinched the electric detonator.

Sparks erupted from wrist, elbow, and shoulder like death screams. Number Two pulled the detonator loose, timer and all, and raised its arm high.

The screen flashed white.

Number Two's fingers blew off where the detonator had burst. Then the robot tilted to the left and, like a lifeless puppet, dropped to the floor. The sensor lights blinked and went out, and the output graph on the monitor blacked out again.

No one said anything for quite some time.

And then the sub-control room rocked with raucous cheers.

—◦◦◦—

The whining of the engine turbines weakened and grew distant.

Higa let out the breath he'd been holding. The nuclear reactor was finally starting to lower its output instead of continuing at a disastrous full-power clip.

He wiped his sweaty forehead with his sleeve and squinted at the laptop screen through dirty lenses. The shutdown process for the two Soul Translators was about 80 percent finished. Over seventeen minutes had passed since the maximum-acceleration phase had been initiated—that would be over 160 years in the Underworld.

By Higa's conjecture, that was over the theoretical life span of the fluctlight. In simple logical terms, it was highly likely that the souls of Kazuto Kirigaya and Asuna Yuuki had disintegrated.

But at this point, Higa also admitted to himself that in truth, he knew nothing about fluctlights in the Underworld. He had planned the simulation, constructed it, and operated it. But within the machine, the alternate world that had been built up by artificial souls had apparently reached heights that no one in Rath could have envisioned.

Right now, the real-world person with the deepest understanding of that world was undoubtedly Kazuto himself. Just a seventeen-year-old high school student, hurled into the Underworld without any preparation. And he had adapted, evolved, and exhibited power greater than that of the four super-accounts meant to be gods.

That wasn't just some preternatural power that Kazuto was born with. It was because Kazuto Kirigaya—unlike the Rath members, who saw the artificial fluctlights only as experimental programs—acknowledged that the fluctlights were just as human as he was. He interacted with them, fought them, protected them, loved them—as human beings.

That was why the Underworld—all the people who lived in it—chose him. To be their protector.

Then perhaps, through some miracle that even Higa could not have anticipated, he might be able to withstand two hundred years.

I bet that's right, Kirito. Now I understand exactly why Lieutenant Colonel Kikuoka was so insistent on working with you. And why you'll continue to be needed.

So...

"...Please come back to us," Higa whispered, watching the shutdown process approach 100 percent.

—⁓—

Rinko was left all alone in the sub-control room.

The other staff members had left to rescue Lieutenant Colonel Kikuoka and restore control to the main control room. For her part, Rinko wanted to rush to the reactor containment unit and find the collapsed Niemon so she could secure its physical memory and the thought-simulation model of Akihiko Kayaba contained on it. But she couldn't leave this spot yet. Not until Higa finished the STL shutdown process and she could confirm the condition of Kazuto Kirigaya and Asuna Yuuki next door.

Rinko had faith that they would wake up as though nothing had gone wrong. She wanted to place Alice's lightcube in their hands and tell them that the Rath team had kept her safe. And she wanted to tell them about the person who had saved the Underworld from the real world—to tell them that Akihiko Kayaba, the man who'd imprisoned them, forced them to fight, and put them through hell, had operated a mechanical body with its battery cable cut and protected the Lightcube Cluster and the *Ocean Turtle.*

She couldn't ask their forgiveness. There was no way to remove the crime of the deaths of four thousand young people from Akihiko Kayaba's story.

But she wanted Kazuto and Asuna to understand the idea that Kayaba had left behind and the goal he'd been striving for.

Rinko placed her hands on the duralumin case containing Alice's lightcube and waited for Higa's voice to come in over the intercom.

"…Rinko, the log-out process is going to be complete in sixty seconds."

"All right. I'll make sure to send someone for you soon."

"Please do. I don't think I can get up this ladder on my own… Also, Kiku went down below to check on things. How is he doing? I think he's got an injury."

At the moment, Rinko couldn't tell him. Nakanishi had gone in to rescue Kikuoka after the gunfight in the hallway to the engine room about three or four minutes ago, but she hadn't heard back from him yet.

But Kikuoka wasn't going to succumb before his mission was complete. He was the man who remained aloof at all times and easily overcame whatever challenges he faced.

"The lieutenant colonel put on quite a show down there. In fact, I'd say he put Hollywood to shame when it comes to action scenes."

"Wow, I can't even imagine that…We got thirty seconds left."

"I'm going over to the STL room now. Get in touch if anything happens. Over."

Rinko switched off her comm and left the console, clutching the case, as she made her way to the adjacent room. Before she touched the sliding door, the speaker in the room crackled with a report from the staff members who'd gone below.

It wasn't from Lieutenant Nakanishi or from the technicians who'd gone to Main Control. It was the security officer who had gone to remove the plastic explosive itself, now that the temperature was dropping in the reactor containment chamber.

"Engine room, coming in! Do you read me? Dr. Koujiro!"

Rinko felt her heart leap in her chest and switched the intercom channel. She shouted, "Yes, I read you loud and clear! What is it?!"

"W-well, ma'am…I removed the C4 safely, but…it's gone."

"Gone…? What's gone?"

"Number Two. I'm not seeing Niemon anywhere in the engine room!"

—∿—

The timer on the cheap digital watch reached zero and beeped.

Critter huddled in a corner of the submersible's passenger bay, listening intently for sound from outside. After many seconds without hearing the death-scream explosion of the megafloat, he exhaled a long and heavy breath.

Even he couldn't say whether it was out of relief or disappointment.

All he knew was that the C4 he'd placed on the *Ocean Turtle*'s reactor had not exploded for some reason, and thus the control-rod drive was not destroyed, and there was no meltdown.

If Hans was still okay back in the engine room, he'd be able to set off the device on his own, so the fact that it hadn't happened meant that he'd been eliminated.

Critter was stunned that a mercenary working for money would choose to stay behind rather than get on the sub. Hans had nearly lost his mind when he'd heard that his partner Brigg was dead; apparently they'd been close enough that he'd chosen to die in the same place.

"People always have a longer history than you think…," he muttered to himself, placing his watch back on a time readout.

In fact, Captain Miller and Vassago, who died before Hans did, had their own motives and circumstances outside of money. And it was those complicating factors that killed them.

In that sense, Critter and the other team members on the submersible had really gotten screwed over by this operation ending in failure. Glowgen DS, their client, had gotten to its current size by undertaking wet works for the NSA and CIA, and they wouldn't think twice about hanging personnel out to dry. They might even be silenced to the very last man the moment they stepped on US soil again.

As a bit of personal insurance, Critter snuck a micro–memory card out of the *Ocean Turtle*, taped to his chest with skin-colored waterproof tape. He had no idea how much good that would do him, but at the very least, if they were going to kill him, they'd just put a bullet in his brain, which was a much better way to go than whatever gruesome fate Vassago and Captain Miller had suffered.

"Good grief." He snorted and glanced unhappily at the two body bags at the back of the passenger section. The sight of Miller's horrible death rictus flashed into his head, and he shivered.

"...Huh? Two?"

He squinted into the darkness at the rear of the craft—there were only two body bags. But that didn't add up. Hans had stayed behind, but there had been three casualties on the team: Captain Miller, Vassago, and Brigg.

"...Hey, Chuck," he said, elbowing a nearby man chewing on an energy bar.

"What?"

"Your team collected the bodies, right? Why are we down one?"

"Huh? We got Brigg from the corridor and Captain Miller in the STL room. Who else died?"

"But...there was another one in the room there..."

"Nope, only found the captain. Gonna remember that goddamn face in my nightmares."

"......"

Critter pulled back and looked around the little cargo section. There were nine men sitting in the cramped space, all of them looking exhausted. Vice-Captain Vassago Casals was not among them.

Critter had definitely confirmed Captain Miller's death in the STL room, but he'd only looked at Vassago. His skin had been totally pale, though, and his hair had been bone white. He couldn't have been alive. If he was alive, why wasn't he on the submersible?

Critter's brain refused to consider this topic any longer. He wrapped his arms around his knees. The loquacious hacker did not say a single word until they returned to the Seawolf-class sub *Jimmy Carter* many minutes later.

—–⁓—

Nineteen minutes and forty seconds after the start of the maximum-acceleration phase, the shutdown of Soul Translator Unit Three and Unit Four in the *Ocean Turtle*'s STL Room Two was complete.

Three minutes later, the acceleration process itself finished, and as the cooling system wound down, quiet returned to the ship interior again.

Dr. Rinko Koujiro and Sergeant First Class Natsuki Aki released the boy and girl from the STLs—but Kazuto Kirigaya and Asuna Yuuki did not open their eyes.

It was clear that their fluctlight output was nearly at a minimum and their mental activity was all but lost.

But Rinko clutched their hands, tearfully calling and calling out to them.

There were the faintest of smiles on Kazuto's and Asuna's faces in the midst of their deep, deep sleep.

3

Tek.

…Tek.

The sound stopped right before me.

Then someone called my name.

"…Kirito."

It was a voice of pure crystal, a voice I never thought I'd hear again.

"As usual, you turn into a crybaby on your own. I know that about you…I know everything."

I lifted my tearstained face.

There stood Asuna, hands behind her back, head tilted a little, smiling down at me.

I didn't know what I should say. So I didn't say anything. I just looked up into those familiar brown eyes of hers and stared and stared.

A little breeze picked up, and the fluttering butterfly between us rode the wind up into the blue sky. Asuna watched it go, then looked back at me and held out her hand.

I had a feeling it would vanish into illusion if I touched it. But the gentle warmth I felt radiating from her white palm told me that the person I loved most of all was right there.

Asuna knew the stakes. She knew this world was going to be sealed shut—and that return to the real world would come only at the end of an unfathomably vast length of time.

And that was why she'd stayed. For me. Just for me, who she knew would probably make the same decision in her situation.

I reached out and squeezed her delicate hand.

With her support, I got to my feet so I could look into those beautiful eyes from up close.

Still I had no words.

But I didn't feel like I needed to say anything. All I did was draw her slender body close and hold her tight. Asuna let her head drop against my chest and whispered, "When we get back there…Alice is going to be angry, isn't she?"

I thought of that confident golden knight, blue eyes flashing like sparks as she scolded me, and I laughed. "It'll be fine as long as we remember her. As long as we don't forget a second of the time we spent with her."

"…Yes. You're right. As long we remember Alice…and Liz and Klein and Agil and Silica…and Yui…everything will be all right," she said.

We ended our embrace, nodded to each other, and looked to the empty shrine together. The World's End Altar had ceased to function, and it slumbered silently beneath the gentle sun at the very edge of the world.

I turned to her, held her hand again, and started to walk down the marble path. We continued past the colorful flowers until we were at the northern end of the floating island. The world seemed to continue forever beneath that deep-blue sky.

Asuna looked at me and asked, "How long do you think we'll be living in here?"

I was silent for a good long while, then told her the truth. "A minimum of two hundred years, apparently."

"Ah," Asuna murmured. She gave me a smile that hadn't

changed for as long as I'd known her. "Even a millennium with you wouldn't feel too long...C'mon, Kirito. Let's go."

"...Yeah. Let's go, Asuna. We've got so much to do. This world is still just a newborn."

Then we joined hands, spread our wings, and took the first step into the infinite blue.

EPILOGUE

1

At the bottom of the sea, where no light could reach, a shadow slowly crawled along.

It looked like a large, flat crab. But it had only six legs, a string extended from its stomach like a spider, and its form was covered in a pressure-resistant metal shell painted gray.

The metal crab was a deep-sea maintenance robot designed to administer to the transpacific optical cable that connected Japan and America known as FASTER.

Since being placed at its sea-floor protective terminal three years ago, the crab had slept without once being called into duty. Until today, when at last it received a wake-up signal, and it stretched grease-crusted joints and left the safety of its home.

The crab had no way of knowing or understanding, however, that the order was not coming from the company that owned it. Following the unofficial orders from this mystery source, it headed straight north, hauling the FASTER repair cable behind it.

A faint, repeating artificial sound was calling the crab. Once a minute, it stopped, ascertaining the location of the sonar signal, then resumed forward progress.

How long did it repeat this process?

At last, the crab determined that it had reached the indicated location. It turned on the light equipped to the front of its body.

The ring of light it produced captured the sight of a silver humanoid machine resting on the sea floor.

A number of brutal holes were opened in its simple aluminum-alloy exterior. Exposed cables were burned and severed here and there, and its left arm was practically ripped loose. The head was even half-crushed, apparently from the water pressure.

But in its right hand, lifted the tiniest bit, was a fiber-optic cable of the same deep-sea line that the crab was pulling from its stomach. The cable stretched straight upward, vanishing into deep darkness, and what it went to was unseen.

The crab stared for a while at the remains of the robot, one of its own kind.

But of course, it did not feel any emotion or fear toward this object. It just followed its orders, extending a manipulation limb to grab the end of the cable held in the humanoid robot's hand. With its other manipulator, it pulled out the endless cable stored around the reel in its own stomach area.

Then the crab pushed the connector ends of the cables together. That was the end of its orders.

It did not spare a single thought for where the cable the humanoid robot held was going. The metal crab just turned around, six legs working in alternation, and headed back to its sea-floor terminal for another long period of hibernation.

Leaving behind it the remains of an utterly destroyed humanoid robot.

The heavily insulated optical cable remained firmly clutched in its metal hand.

2

Two PM, Saturday, August 1st, 2026.

A typhoon had passed over the Kanto region the previous night, and blue skies abruptly returned when the morning came. At Roppongi Hills Arena in Minato Ward, media companies of all kinds from within and outside of Japan had gathered, waiting for their now-delayed payoff.

TV variety shows and online live streams were already covering the press conference. Reporters and commentators breathlessly spoke over the murmuring of the crowd.

The talking heads' tone was skeptical. *"You see, no matter how close you get to the real thing, a fake can never be real. It's like alchemy in the Middle Ages. No matter how you burn or boil iron and steel, you can never turn it into gold!"*

"But, sir, according to their press release for this conference, they've succeeded at re-creating the structure of the human brain itself…"

"And I'm telling you that what they're saying is impossible! Listen, our brains are made up of tens of billions of brain cells. Do you think that a piece of electronics, or some computer program, can re-create that kind of complexity? Do you?"

"Pshh, listen to this guy…acting like he knows what he's talking about before he's seen it in action," sneered Klein, nursing a midday gin and tonic, his tie loose around his neck.

The coffee shop and bar known as Dicey Café, located in a back alley of Okachimachi in Taito Ward, was so packed that there almost wasn't any standing room. They didn't need the CLOSED FOR PRIVATE PARTY sign out; nobody would want to squeeze in anyway.

Sitting at the counter, across from Agil, the proprietor, were Sinon, Leafa, Lisbeth, Silica, and Klein. The four tables were packed with *ALO* leaders, like Sakuya, Alicia, and Eugene; the Sleeping Knights, like Siune and Jun; and former *SAO* players, like Thinker, Yuriel, and Sasha.

Every person had their own beer, cocktail, or soft drink as they watched the large TV on the back wall.

Lisbeth sighed as Klein continue to kvetch. She told him, "I don't blame the guy. I didn't even believe it until I saw it for myself. How could I believe that those people were artificial intelligences and that world was just a virtual creation on some server?"

Sinon brushed the temple of her glasses and murmured, "I know. The smell of the air, the texture of the ground—in a sense, it was almost *more* real than real life."

Leafa nodded in agreement, and Silica winced. "That's only because you had the privilege of diving with those...STLs? Those machines. We were stuck using our AmuSpheres, so to us, the environment and items were just normal polygonal models."

"But nobody ever believed that the Underworlders themselves were just NPCs, did we?" Agil said, the most crucial point of all.

Just then, the sound of the newscaster's voice on the TV rose in pitch. *"Ah, it looks like the conference is about to start! We're going to return you to the media center so you can watch it live!"*

The building went quiet. Over a dozen VRMMO players held their breath as the camera flashes went off at the conference. They were about to witness the moment that the thing they'd worked so hard to protect was revealed to the public at last.

The first person to appear before the rows of TV cameras and photographers was a woman in her late twenties wearing a relaxed pantsuit. Her makeup was reserved, and her hair was tied back in a ponytail.

She came up to the podium and the dozens of microphones arrayed there, where a placard read DR. RINKO KOUJIRO, OCEANIC RESOURCE EXPLORATION & RESEARCH INSTITUTION. She squinted at the flood of light from the flashing cameras but bowed firmly to the crowd before speaking.

"I appreciate your time in the midst of your busy schedules. Today, our institution announces the birth of what we believe is the world's first true artificial general intelligence," she said, getting right to the point. The crowd buzzed.

The scientist lifted a hand to point to the other side of the stage and coolly announced, *"And now I would like to introduce you... to Alice."*

Into a maelstrom of attention both hopeful and skeptical, a figure emerged from behind a silver partition set up on the stage.

It was a girl in a navy blazer. She had long, shining golden hair. Skin whiter than snow. Long legs and a slender build.

On the TV, there were so many flashes going off that the image was practically blanked out. The girl didn't even turn to the reporters, much less bow to them. She just walked forward, her back straight, looking proud. The stream of shutter sounds and the murmuring of the crowd drowned out the faint mechanical whirring that her steps produced.

She crossed the stage smoothly and came to a stop next to Dr. Koujiro. It was at this point that the girl finally turned. Her blond hair gleamed as it swayed in the spotlight.

The girl stared down at the reporters in silence. Her eyes were a brilliant crystal blue.

Her beauty had an almost unearthly quality, not quite Western and not quite Eastern. The crowd steadily began to fall silent.

The intuition of everyone at the conference and of the countless viewers at home said that this was not the appearance of an organic human being. It was most definitely something created by humans—a robot with a metal skeletal structure covered in silicone skin. You could go to the closest theme park or event hall to see similar feminine robots.

But the smoothness of her walk and the perfect posture, plus something about that golden hair, shocked the audience into silence for some reason no one could articulate.

Or perhaps it was the deep brilliance that illuminated those blue eyes. It was a sign of intelligence, something that could not reside in a simple optical lens.

When the reporters fell completely silent, the girl's mouth curled into a suggestion of a smile, and she performed a strange gesture. She made a soft fist with her right hand, then touched it level to her left breast. Her left hand hung down and brushed her side, as though resting atop the hilt of an invisible sword.

Then she returned to a neutral posture, swept the hair off her shoulders and over her back, and parted her light-pink lips. A clear, clean voice with a hint of sweetness traveled over the speakers in the hall and those of countless television sets.

"It's a pleasure to meet you, people of the real world. My name is Alice. Alice Synthesis Thirty."

"Oh…hey, that's our school uniform!!" shouted Silica. She looked from her own blazer to the one Alice was wearing on the screen, stunned.

"She asked for it specifically," Lisbeth noted, tweaking the ribbon of her own uniform. "She wanted to wear the uniform of the knight brigade that came to the aid of the Human Guardian Army, apparently. But her first choice was the same golden armor that she was used to wearing over there."

"Even Rath can't make something like that happen," Leafa said, sending chuckles through the room.

On the screen, Alice had taken a seat just behind Dr. Koujiro's podium. In front of her was another nameplate, reading A.L.I.C.E. 2026—ALICE SYNTHESIS THIRTY.

"…The level of detail in her re-creation is amazing. I only spoke with her a bit in the Underworld, but I can barely tell the difference, looking at her now," Sinon remarked.

Dr. Koujiro cleared her throat and addressed the crowd. *"Now, while this might seem a bit exceptional, I would actually like to start with a question-and-answer demonstration."*

Hands shot up from the reporters' seating area; they had been briefed on this already. The first man Dr. Koujiro called on was from a major newspaper.

"Well, uh...I'd like to ask you something basic, er...Alice. How are you different from other programming-dependent robots?"

Dr. Koujiro stepped in to answer that one. *"At this conference, Alice's physical appearance is not the primary concern. It's her brain...or what we're calling her brain. Her consciousness, which is stored in the photonic brain contained inside her skull, is not a program that is compiled from binary code, but in essence works the same way that human brains do. That is the absolute difference that separates her from existing robots."*

"In that case...it would be nice to have that demonstrated for us and our viewers in an easy-to-understand way..."

Dr. Koujiro's eyebrows knit in annoyance. *"I believe you have the Turing test results in the materials we distributed."*

"No, ma'am, I'm referring to her head...If you could open her skull and show us this photonic brain you're talking about."

The scientist looked stunned for a moment, and she would have said something rather cross if Alice had not answered for herself.

"Of course. I don't mind," she said with a natural smile. *"But before I do that, can you prove to me that you are not a robot?"*

"Huh...? I-I'm a human being, of course...I don't know how to prove that."

"It's simple. Just open your skull so you can show me your brain."

"Oh, wow...Alice is *pissed!*" Leafa giggled, her shoulders shaking.

All the players at Dicey Café had already had a chance to interact with Alice in *ALfheim Online*, so they understood her dignified and sometimes acerbic personality.

Naturally, because Alice needed to generate a new *ALO* account, her avatar's appearance was a bit different from how she looked now. But she still had her superhuman technique with the sword, and her innate knight's pride and honor struck fear and awe into the hearts of many players.

On the TV, the reporter sat back down with a disgruntled look, giving the next person a chance to stand.

"Uh, this question is for Dr. Koujiro. We've heard concerns from some labor unions about a side effect of advanced artificial intelligence in the industrial space leading to a rise in unemployment…"

"Those suspicions are unfounded. Our institution has absolutely no intention of providing true AI for use in simple labor," she said flatly.

The reporter mumbled for a moment but regained her poise and continued, *"It seems as though the financial world has its hopes fixed on this, however. The stocks of industrial-robot manufacturers shot upward on the news. Any comment about that?"*

"Unfortunately, these true AIs—or 'artificial fluctlights,' as we call them in the notes you've been provided—are not the kind of thing that is mass-produced on a short turnaround. They are born as infants, as we are, and grow into unique individuals under the care of their parents and siblings as they age from children to adults. We believe that it would be wrong to place intelligence of this kind into industrial robots to force them to perform repetitive labor."

The conference hall went silent. Eventually, the reporter asked, more than a little harshly, *"Doctor, are you saying…you acknowledge this AI as having human rights?"*

"I'm well aware that this is not the kind of topic that can be argued to a conclusion in a day," said Dr. Koujiro. Her voice was soft and even, but there was the firmness of resolute purpose at its core. *"But we must not commit the mistakes of the past again. That much is very clear. Years ago, many of the developed countries we called the Great Powers used colonization to impose their*

will on undeveloped countries, selling their people as products and forcing them into labor. Even now, a hundred, two hundred years later, this history casts a long shadow on international relations. I'm sure the majority of people listening right now would take umbrage at the suggestion that we should immediately accept artificial fluctlights as human and give them full rights. But in one or two hundred years, we will live in an equal society that accepts them as ordinary. We will interact with them, even marry and start families with them. That is my personal view, but I am certain of it. Will we need to experience the same bloodshed and sorrow that came with the process the last time? Do you want human history to contain another chapter that no one wishes to remember—that we try to hide?"

"*But, Doctor!*" the reporter cried, unable to help herself. "*Their existence is too different from ours! How are we supposed to accept a common humanity with something that has a mechanical body without warmth of its own?!*"

"*Earlier I said that Alice's physical body is not the point,*" Dr. Koujiro answered calmly. "*We are different beings with bodies that work on different mechanisms. But that is only here, in this world. We already have a place where we and the artificial fluctlights can entirely accept one another as equals.*"

"*What…place is this?*"

"*The virtual world. A very large percentage of general-use VR spaces that we use in society today are shifting over to the system of standards supported by The Seed Package. In fact, much of the press requested that we conduct this conference today in a VR environment, but at our institution's insistence, we held it here in the real world. That is because we wanted you first to be aware of the differences between the artificial fluctlights and us. In virtual reality, it will not be this way. The photonic brains of artificial fluctlights like Alice are built to be perfectly compatible with The Seed's VR spaces.*"

The conference room buzzed again. Many of the reporters understood correctly that if an AI could dive into a virtual space, then there would be no way to tell the difference between a human and a sufficiently advanced AI.

The reporter sat down at last, speechless, and a third person rose. The man wore lightly tinted sunglasses and a flashy jacket. He was a well-known freelance journalist.

"First, I'd like to confirm something. I'd never heard of your Oceanic Resource Exploration & Research Institution—I assume this is an independent entity within the Ministry of Internal Affairs? Meaning that the funds you used to complete your research came from taxpayers' pockets. Wouldn't that make the product of your research, that...artificial fluctlight...the property of the citizens of this country? Why is it your institute's decision whether to use this true AI for industrial robots, and not up to the people?"

Dr. Koujiro had handled all the previous questions with grace, but this was the first point at which her mouth pursed with displeasure. She leaned into the microphone, but a pale hand stopped her. It was Alice, who was ready to break her long silence.

The girl with the mechanical body bobbed her head, making her long blond hair shift. *"I accept that you real-worlders are our creators. I am grateful to you for creating us. But another person born in my world once said, 'What if the real world is also just a creation? What if there is yet another creator behind it?'"*

Lightning flashed in the depths of her cobalt-blue eyes. The journalist pulled back, intimidated. Alice stared at him and the other members of the press and rose to her feet.

She puffed out her chest and folded her hands in front of her, looking for all the world like the knight she was, despite her high school girl's uniform. Her eyes were downcast, and in a clear, crisp voice, the world's first true AI continued, *"What if one day, your creator appeared to you and ordered you to become their property? Would you place your hands upon the ground, pledge your allegiance, and beg for mercy?"*

Then the fierce look in her eyes subsided, and a hint of a smile appeared on her lips.

"...I have already spent time with many real-worlders. They

have helped encourage and support me as I find myself all alone in a strange world. They've taught me many things and taken me places. I like them. And not just that...There is one real-worlder whom I love. The fact that I cannot see him now...is a thought that tears even this metal breast apart..."

Alice paused, closed her eyes, and hung her head. Although her body wasn't equipped with the function, many people swore they could see a drop run down her cheek.

Then her golden eyelashes swiftly rose, and her gentle gaze pierced the conference room. The golden knight smoothly lifted her hand and said, *"I have a right hand, as you can see, for reaching out to the people of the real world. But I do not have knees meant to fall upon or a forehead for grinding into the dirt. I am a human being."*

3

Takeru Higa watched the conference from Rath's Roppongi office, not far from the building where it was being held.

His gunshot wound from the attack on the *Ocean Turtle* was healing up at last, and his cast had come off. But he still had an ugly scar from where the pistol bullet had passed through his shoulder. Another round of plastic surgery would get rid of that, apparently, but Higa was planning to leave it the way it was.

The TV station switched from their live feed back to the studio, where the newscaster began to deliver an explanation of the "incident."

"...The Oceanic Resource Exploration & Research Institution in question was conducting research with autonomous submersibles for exploring the sea floor on the Ocean Turtle *megafloat, but in recent days it's been much more famous for the reporting on the attempted armed takeover that happened there."*

The commentator nearby nodded and added, *"Yes, and according to some, the purpose of that invasion was to steal this artificial intelligence. It's very hard to say what the truth is, however, when the invading group hasn't even been identified...*

"Also, the state-of-the-art defense ship Nagato *was roaming that stretch of sea at the time, which raises the question of why it did not rush to help for an entire twenty-four hours. The minister of defense*

claimed that they were prioritizing the safety of the hostages, but apparently that did not save the life of one security member who perished in the attack..."

The program displayed a photograph of a man. He was dressed in the pristine primary formal wear of the Japan Self-Defense Force. With his hat pulled low and his black-framed glasses, it was hard to make out his expression.

Next to the photo was a caption.

Killed in the attack: Seijirou Kikuoka.

Higa let out a long breath and murmured, "It's hard to believe that if there was going to be a single casualty…it would be you, Kiku…"

The person standing next to him shook his head. "Yeah, no kidding…"

The man wore sneakers, cropped cotton pants, and a hideous patterned shirt. His hair was cut short, and a fine layer of stubble covered his face from his ears to his chin. He wore reflective sunglasses to hide his eyes.

The mystery man pulled a cheap little plastic tin of hard candies out of his shirt pocket, popped one in his mouth, and grinned. "This was for the best, Higa—it really was. Either they were going to haul me in front of a court to put everything on me, or they were going to make sure I was never seen again. Plus, having an official casualty as a result of the attack is what allowed us to put so much public pressure on the domestic forces trying to sabotage our goal. Though I didn't expect that it would go all the way up to the administrative vice-minister of defense."

"Sounds like he was getting quite a lot of money from the American weapons companies. But…that aside," Higa said, shrugging and looking at the screen again, "are you sure it's a good idea to announce the artificial fluctlights this publicly? This is totally going to screw up Rath's ultimate plan of putting them on drone weapons, Kiku."

"It's fine. The real point is that we want the Americans to know that we can do it." Kikuoka grinned. Rath's commanding officer had taken an assault rifle bullet through the side of his protective vest but had recovered sooner than anticipated, because he'd luckily avoided any organ damage.

"Now their weapons manufacturers won't be able to force us to hand over our tech under the guise of 'joint development,'" he continued. "We've already perfected the artificial fluctlights, so we don't need their help. They'll have to give up after this press conference…and my word, but Alice's beauty goes beyond that of any human being's…"

His narrow eyes squinted through the sunglasses when Alice showed up on the TV screen again.

"That's true…She truly is the jewel of Project Alicization…"

They said nothing for a time after that, giving Higa a chance to think.

Their finished project was code-named A.L.I.C.E. after the specific kind of highly adaptive artificial intelligence Rath was hoping to bring into existence. Was it just a miraculous coincidence that the girl who ended up fitting that definition was given the name Alice as a child in the Underworld?

If it wasn't sheer coincidence, there must have been a reason for it. Was it the result of some staff member secretly interfering with the project, the way Yanai had? Or was it someone not on the staff…like the one man who had logged into the Underworld all alone…

Higa turned to look at the two Soul Translators at the back of the spacious lab room. Resting on the very same unit he'd used for a three-day dive just two months ago was none other than Kazuto Kirigaya.

There was a drip-feed catheter in his left arm. EKG electrodes were stuck to his chest. During the three weeks of his comatose state since being shipped here from the *Ocean Turtle*, his face had become even more sunken than before.

But his sleeping face was peaceful. It even looked like he was smiling with satisfaction, maybe.

The same could be said of the girl sleeping next to him: Asuna Yuuki.

The STLs were continually monitoring their fluctlight activity. Not all brain signals had vanished. If their fluctlights were totally destroyed, they ought to stop breathing entirely. But their mental activity was at an extreme minimum and hopes of a recovery were dying out.

It wasn't a surprise. Kazuto and Asuna had experienced an unbelievable two hundred years before the maximum-acceleration phase ended. Higa had lived for only twenty-six years; he couldn't imagine that length of time. It was already a biological miracle that their hearts were still beating after they had long since passed the theoretical life span of the fluctlight.

Higa and Dr. Koujiro had gone to explain and apologize to Kazuto's and Asuna's parents as soon as the two had been transferred to Roppongi. They'd told the parents what they considered to be the truth—all except for the part where Rath was partly staffed by elite researchers connected to the SDF and the national defense industry.

Kazuto Kirigaya's parents cried, but they did not fly out of control. They'd already heard most of the story from his sister. The real problem was the father of Asuna Yuuki.

For one thing, he was the former chief director of RCT, a major Japanese company. His anger was considerable, to the point of threatening to take them to court that very day. Surprisingly, it was Asuna's mother who stopped him.

The college professor had stroked her sleeping daughter's hair and said, *I believe in my daughter. She would never simply get up and leave without telling us. I know that she will come back to us safe and sound. Let's wait a little longer, dear.*

Their parents were probably watching the press conference now, seeing the new form of humanity that their children had fought so hard to protect. It wouldn't be right for this momentous day, the first step for Alice and all future artificial fluctlights into the real world, to be crowned with sadness.

Please, Kirito, Asuna…just open your eyes, Higa prayed, lowering his head. Suddenly, Kikuoka elbowed him.

"Hey, Higa."

"...What, Kiku? I'm focusing on something right now."

"Higa. Higa. Look...look at that."

"The conference is basically over. I can already guess what all the questions will be," Higa grumbled, looking up. Then he saw that Kikuoka was gesturing with the candy container not to the TV screen but to the little sub-monitor to the right.

The two windows on the screen were displaying real-time data from the two STLs. A faint, white ring was floating against a black background. That unmoving, faint shape gleamed with the light of the sleeping boy's and girl's souls...

Bink.

A little tiny peak rose from a part of the ring and vanished.

Higa's eyelids blinked violently, and he gurgled as something caught in his throat.

———

Dr. Koujiro's voice filled the vast conference hall again.

"...It will require a tremendous amount of time. There is no need to rush to a conclusion. We want you to get to know the artificial fluctlights who will be born through new processes and methods in the future. Interact with them in the virtual world. Feel and think. That is all this institute truly wants the people of the world to do."

She took her seat at the end of this speech, but there was no rousing round of applause. If anything, the reporters looked even more concerned than before.

The next person promptly raised a hand and stood. "Doctor, what can you tell us about the potential dangers of this development? Can you guarantee that these AIs will never attempt to wipe out humanity and take over the planet?"

Dr. Koujiro stifled an exhausted sigh and said, "It absolutely will not happen, *outside* of one possibility. And that would be the case that we attempt to exterminate them first."

"But it's been a longtime trope in books and movies…," the reporter protested, until Alice suddenly shot to her feet. The man backed away in alarm.

Alice's blue eyes were wide and staring at nothing, as though she were listening to some faint, far-off sound. After a few seconds, she said, "I must go. I will leave you now."

Then she spun, golden hair swaying, and made her way to the edge of the stage and vanished at the maximum speed her mechanical body could manage, leaving behind a speechless room full of reporters and a national TV audience.

What could be more important to Alice than this very conference, her introduction to the world? Even Dr. Koujiro seemed to be alarmed by the interruption, but she quickly altered her expression, coming to an apparent understanding. She inhaled, then exhaled, and not one of the reporters noticed the faint smile on her lips.

———

It was no trick of the eyes.

There was a pulse in both Kazuto's and Asuna's fluctlights, happening at distinct intervals of about ten seconds and getting slightly higher each time.

"K…Kiku!" Higa exclaimed, turning around to look at the STLs.

There was no change in their sleeping faces. Except…

Even as he was watching them, the blush of blood seemed to be coming back to their cheeks. Their pulses were growing stronger. The monitoring equipment was indicating that their internal temperatures were rising slowly, too.

Could he dare hope? Through some miracle, they were waking up. Their souls were being resurrected from the dead.

The ten minutes from that point on felt as long to Higa as the maximum-acceleration phase had while it'd been happening. He summoned spare staff from around the office and checked the monitors frequently to ensure that the fluctlights were returning to a normal condition while they made preparations. It felt like the pulsating rainbow ring was going to vanish like some vision in the desert if he didn't keep an eye on it at all times.

They got oral rehydration solution, nutrient-replenishing gels, and whatever else they might need ready. Then, when there was nothing left to do but wait, the entrance door slid open, and a person no one expected to see entered the lab. Higa and Kikuoka yelped in unison.

"A...Alice?!"

The young blond woman was supposed to be in the middle of the press conference of the century at Roppongi Hills. But here she was, actuators whirring as she hurried to the two STLs.

"Kirito! ...Asuna!" Alice called out, her voice just a bit tinny and electronic. She knelt beside the gel beds.

Higa swiveled to the TV screen, dreading what he might see there. The program had cut to the studio, where the newscaster was breathlessly describing how the star of the conference had suddenly vanished.

"...Well...I'm sure Dr. Koujiro will manage for us," Kikuoka said with a stiff grin. He turned off the TV. It wasn't the time to be watching the conference. Higa checked on Kazuto's and Asuna's vitals first, then watched Alice as she performed what seemed to be a prayer for the two.

While she'd hibernated within her lightcube package, Alice had been taken from the *Ocean Turtle* to the Roppongi office. They had produced a modified version of Niemon that was meant to approximate Alice's appearance called Number Three and had loaded her in, and that was when she woke up in the real world.

As she had said at the press conference, the shock of suddenly waking up in an unfamiliar world must have been great. The fact that she'd adapted so well to a dramatically different environment in just three weeks was surely due to the single powerful drive that possessed her: to see Kirito and Asuna again.

And now that time had come.

Alice's hands rose, motors whirring faintly, until they enveloped Kazuto's right hand where it lay on the gel bed.

His bony fingers curled slightly.

His eyelashes twitched.

His lips opened a bit, closed, opened again...

Then his eyelids slowly, slowly rose.

His dark eyes reflected the dimmed lights of the room, but there was no conscious focus to them. *Speak—just say something,* Higa prayed.

A breath escaped through his parted lips, almost like a sigh. In time, the vibration of his vocal cords gave it voice.

"...I...dil..."

A sudden chill colder than ice ran up Higa's spine. The sound he made was eerily similar to the creepy utterances made by fluctlight copies shortly before they collapsed.

But this time...

"...be...all...rie."

...different sounds followed.

It'll be all right. That was what Kazuto said. It had to be.

There was utter silence in the lab room until another quiet voice replied.

"Sure."

That one belonged to Asuna in the other STL. Her lids were rising slowly.

Their eyes met, and their heads tilted.

Then Kazuto turned to face the other direction and smiled at Alice, who was holding his hand. "Hi...Alice. It's been a while."

"...Kirito...Asuna...," she whispered, smiling back at them. She blinked furiously—almost like she was chagrined that her body did not have a crying function.

Kazuto gave her a benevolent look and said, "Alice, your sister, Selka, chose to go into Deep Freeze to wait for your return. She's still sleeping even now, atop that hill on the eightieth floor of Central Cathedral."

"...!!"

Higa didn't understand any of that, but Alice's body jolted

with shock, and her blond hair fell onto her shoulders, hiding her expression.

She placed her face against the sheet. Kazuto rested his hand on her back—and looked at Kikuoka and Higa for the first time.

At that exact moment, Higa experienced a very mysterious feeling somewhere deep in his consciousness. It wasn't emotion. It wasn't fascination. It was…awe?

Two hundred years.

A soul that had experienced almost endless time.

Kazuto told the frozen man, "Go on, Mr. Higa. Delete our memories. Our roles have ended."

4

My eyelids rose.

Like always, I was hit by momentary hesitation—where and when was I?

But that strange feeling was growing weaker by the day. Like flowing water, the past was drifting further and further away from me. It was a sad, lonely thing.

I looked up at the clock on the wall across from my bed. Four in the afternoon. I'd finished my after-lunch rehab session, showered, and fallen asleep for about an hour and a half.

The sunlight filtering through the white hospital curtains cast a clear contrast on the room's interior. If I listened hard enough, I could hear the buzzing of cicadas in the distance—as well as the dull roar of the city, with all its machines and humans.

I breathed in deep the scent of sunny linen and disinfectant, slowly exhaled, and got out of the bed. The room wasn't very large, so it took me only a few steps to reach the southern-facing window. I spread the curtains with my hands.

The western sun was blinding. I squinted and beheld the massive city below me. The real world, which continued to function in complex and turbulent ways, consuming vast resources. The world where I was born.

It filled me with a feeling of return and wholeness yet also a wish to go back to the other world. Would there ever come a time when I wasn't grappling with homesickness of some kind again?

There was a faint knock at the door behind me. I called out an invitation to open the door, turning around to see it slide open and reveal my visitor.

She had long chestnut-brown hair collected into two bundles. She wore a white knit top, an ice-blue flared skirt, and white mules. I couldn't help but stare. She looked like the summer sun, lingering in the air.

Three days ago, Asuna had left the hospital ahead of me. She carried a small bundle of flowers and grinned. "Sorry, I'm a bit late."

"Actually, I just woke up," I said, returning her smile. Asuna walked into the room, and we embraced. She rubbed my arms and back with her free hand. "Hmm, still only about ninety percent of the normal Kirito. Are you eating enough?"

"I am. Tons. It's just going to take a while; I was bedridden for two whole months," I said with a wince and a shrug. "In better news, I've got a leave date now. Three days from today."

"Really?!" Asuna's face lit up. She walked over to the flower vase on the side cabinet. "Then we'll have to celebrate. First in *ALO*, then in real life."

She deftly changed the water in the vase, took out the wilted flowers, and added the two new pale-purple roses she'd brought before putting the container back on the cabinet.

The roses seemed to be doing their best to reach a pure-blue color, but they weren't quite there yet. I murmured my agreement, staring at the flowers.

I sat on the bed, and Asuna plopped down next to me. Another wave of homesickness hit me. But it didn't have the same sharp pain that I'd felt moments ago.

Asuna leaned against me, so I put my arm around her shoulder and let my mind wander through distant memories.

On the day we'd been left behind in the Underworld as it plunged into the maximum-acceleration phase, we'd flown off the World's End Altar with its abundance of flowers, crossed the black deserts and strange reddish rocks, and first rejoined the Human Guardian Army at the ancient ruins where the last battle had taken place.

Already Klein, Agil, Lisbeth, and the other players from the real world were gone. They'd been booted off the simulation when the acceleration resumed.

I calmed down the weeping Tiese and Ronie, then got an introduction to the young Integrity Knight named Renly, courtesy of Sortiliena. He and I reformed the group, then led them back north along the path until we reached the Eastern Gate again.

Vice Commander Fanatio, Deusolbert, and the apprentice knights Fizel and Linel were still stationed there at the gate. We shared a nervous reunion, and I also met the knight named Sheyta for the first time. She gave me a message from a man called Iskahn, who was the champion of the pugilists and temporary commander of the Dark Army.

He said that the Dark Army would be pulling back to the Imperial Palace far to the east, and once the surviving generals had finished cleaning up and reorganizing after the war, they would come seeking peace with the human army in one month's time. Sheyta volunteered for the role of envoy. Once she had left on her gray dragon for the east, the remaining members of the Human Guardian Army resumed marching back to Centoria.

Somehow, the people at the towns and villages on the return trip already knew that peace had arrived. We received great cheers and welcomes from local residents wherever we went.

When the trip to Centoria was finished, the days passed in a blur. We helped Fanatio, now the highest-ranking Integrity Knight in the wake of Bercouli's passing, to rebuild the Axiom Church, offer reparations to the families of the soldiers who had died in the war, and rebuff the attempts of the four imperial families and other high nobles to seize power in the chaos and vacuum of the postwar order. A month passed by in a flash.

When we returned to the site of the Eastern Gate for the peace talks, Asuna and I were introduced to Iskahn, who was now the official commander of the Dark Army.

The warrior was a bit younger than I was, with fiery-red hair. He said to me, "You're the brother of Leafa, the Green Swordswoman? I hear you cut Emperor Vecta in two. Not that I doubt your story...but let me test you with just a single punch."

And for some reason, Iskahn and I decked each other in the cheek, right there in the midst of peace talks. He seemed satisfied by it, though. Then he said, "Yeah...you're tougher than the emperor...and even me. I hate to admit it, but I will...You're the...first..."

That was where my memory cuts off.

The next scene I could recall was waking up on the STL's gel bed as Takeru Higa announced, "I've finished the process of deleting your memory."

According to Dr. Rinko Koujiro, from the day that we established peace in the Underworld, Asuna and I had apparently remained active for two hundred years, well beyond the capacity of the fluctlight. But I couldn't recall a thing about what we did during all those years or how we avoided the destruction of our fluctlights. Even more frightening, I had completely forgotten the conversation I'd had with Higa and Kikuoka right after waking up in Roppongi.

The same was true for Asuna. But she just gave me one of her usual fluffy smiles and said, "Knowing you, I'm sure you stuck your head into all kinds of squabbles and had to go on the run from the advances of girls everywhere."

That sapped any interest I had in trying to remember, but no matter what, the painful sense of loneliness never went away. That was because as the Underworld ran (in real time) to this very moment, Fanatio, Renly, and the other Integrity Knights; Iskahn and the dark lords; and Ronie, Tiese, Sortiliena, and Miss Azurica were no longer alive...

Asuna sensed what I was thinking and whispered, "It's all right. Your memory might have vanished, but the *memories* still linger."

That's right, Kirito. Don't cry...Stay cool, said a tiny, familiar voice deep in my ear.

The voice was right. Memories weren't saved only in the areas of the brain dedicated to storing information. They were a part of the fluctlight network that spread across all the cells of the body.

I blinked to blot away the tears in my eyes and caressed Asuna's hair. "Yes. I'm sure…I'm sure we'll see them again someday."

A few minutes of gentle, silent tranquility passed. The sunlight began to color and darken against the white wall. Every now and then, the shadows of birds returning to the nest crossed its surface.

It was another knock on the door that broke the silence.

I looked over, curious; there weren't any scheduled visitors at this hour. Eventually, I let go of Asuna's shoulder and said, "Come in."

The door slid open, right as a familiar—and obnoxious—voice said, "Well, well, I hear you're going to be released soon, Kirito! We'll have to throw you a party— Oh! Oops! Am I interrupting something?"

I sighed and replied, "I'm not going to demand you tell me how you already know my discharge schedule when Miss Aki *just* told me about it…Mr. Kikuoka."

The former Ministry of Internal Affairs Virtual Division official, former Ground SDF lieutenant colonel, and former commanding officer of the fake company Rath was thankfully not wearing the same hideous shirt he'd had on the other day. Seijirou Kikuoka slipped into the hospital room.

He was dressed in a sharp, expensive suit with a necktie, despite the summer heat. His short hair was in perfect order, and there wasn't a drop of sweat on the skin behind his narrow, frameless glasses. From every angle, he was an elite businessman working at a foreign capital firm—if not for his usual smirk and the cheap paper bag he was carrying.

Kikuoka lifted the bag and said, "This is for you. We need you to build up your strength again. I was really thinking hard about what to get you, but Dr. Rinko demanded that I bring you proper store-bought products. At any rate, to get your energy back, you need fermented food—that's a must. So I've got a grab bag here.

First is some salted and fermented goldfish sushi from Lake Biwa, and they're hard to find, because they don't catch many anymore. Then there's some fermented tofu from Okinawa. That's perfect with some aged *awamori* to drink. But the best is the cheese—and it's no ordinary cheese. This is super-fancy washed-rind cheese straight from France called Époisses! They wash it in marc every day during a long aging process, until it begins to support a wonderful array of microorganisms on its surface, giving it the most stunning bouquet of—"

"The refrigerator's over there," I said, pointing to the corner of the room to stop Kikuoka from going on.

"Huh? Why?"

"Thanks for the souvenirs. The fridge is over there."

"C'mon—let's open them up."

"The windows are sealed! What do you think will happen if you open all that stuff in here?"

There was already a peculiar fragrance coming from the paper bag, and Asuna began to inch away with a look of terror on her face.

"I think it smells nice…Also, I know I keep saying this, but you don't have to be so stuffy around me. It feels awkward," Kikuoka said casually, sticking his food in the refrigerator and moving to the chair for guests.

The grin returned to his face. He crossed one leg over the other and steepled his fingers atop them. "I'm really very glad about all of this. I mean, you were in a physically comatose state ever since the Death Gun accomplice attacked you at the end of June. I suppose it's a sign of your youth that you're doing this well after just a single week of PT."

"Well…uh…I suppose I should thank you for the help," I admitted, crossing my arms. It was the STL's fluctlight-stimulation therapy that had helped heal me when I fell into cardiac arrest after the attack. This man had used a falsified ambulance to ferry me from the hospital to a helicopter that took me all the way to the *Ocean Turtle*, out at sea near the Izu Islands.

I understood why he couldn't use official methods. I needed STL treatment at the soonest possible moment, and Rath was a secret organization that couldn't be made public. If anything, Kikuoka deserved my full gratitude for going to such dangerous lengths to save my life.

And yet...

"...Mr. Kikuoka, when I dived into the Underworld the second time, and I woke up in that little northern village without having my memory blocked—was that really an unexpected accident?"

"Of course," Kikuoka said, his smile waning. "There would have been no point to dropping the real-world you into the Underworld. It would have contaminated the simulation. In reality, of course, Yanai had already corrupted it, and you ended up putting the world back on the proper track..."

"To think that someone who worked for Sugou was hiding in plain sight at Rath," I said, glancing over at Asuna. She was rubbing the back of her arms with disgust, this time over something other than smells.

"It gives me chills to think that I was in a dive for hours while that slug-man was in the next room over. And then he shot Mr. Higa...I wish that we could have arrested him and forced him to admit to all his crimes..."

"It may have been for the best that he died that way, actually," Kikuoka said quietly. "If Yanai had met up with the attackers like they planned and managed to flee to America, I can't imagine that his clients in the NSA and Glowgen Defense Systems would have kept their agreement with him. If anything, they'd probably use whatever means necessary to make him spill everything he knew about the STL and artificial fluctlights, and then they'd dispose of him. No one man can hold his own against the darker side of the American military business."

"Is that why you're officially dead, Mr. Kikuoka?"

"You could say that," he said, admitting that when it came to facing a massive enemy alone, playing possum was the obvious choice.

Asuna was concerned about his aloof manner, given the very

serious topic. "What are you planning to do next? Dr. Rinko's been put in charge as Rath's public face. You can't really hang out around the Roppongi office anymore, can you?"

"No need to worry. There are still many things for me to do. For now, I need to pour all my efforts into securing the *Ocean Turtle* and the Underworld."

That was the topic I wanted to know about most, and I leaned forward with interest. "Yes, that! What's going to happen to the Underworld now...?"

"We can't be too optimistic about the current momentum," Kikuoka said, rearranging his legs and looking out the window. "The *Ocean Turtle* is still in the Izu Islands, anchored and locked down. There are only a few people on board to maintain and protect the reactor. There are defense ships patrolling the area constantly...which all sounds good, but that's just a holding pattern. The country doesn't know what to do next."

"In all honesty, the government would love to immediately shut down Rath, or the 'Oceanic Resource Exploration & Research Institution,' and assume control of all artificial fluctlight tech. If you mass-produced them, you could create all the ultra-low-cost labor you would ever need. Even the biggest factories on mainland Asia couldn't keep up. But if they do that, it will retroactively reveal the truth of the assault on the float. It would be a massive scandal—an attack by the NSA and American military contractors, with the acting administrative vice-minister of defense taking dirty money to delay a military response for twenty-four hours. That money also trickled to Diet representatives of the ruling party—men who have financial connections to major domestic weapons companies. If all of this goes public, it will rattle the current administration to its core."

But despite the force of his words, Kikuoka's expression was anxious.

"Rattle...That's it?"

"Exactly. It will rattle them but probably not be enough to overturn them entirely...The party will simply decide to cut loose the vice-minister and a few Diet members. Rath will be dismantled, and its property will be absorbed by one of the major zaibatsu conglomerates. Alice will be taken, and there's no way they won't reinitialize the Lightcube Cluster on the *Ocean Turtle*…"

"No…no, they can't!" cried Asuna. Her hazel eyes flashed with righteous fury.

I pressed my fingers against her arm and urged Kikuoka to continue. "You've got a plan in mind for how to head this situation off, don't you?"

"It's not a plan…as much as a hope," Kikuoka said. His smile had a rare honesty to it. "The hope is that while the government grapples internally with the decision, we are able to formulate an effective public argument…That's it. In other words, to convince people that artificial fluctlights deserve human rights. And to do that, we need as many real people in the real world as possible to have as much contact with artificials as possible. That, in fact, is the very purpose of The Seed Nexus, you might say."

"…Yeah…I see."

"But for that to be feasible, the Underworlders will need high-capacity connections to The Seed Nexus first. The government shut down the satellite connection on the *Ocean Turtle*. I'm going to try to get that restored next. We took the initiative with that press conference. That's given us a bit of time to work with for now."

"The connection…," I murmured, gazing at the orange sky outside the window.

Beyond the sunset were countless communication satellites, each traveling its own orbit. But only a few of them would have the kind of throughput needed to communicate with the Underworld. I didn't have to think about it very hard to understand that Kikuoka's plan was going to be tremendously difficult.

But now that it had come to this, there was nothing that a mere high school student like me could do. My only option was to have faith and leave it in more-capable hands.

I turned away from the window, took a step forward, and bowed my head.

"Mr. Kikuoka…please. Please save the Underworld."

"You don't need to ask me," Kikuoka said, standing and smiling. "The Underworld is a dream I'm willing to put my life on the line for, too."

Former lieutenant colonel Seijirou Kikuoka left as quickly as he arrived, leaving behind his tempting bag of delicacies.

Asuna exhaled and said, "His statements and attitude are very bold and reassuring…but I guess it wouldn't be Mr. Kikuoka if I didn't feel like there was something else behind it…"

"Oh, I'm sure there's more. Several layers." I chuckled, sitting back down on the bed. "Despite what he says, I'm sure that he hasn't given up on the idea of giving the SDF domestic jet fighters with artificial fluctlights for pilots."

"Wh-what?!"

"Of course, he wouldn't think of forcing AI to operate them without free will—not anymore. But what if the Underworlders voluntarily agree to serve? The Integrity Knights and dark knights are born to be warriors, for example."

"Oh…that's true…Hmm."

While Asuna pondered that, I got to thinking as well. What was Seijirou Kikuoka's true intention? It was probably something I couldn't even imagine at this point. Something vast and distant beyond the boundaries of government and national defense, something like Akihiko Kayaba's vision…

"Ah! Oh no! Look at the time!"

"Hmm? Visiting hours don't end soon…"

"No, I mean…it's today! The meeting of the nine fairy leaders of *ALO*!"

"Oh…that's right," I said, clapping my hands together.

In the invasion of the *Ocean Turtle* last month, about two thousand Japanese VRMMO players had attempted to fight back against PoH's plot to insert a large number of foreign players into the Underworld, by converting their own avatars in a suicide rescue operation. Except for a few hundred survivors, all the rest of those characters had died.

Today there was going to be a major meeting within *ALO* for the purpose of revealing the full truth to those players who had served as heroic volunteers. Since Asuna and I were in the center of that whole situation, we had to be in attendance, of course.

"Hmm, I don't think I have time to get all the way home," Asuna said, rather unconvincingly, and pulled an AmuSphere unit right out of the tote bag she was holding. "Guess I'll just have to dive from here."

"..."

I blinked a few times and noted, "Um, Asuna...it would seem to me that you fully intended to do this..."

"Oh, no, this was just a precaution. Let's not get hung up on minor details!" she insisted. Then she smiled and suddenly flopped onto the bed on top of me. Despite being alarmed at the thought of what would happen if Miss Aki came in to take my temperature, I put my arm around her waist and squeezed.

The only sound in the silence was our breathing.

There was no way for us to know how we'd gotten through two hundred years in the Underworld—longer than the supposed limit of the fluctlight itself. Perhaps, like Administrator, we'd spent a very long time sleeping, or perhaps we'd been able to manipulate the STL from within to continually organize our memories. But one thing I could say for certain: I made it back to the real world only because Asuna was at my side.

I thought I could hear her voice through our skin contact.

No matter what world we're in or how much time passes...we'll always be together...

"Yeah...that's right," I said out loud, stroking Asuna's hair as she beamed. I placed the AmuSphere over her head.

Once the harness was locked, I did the same with my own.

We shared a look, nodded, and spoke our command together.

"Link Start!"

5

"Papa!!"

A small person leaped onto me the moment I logged in to *ALO*. I caught her with both hands, lifting her high up first, then clutching her to my chest. She rubbed her cheek against me, purring like a cat.

Yui was an advanced AI of the top-down variety—and my adopted daughter with Asuna. Since I'd been allowed to use an AmuSphere for a week now, I'd been seeing her every day. It seemed like she was more needy and affectionate each time I saw her.

I wasn't going to scold her for that, of course. Yui had helped track down my location after I vanished, predicted that the people who attacked the *Ocean Turtle* were going to use VRMMO players from other countries, and helped set up countermeasures. She'd played a massive role.

Once she had gotten her fill of physical contact, her childlike form in the white dress vanished in a burst of light, replaced by a palm-sized pixie. She fluttered translucent wings and rose to alight on my left shoulder, her favorite seat.

I took another look around my house: the log house on the twenty-second floor of New Aincrad within *ALO*. This place, too, I had visited every night, and the wave of nostalgia it gave me hadn't dimmed yet.

Perhaps it was because it was a bit similar to the cottage on the outskirts of Rulid in the Underworld where I had lived with Alice for half a year. At the time, I was in a largely unconscious state, so my memories of it were vague, but the gentleness of that period of time still lingered in my heart.

Alice's sister, Selka, had come with food just about every day. Apparently, she had chosen to be frozen long-term so that she could see Alice again one day, and that was the one thing I had told Alice before my memories were deleted.

Since then, Alice had been awaiting an opportunity to return to the Underworld, although she did not speak of this. I wanted to make it come true for her. But as of this moment, the *Ocean Turtle* was on lockdown near the Izu Islands, and there was no satellite connection to reach it. We could only wait for Kikuoka's plan to bear fruit.

I sighed, putting the thought out of my head, and turned around, Yui still sitting on my shoulder. Asuna met my gaze with a gentle, all-knowing smile. The blue-haired girl took my hand and led me out of the house.

Alfheim's curtain of night was beginning to fade. We spread our fairy wings and took flight into the first rays of sun peeking through the outer aperture.

Many players were already together at the open space before the massive dome at the roots of the World Tree. I spotted a group of familiar faces and sped over to land among them.

"You're late, Kirito!"

I lifted my fist to strike Klein's incoming knuckles, which shot at me the moment I made contact with the ground. The katana user was grinning, wearing his usual ugly bandana. "You can't go teleporting around here, so you gotta give yourself more time for travel, hero!" he teased.

"That wasn't teleportation. It was ultra-high-speed flight."

"Same damn thing!!"

He smacked me on the back. Next to him, Agil unfolded his

arms and extended a huge fist toward me. I gave him a knuckle salute, and the bearded man smirked and added, "Did you get too used to that superpowered character, and now you've gone on us? We can give you a little refresher after the meeting."

"Ugh," I grunted guiltily. If I fought in *ALO* now, I would probably forget I didn't have Incarnation attacks and element generation, and I would end up trying to block sword blows by yelling at them.

"A-actually, you'd better prepare yourself, because I've got some Underworld tricks you haven't seen yet," I bluffed back. Then I turned and saw Leafa, her long ponytail glimmering in the morning sun, and Sinon, who was smiling with a huge bow slung over her shoulder. We traded quick high fives.

I'd seen both of them several times since waking up, too, of course. Leafa—Suguha—told me how she'd saved Lilpilin, chief of the orcs, and fought at his side. I rubbed her head and told her she did well, and she scrunched up her face and cried. It was hard for me to reconcile that with the mental image of the furious Green Swordswoman whom the Dark Territory soldiers would go on to speak of in legend. But at the same time, I could totally buy it. Suguha was the one who'd continued with kendo long after I'd dropped out. She was a true devotee of the sword, unlike me.

At the peace talks, the orcs announced that they would wait eternally for the return of the one they called the Green Swordswoman. I was certain that even now, two hundred years later, that tradition was continuing strong.

Sinon described her one-on-one combat with Gabriel Miller in brief terms and revealed that he was none other than Subtilizer, who'd defeated her in the fourth Bullet of Bullets tournament. Gabriel's Incarnation attacks numbed her and nearly sucked her mind away, except that her good-luck charm protected her—and she wouldn't tell me what that was when I asked.

I told her about the path of my battle with Gabriel, too, as well as the fate of the man in the real world. After the attackers fled in their submersible, Gabriel and the other enemy—PoH, leader of Laughing Coffin—were not found in the STL room, but the STL logs told some of the story.

After Gabriel Miller's duel with me, the majority of his fluctlight was lost in the pressure of a tremendous flood of information. His heart stopped immediately after that; he was surely dead.

PoH's situation was a bit more complex. His mental activity was retained for about ten years of internal time after the maximum-acceleration phase began. From that point on, his fluctlight activity lowered over time, until he essentially lost all conscious thought around the thirty-year mark.

It was frightening to consider, but after I had defeated PoH, I transformed the structure of his avatar into a simple tree, to prevent him from logging back in to use it, and left him there. In other words, he spent decades with no sensory inputs beyond the sensation of "skin." Of course his fluctlight would break down; Higa said that even if he was physically alive, his mind would no longer be present.

Although it was only an indirect consequence in each case, I was clearly responsible for taking their lives. I could accept that sin, but I did not want to regret it. To do so would be an insult to Administrator, whom I'd also killed, and the many Underworlders who'd died in the course of acting on their beliefs.

After greeting Sinon and Leafa, I shook hands with Lisbeth and Silica next.

"I heard you were the one who recruited the Japanese players, Liz? I wish I could've heard that speech," I said.

Lisbeth just chuckled nervously. "Speech? Oh, gosh, it wasn't anything that fancy. Honestly, I wasn't even conscious of what I was saying…"

"It was amazing!" Silica interjected. "Her speech was masterful!" Lisbeth grabbed her triangular animal ears and pulled.

"Thank you, too, Silica," I said, bowing to the little beast-tamer. She grinned, revealing small, sharp fangs.

"Um, in that case, give me a present," she said, rushing to hug me. Her little blue dragon, Pina, trilled and leaped off her shoulder to land on my head.

"Hey, you! What do you think you're doing?" Lisbeth demanded, pulling Silica's tail this time. The smaller girl let out a bizarre yelp like "*Hgyuh!*" sending the others into fits of laughter.

There were several groups of players nearby, in fact. Lady Sakuya and the sylphs. Alicia Rue and the cait siths. Eugene and the salamanders. Plus Siune, Jun, and the Sleeping Knights.

I'm back.

It was the strongest I'd ever felt that statement to be true since waking up in Rath's Roppongi office.

This wasn't a complete and total happy ending, not at all. The route back to the Underworld was unclear at best; repairing the damage in online relations with American, Chinese, and Korean VRMMO players was crucial; and there were other problems beyond that.

Lisbeth hung on my other arm in playful competition with Silica. I asked her quietly, "Do you think there's any way to get back the items that were lost in the Underworld?"

"Oh…um…"

Her cheerful face clouded over a bit. Thankfully, the accounts of the players who'd converted over from *ALO*, *GGO*, and other Seed worlds hadn't been totally lost after death, and they were able to convert back to their original VRMMOs.

Unfortunately, however, their weapons and armor that were destroyed or stolen in the battle did not come back. As they'd gone in with their finest gear, these were items that could not be easily replaced, and Lisbeth was leading a group of players negotiating with the operators of the different VRMMOs to try to find a way to restore that data.

"Most of the developers have a hands-off stance that says, if you lost items as a result of conversion, it's your own responsibility. But Mr. Higa from Rath says that if the data is still on the Underworld server, it might be recoverable, so I asked him to check that out when he can. That just means waiting for the connection to come back online…"

"I see…I'm sure Higa will find a way to work it out. And…what about the Chinese and Korean players…?"

"It's a very bad situation," Lisbeth said, looking gloomy. "It was a really awful battle…But people are agreeing that we bear some responsibility for things being that bad before the incident. I mean, The Seed Nexus cuts off all connections from outside Japan. There's some discussion about opening *ALO* as a means of facilitating talks with them. I'm sure it'll be a topic of debate today."

"That sounds good. Walls can make relations worse, but the reverse is never true," I replied, thinking of the End Mountains, which had separated the human realm and the dark realm in the Underworld for hundreds of years.

I gazed at the hazy horizon of Alfheim for a while, then turned back to the roots of the World Tree. The marble gates were wide open now, ushering the players into the dome within.

"C'mon—let's go," I said to my friends. But before I could take a step toward the doors, I noticed a flashing icon that indicated I was getting a voice-chat signal from outside *ALO*. "Oops, I'm getting a call. You guys go ahead."

Asuna and the others continued onward while I took a few steps in the other direction and tapped the icon. "Hello?"

A very familiar voice answered. "Kirito…it's me…Alice."

"Alice! Hey…it's been a while. I heard that you were coming to the meeting in Alfheim, too…"

"I'm sorry…I can't. This party isn't going to be ending anytime soon…Tell everyone that I'm sorry."

"…Okay," I murmured.

But I was a bit perturbed. As the first true artificial general intelligence, Alice was put on a busy schedule that had her in attendance at receptions and parties every single day in an attempt to place her at the forefront of society's attention. Dr. Koujiro apologized for it, and Alice seemed to know that she didn't really have a choice anyway, but I knew there was no way the proud knight would enjoy being treated like some sideshow.

"All right, I'll let everyone know. Don't hold it in too much, Alice. If you don't like something, let them know."

"...I am a knight. I exist to fulfill my duty," she said rigidly, although not with her usual crispness. Still, there was very little that I could do for her at this point in time.

"Well, Kirito...until later."

"All right...talk to you then," I replied, waiting for her to disconnect the call.

Instead, there was a brief silence, and then I heard her say faintly, "Kirito...I feel...as though I may wither away."

The voice chat disconnected before I could answer.

6

Takeru Higa spent the better part of an hour racked with indecision.

An aged keyboard rested on his knees. The question was whether to hit the smooth, worn-down ENTER key at the end of it.

His apartment in the Higashi-Gotanda district was stuffed full of electronics that he'd been collecting since his student days. The room was miserably humid, the air conditioner unable to keep up with all the heat exhaust. He kept the lights off to limit whatever sources of heat he could, meaning that he sat in darkness, surrounded by red, green, and blue LEDs flickering in different patterns.

Across from Higa and his padded floor chair was a glowing thirty-two-inch monitor placed atop his *kotatsu*, a low table covered by a blanket with a heater underneath for the winter. Nothing was happening on the desktop—just a single plain window displaying nothing.

Higa sighed, something he'd done dozens of times without moving, and leaned back into the chair. Its rusty frame creaked.

He'd told his coworkers that he was going home to get a change of clothes, so he'd have to go back to the Roppongi office in thirty minutes. Dr. Koujiro was busy handling all the external business, now that Lieutenant Colonel Kikuoka was officially "dead." Higa was now, for all intents and purposes, the one in charge of Project Alicization.

But if anyone found out that he'd abused his position to take something out of the office, he would certainly be scolded, if not demoted entirely.

The thing he'd taken was now resting on the right end of the *kotatsu*, connected to an extremely complex and strange device. The device's handmade frame was stuffed with boards and wires—and was easily the most expensive and advanced piece of tech in the room. It was something that could not be found anywhere outside of the *Ocean Turtle*, except in Alice's machine body: a lightcube interface.

And the object connected to that device was a metal package two and a half inches to a side. Higa stared at its cold, gleaming surface and muttered, "Of course it's not going to work."

He withdrew his index finger from the space above the ENTER key.

"It's going to fall apart at once, obviously. That's what happened to the copies of Kiku and me. Human souls saved onto lightcubes cannot bear the knowledge that they are replicas. Even if…even if they're…"

He couldn't finish that sentence. Higa sucked in a deep breath, held it in—then stretched out his finger again and tapped the ENTER key.

A program sprang to life. The large fan in his PC tower picked up in intensity. In the middle of the dark window on the screen, a radiating circle of rainbow-gradient color appeared, like the birth of a star.

Many little spikes jabbed out into the darkness surrounding it. It shook, quivered, sparkled.

Eventually, out of the speakers to the sides of the monitor emerged a quiet, familiar voice.

"……*Mr. Higa, I presume?*"

He swallowed and replied, "Th…that's right."

"*So you didn't delete me. You just…copied me, I suppose.*"

"I couldn't…I couldn't delete you!!" cried Higa, arguing in

defense of his own actions. "You're the first fluctlight to survive a span of two hundred years! I mean...you're the longest-living person in human history! I couldn't delete you...I couldn't be the one to do that, Kirito!!"

Higa felt sweat dampen his palms. In the upper part of the window, a digital timer that measured the time from activation was spinning rapidly. Thirty-two seconds...thirty-three.

Kazuto Kirigaya—or at least, the copy of his fluctlight after awakening following a two-hundred-year stay in the Under-world during its maximum-acceleration phase—was aware that he was a replica.

In these experiments, every copy faced with that fact quickly lost rationality, falling into madness and emitting bizarre squeals as they collapsed. Without exception. Higa gritted his teeth and waited for an answer from the speakers.

Seconds later...

"...*I had a feeling that something like this might happen...*," said the voice, almost muttering to itself. "*Mr. Higa...was it only my fluctlight you copied?*"

"Y...yeah. Yours was the only one I could sneak out from under Kikuoka's and Dr. Koujiro's noses while I was performing the memory-deleting operation..."

"*I see...*"

There was another silence. The replicated consciousness within the lightcube remained gentle and in control.

"*I've talked to Her Majesty...to Asuna about this. About what we would do if something like this happened. Asuna said if it was just she who was replicated, she would want it deleted at once. If both of us were replicated, we would use our limited time remaining for the purpose of harmony between the real world and the Underworld...*"

"And...if it was just you? What would you do then?" Higa asked, unable to stop himself. The answer chilled him.

"*Then I would fight only for the Underworld. I am the protector of that world, after all.*"

"F...fight...?"

"*The Underworld is currently in an extremely precarious state. Isn't that right?*"

"Well...that's true..."

"*In the real world, it is tragically powerless. The energy costs, hardware, maintenance, network...It is utterly dependent on real-world people to keep its infrastructure intact. There is no way to ensure long-lasting stability and safety.*"

The conversation had already lasted two minutes. But the replica's manner was very calm and showed no hints of disaster.

Higa leaned back in the chair and, without really intending to, argued back, "There's no way around that, though. The actual Underworld—the Lightcube Cluster—can't even be moved out of the *Ocean Turtle*. The ship is under government supervision now. The government could order the power cut tomorrow and wipe the entire cluster clean..."

"*How long will the reactor fuel last?*" said the voice, rather unexpectedly. Higa blinked in surprise.

"Uh...well, that's a pressurized water reactor for submarines, so...if it's just maintaining the cluster, another four or five years, maybe..."

"*Then roughly speaking, for that time, there is no need to replenish the fuel. In other words, as long as we prevent interference from the outside, the Underworld will continue to exist, correct?*"

"P-prevent interference...? The *Ocean Turtle* doesn't have any weapons systems to begin with!"

"*I said that I would fight,*" said the voice, quiet and gentle, but with a steel edge.

"F...fight...? But the satellite connection is down, and we can't even contact the *Ocean Turtle*..."

"*There is a line. There must be.*"

"Wh-where?!" Higa said, leaning forward. The answer was not what he expected to hear.

"*Heathcliff...Akihiko Kayaba. We need his power. First we must search for him. I trust...we'll have your help?*"

"K…Kayaba…?!"

That man was dead now…In fact, he'd died *twice*.

The first time was at the retreat in Nagano. The second time was in the engine room of the *Ocean Turtle*.

But Niemon's mechanical body, where Akihiko Kayaba's thought-mimicking program was lurking, had vanished from the ship.

"He's still…alive…?" Higa gasped. He was in a daze—he had completely forgotten about checking on the timer at the top of the window.

What was going to happen?

Former archenemies, a copy of Akihiko Kayaba and a copy of Kazuto Kirigaya. If these two ever came into contact…what would happen?

Maybe…I've actually opened some kind of horrible Pandora's box…

But the trepidation lasted for only a moment in his mind before it was pushed out by a cavalcade of excitement.

I want to see that. I want to know what will happen.

Higa inhaled deeply, exhaled, then said, "All right. I've got a few old contacts…I'll try sending out some encrypted messages…"

There was no going back now.

Higa squeezed his eyes shut, wiped his sweaty palms on his T-shirt, then began to type furiously at his keyboard.

On the monitor, the massive glowing cloud that stretched beyond the boundary of the window frame flickered and pulsed periodically, gently observing the movements of Higa's fingertips.

7

I looked around my room for the first time in two whole months.

A very plain computer desk and wall rack. A pipe-frame bed and simple curtains.

I would have found it nostalgic…if I hadn't been put off by how barren it all was. In subjective terms, it had actually been two years and eight months since I was last in here—I'd spent two and a half years in the Underworld.

My room at the North Centoria Imperial Swordcraft Academy had had heavy wooden furniture, beautiful carpet, painting frames, flower arrangements, and all manner of pleasing and comfortable details. And of course, I'd always had Ronie, Tiese…and Eugeo's smile nearby.

Though they were just memories now, a painful and vivid sting hit my chest and put a lump into my throat.

I dropped my bag full of clothes onto the floor and walked a few steps to sit down on the bed. I lay down on my side and smelled the fresh linen of the sheets. They must have just been cleaned.

I closed my eyes.

I heard a faint voice.

If you're going to nap, you should finish your sacred arts lesson first. Or are you going to copy mine again?

Oh, listen, I added a wrinkle to that technique you taught me. Let's go to the training hall later.

Hey, you snuck out to buy sweets again! You'd better have some for me!

C'mon, wake up, Kirito.

Kirito...

I rolled over slowly and buried my face in the pillow.

Then I did something I'd been resisting ever since I woke up in the Roppongi lab.

I clutched my sheets, gritted my teeth, and cried. I bawled like a baby, the tears coming and coming, my body shaking.

Why...?

Why couldn't I have had *all* my memories removed?!

All of those two and a half years, starting from waking up in the forest, walking along the brook, hearing the ax, and meeting that boy at the foot of the great black tree!

I cried and cried and cried, and still the tears wouldn't stop.

At last, there came a soft knocking on my door.

I didn't reply. The knob turned, and I heard quiet footsteps. My face was still pressed into the pillow. Then the bed sank a little.

Fingers hesitantly stroked my hair.

I didn't want to lift my head. A voice spoke that was gentle and soft but with a firm insistence at its core.

"Tell me, Big Brother. Tell me what happened there—the fun things, the sad things, all of it."

"........."

I held my silence for a few moments more. Eventually, I turned my face to the right and, through teary vision, saw Suguha—my only sister—smiling at me.

I was back. Back home. With my family.

The past gets further away, and the present continues. Onward and forward.

I shut my eyes, wiped the tears, and through trembling lips said, "When I first met him...right at the start, in the deepest part of the woods...he was just a lumberjack. It's impossible to believe, but they'd spent generations—over three hundred years—trying to cut down a single cedar tree..."

It was August 16th, 2026, when I finished my physical therapy and returned home to Kawagoe in Saitama Prefecture. I spent that entire night telling Suguha about the things that had happened in the Underworld.

The next morning, I was awakened by a phone call.

It was an alert that Alice had vanished from Rath's Roppongi office.

Monday, August 17th, nine AM.

"V...vanished?! Like...electronically speaking?!" I said into the phone, dressed in my nightwear of a T-shirt and boxers.

Dr. Koujiro was on the other end of the line. She kept her voice level, but there was clearly a considerable amount of anxiety in it. *"No...I mean her entire machine body. According to security footage, she undid the security locks herself at nine o'clock last night and snuck past the guards to get outside."*

"All by herself...?" I asked, letting out the breath I'd been holding.

There were enough formal organizations and loose groups in Japan who did not think highly of Alice that you couldn't count them on just two hands. Beyond that, I couldn't begin to guess how many individuals might seek to destroy her for practical, religious, moral, or emotional reasons. She didn't have a sword or sacred arts to defend herself; if someone like that captured her now, she would be helpless.

Rath had upped their security protocol at Roppongi to fortress-like tightness in recognition of the danger. The one thing they hadn't counted on, apparently, was Alice vanishing on her own.

The only other question was why Alice would do such a thing. I recalled something I'd heard her mumble a week earlier, right before our voice chat was cut off when I was in *ALO*.

With great distress, Dr. Koujiro said, "*I was worried that we were putting too much stress on Alice. But every time I asked her 'Are you tired? Do you need a break?' she would just smile and shake her head...*"

"Well...of course. She's a proud and noble knight—she would never admit weakness to anyone."

"*Except for you, that is. Kirigaya, I think that she's going to contact you. So...I hate to ask this, considering that you just got out of the hospital, but...*"

As she trailed off, I stepped in and said, "Yes, of course, I understand. If I hear from Alice, I'll rush to her location. But, Doctor...is it even possible for her to get that far?"

"*That's what we're worried about. On her internal battery, a full charge will last for about eight hours of walking, and half of that if she runs. If her power runs out somewhere around Roppongi...and some unfriendly person happens across her...*"

"And she does stick out," I noted, grimacing. That was another thing to worry about: Alice's bright-blond hair, pure and pale skin, and painstakingly crafted features made her quite visible in a crowd, even before you got to the robot part.

"*We have every available employee out searching the area now. We're tracking Internet posts, too, and even have a bot infiltrating public camera networks and looking at the recordings.*"

"Then I'll just go to the office for now. If anything happens, I want to be able to get there ASAP."

"*That would be a great help. Thank you, Kirigaya,*" she said and promptly hung up.

I pulled a random outfit out of the closet; stuck my arms and legs through it; grabbed my backpack, smartphone, and motorcycle key; and rushed out of my room.

Down the stairs, the first floor was quiet. My dad and mom were on vacation for the Obon holiday and had gone somewhere together, and Suguha was probably at morning kendo-club practice. We were supposed to be celebrating my discharge from the hospital as a family tonight, but this was more important.

I chugged some orange juice straight from the bottle while standing by the fridge, popped the bagel sandwich Suguha must have left for me into my mouth, and raced for the door. I stuck my feet into my riding shoes and was just turning the doorknob when the intercom right next to me on the wall rang.

My heart nearly skipped a beat. Had Alice somehow found a way to get to my location on her own?

"Ali..."

I opened the unlocked door, the name catching in my throat.

Instead, it was a young man in the blue uniform and cap of one of the major delivery companies. It was exquisitely bad timing, but I couldn't help but notice the beads of sweat on his face as he said "Hello, home delivery!" so I couldn't just ask him to come back later.

I leaned over to grab the official family stamp left on top of the shoe cubbies to stamp his shipping forms, but then he delivered the bad news: "Payment on delivery!"

"Oh...right."

I started to get my wallet out of the backpack but then remembered that this world had a convenient thing called electronic funds. Instead, I pulled my phone out of my pocket and held it up to the tablet the man was carrying.

"Thanks!" he said, trotting off. I took a look at the box he'd left in the doorway.

It was surprisingly large. The cardboard box had to be over two feet to a side. If it wasn't perishable, I was going to leave it and continue on my way, but I checked the sender just in case. It was labeled ELECTRONIC GOODS. And the sender...

"What...?"

OCEANIC RESOURCE EXPLORATION & RESEARCH INSTITUTION. That had to be one of the shipping labels they kept around the Roppongi Rath office. My address was right there in the destination field. I didn't recognize the awkwardly angular handwriting.

If Dr. Koujiro had sent this, she would have mentioned it in the call. So perhaps it had come from Kikuoka or Higa. Which would mean…it was some kind of electronics related to the Underworld or the STL?

I bit my lip, made up my mind, and reached for the edge of the tape seal, carefully peeling it off. Then I lifted the two flaps out to the side, and…

"…Aaaaah!!"

…screamed in horror.

Packed tightly into the box, bent at awkward, unnatural angles, were human hands and feet. I bolted backward, eyes bulging, and then screamed a second time.

"Eyaaaaaa?!"

In the shadows beneath the hands and feet, a single eye stared back at me.

I flopped backward, but my right hand was still holding the edge of the cardboard box. A pale hand reached up out of the box and grabbed my wrist.

Before I could scream a third time, an annoyed voice said, "Stop making noise and pull me out already, Kirito."

Three minutes later, I was sitting on the lip of the wood floor in our entranceway, holding my head in my hands.

I was valiantly attempting to come to grips with the real-life actualization of that trope from popular fiction, "beautiful girl robot delivered to your door." But it was not going well.

"…I can't!!" I shouted, giving up and jumping to my feet.

I turned around to see a beautiful girl robot dressed in a familiar uniform rubbing the pillar in the hallway with a finger out of great curiosity.

Eventually, the robot—Electroactive Muscled Operative Machine #3—housing a true bottom-up AI, the third-ranked Integrity Knight of the Axiom Church, Alice Synthesis Thirty, smiled at me.

"This house is built of wood," she said. "It's just like the house in the woods of Rulid. But much, much larger."

"Ah…yeah…It's probably been around for seventy or eighty years," I said weakly.

Her blue eyes widened. "I am amazed that its life lasts for so long! They must have used quite a mighty tree…"

"I suppose…I mean…Hang on!"

I stomped across the hallway, grabbed Alice by the shoulder, and tried to ask her what the hell was going on, when she gave me a smile like a flower blooming.

"Speaking of life, might I recover the life of this steel-element body? Let's see…I believe that in your words, it is called 'recharging.'"

Allow me to elaborate on my earlier point: beautiful girl robot delivered to your door who recharges using a standard home power socket.

While I'd been away in the Underworld, the real world had apparently advanced quite a ways into the future.

"Oh…you need to recharge…? Go ahead, take as much as you need…," I said, prodding her shoulder toward the living room.

She pulled a charging cable out of her uniform pocket; stuck one end into her left hip, near the waist, and the other end into the wall socket; then sat on the sofa with her back perfectly upright. From there, she continued to swivel her head, looking around.

I guess I should make some tea for her, I thought, getting up—and then I realized that Alice couldn't eat or drink anything here. I was still rattled by this experience, I could tell.

The best way to calm down would be to solve some of the more basic questions, so I asked, "Um…first of all, can you tell me how exactly you pulled off the feat of putting yourself through the mail…?"

The golden-haired, blue-eyed girl shrugged her shoulders as if this was a very stupid question and said, "It was simple."

According to her, she found pay-on-delivery shipping forms, packing tape, and a reinforced cardboard box at the Roppongi office, and then she made sure the security cameras recorded her leaving her living quarters.

Later, she put the box together away from the view of the camera at the entrance, filled out the shipping form with my address, pasted it on, then undid the joint locks of her body and got inside the box. She placed the tape on just one side of the top lid, then pulled it down from the inside to seal it and ran another line of tape on the underside for reinforcement.

Then she sent a message to the shipping company, announcing a package for pickup. The deliveryman would have stopped at the security gate, but the message was sent from the building's premises, and the package was there at the entrance. Without realizing that a beautiful robot was hiding inside, the courier redid the insufficient tape job and placed the box in his truck, where it waited until it was delivered in Kawagoe, Saitama, the next morning…

"……I see……," I murmured, sinking back into the sofa.

Now it made sense that they hadn't been able to track her. She hadn't actually taken a step outside the Roppongi building. What was most surprising to me wasn't the sophistication of the trick but the fact that Alice had come up with the idea after spending only a month in the real world. When I brought that up, the uniformed girl just shrugged again.

"When I was a newly minted novice knight, I once snuck out of the cathedral and went to visit the city."

"…I…I see."

What would happen once Alice was intimately familiar with information technology? She could dive into virtual spaces without an AmuSphere; in a way, she was already a child of the network.

But I pushed that frightening thought aside and sat up on the couch. It was time to get to the real question.

"But…Alice, why did you do this? If you just wanted to visit my home, you could have told Dr. Rinko, and she would have set aside time for you."

"I suppose so. She is a good person…She is very concerned for my well-being. And therefore, if she had given me the chance to visit your home, it would have been with a small squadron of men-at-arms in black."

Her long, delicate eyelashes lowered. It was hard to believe that they were artificial.

"…I feel bad that I essentially fled from there. I'm sure that Dr.

Rinko is very worried and searching for me now. I will make whatever apologies are necessary when I return. But...I just wanted this bit of time very badly. Time to be with you...not in an assumed form, but in your real body, face-to-face, where we can speak to each other alone."

Her large blue eyes were staring right into me. I knew that they were just optical devices made of CMOS image sensors and sapphire lenses, but there was something breathtakingly beautiful about them. Perhaps it was the light of her fluctlight itself, shining through the brief circuit to those eyes.

Alice stood up in one smooth motion, motors whirring quietly. She rounded the glass table and approached me, step by step.

Then the charging cable plugged into the wall went taut, preventing her from walking farther. A faint look of frustration settled over her features.

I breathed in deep and stood up as well. Two steps put me right in front of Alice.

Her eyes burned and flickered with intent, just below the level of mine. Her lips moved, emitting a voice that was sweet and clear, but with a slightly electronic aspect to it.

"Kirito. I am angry."

I didn't have to ask her what she was upset about. "Yes...I suppose you are."

"Why...why did you not tell me? Why did you not tell me there was a possibility that we would never see each other again? That it could have been an eternal farewell? If you had simply said that we would be separated by a wall of two centuries, never to see each other again, when I was there at the World's End Altar, then I...I would not have fled on my own!!" Alice shouted at me. Her expression was such that if her body had had the ability to cry, tears would have adorned her cheeks.

"I am a knight! To fight is my lot in life! So...why did you choose to face that terrible foe alone, and why did you not wish to have me there beside you?! What am I...what is Alice Synthesis Thirty to you?!"

She lifted a small fist and smacked it against my chest. And again. And again.

She tilted her small head down, trembling, and bumped her forehead against my shoulder.

I enveloped the back of her golden hair with my hands.

"You are...my hope," I muttered. "And not just mine. You're the irreplaceable hope of all the people who lived and died in that world. So I just wanted to protect you. I didn't want to lose you. I wanted to make sure that hope lasted...into the future."

"...The future...," she repeated tearfully in my arms. "And what exactly does the future look like? When I have suffered and persevered through the meaningless banquets and events of the chaotic real world, in this inconvenient steel body, battling endless loneliness, what will I find?"

"...I'm sorry. Even I don't know that yet."

I squeezed her body harder and tried to put everything I was thinking and feeling into whatever words I could find.

"But your being here will change the world. You will change it. And wherever that leads, there will come a time when Cardinal's and Administrator's and Bercouli's and Eldrie's...and Eugeo's wishes will be fulfilled. That's what I believe."

And it didn't stop there. That other alternate world, the castle that floated in a virtual sky, where many young people lived and fought and died—it was connected to this place and this moment, too.

Alice left her forehead on my shoulder and held her silence for a long, long time.

Eventually, the otherworldly knight pulled away from me and gave a slight but noble smile, just like she had when I'd met her at that chalky-white tower.

"...I must make contact with Dr. Rinko. It would not be good to cause her to worry," she said.

I continued staring into Alice's eyes. It didn't feel as though the tension within them was resolved yet. But what more could I do?

Perhaps it was a problem that could be solved only through the passage of time.

"...Yeah, good idea," I said, pulling my phone out of my pocket.

When I told her what had happened, Dr. Koujiro was indeed stunned for a good five seconds, but her first words when she found her voice were an apology to Alice. She really was a good person. I could see why she was the one woman to whom Akihiko Kayaba had ever opened his heart.

"I suppose I was taking things for granted," Dr. Koujiro said. "If anything, we've been relying on Alice too much."

She followed that by giving me surprising instructions. After I hung up, I gave Alice a reassuring smile—she was looking at me with concern.

"It's all right—she wasn't mad. If anything, she was sorry about the situation. She also said that you could spend the night tonight."

"R-really?!" Alice's face lit up.

"Yup. But she asked that you turn your GPS tracker on, just in case."

"That would be a very small price to pay," Alice agreed. She blinked slowly and got to her feet. "Now that that's decided, please guide me around your home and yard. This is my first time seeing traditional buildings in the real world."

"Yeah, of course. But...this is just a normal family home—there's not much to see...," I mumbled. Then I had an idea. "Oh, hey, let's go outside, then."

Once Alice had put away her cable—she was done charging up—we headed out the front door and around the gravel-covered yard. I showed the knight our pond with koi and goldfish—and the gnarled pine tree, which she seemed quite interested in.

But eventually, we wound up at the aging dojo building sitting quietly in the northeast corner of the lot. As soon as she took off her shoes and stepped up onto the wood-slat floor, Alice seemed to intuit what this building was for.

She turned to me and asked breathlessly, "Is this...a training hall?"

"Yeah. We call it a dojo here."

"Doe-joe...," Alice repeated. She faced the back wall and performed the knight's salute of the Underworld: right hand to her chest, left hand to her waist. I bowed in the Japanese style and stood beside her.

My late grandfather had built this kendo dojo, and only Suguha used it now. The floor was polished to a shine. Despite it being midsummer, the wood was cool on the underside of my feet. Even the air seemed to be different in here.

Alice first examined the hanging scroll on the wall, then walked to the shelf set up next to it. She reached out and carefully lifted an aged *shinai* from it.

"This...is a wooden sword for practice. But it's quite different from those in the Underworld."

"That's right. It's made of bamboo and built so that it won't injure you if you get hit with it. The wooden swords over there could knock out a third of your life if they landed in the right spot."

"I see...You have no instantaneous healing arts here, after all. I suppose that training with the sword must involve quite a lot of difficult work...," Alice murmured. She paused, thinking, for several moments.

Then, without warning, she spun around and, to my shock, pointed the *shinai* handle right at me.

"Huh? What are you...?"

"Isn't it obvious? There's only one thing to do in a training hall."

"Wh...what?! Are you for real?!"

Alice already had another *shinai* in her left hand. I had no choice but to grab the handle she was offering me.

"B-but, Alice, in that body you've—"

"No need for a handicap!"

Crack! She had thrown down the gauntlet.

My mouth hung open as the mechanical girl walked across the wooden floor.

Yes, Alice's machine body was an extremely high-quality example of what was possible by the standards of the year 2026. Her mobility was far greater than that of the first and second test models on the *Ocean Turtle*. Apparently, the big secret to how the third was so much more advanced was the fact that her presence in it removed the need for a balancing function.

Every moment that human beings stand on their feet, they unconsciously balance their center of gravity between their right and left feet. If that function is re-created in a mechanized program with sensors and gyros, the size of the devices involved no longer fits within a realistic human form.

Alice was not subject to those limitations, however. Her fluctlight already contained the same auto-balancing function found in any human being. All that the actuators and polymer muscles in her frame needed were the fine control signals from her lightcube.

And yet...

At present, she still couldn't keep up with the ability of a flesh-and-blood human. I could tell as much from the clumsiness of the writing on the package's shipping form. It was unimaginable to me that she could control swinging a *shinai*—a practice sword—with the complex and speedy motions the action required.

That was my snap judgment, and it left me concerned. But Alice took a position with absolute assuredness five yards across from me and held the *shinai* above her head in both hands, perfectly still.

That was the stance for Mountain-Splitting Wave, from the High-Norkia style.

Suddenly, a chill wind brushed my skin. I gulped and pulled back half a step.

Sword spirit.

Before I could even think about how impossible this was, my body was moving on its own. I had my *shinai*, also doublehanded, at a level grip on the right. Then I dropped my center of gravity and pushed my left foot forward. That was the stance for Ring Vortex, from the Serlut style.

On the other hand, I was not only physically recovering, I was also just a weakling gamer in the real world. I wasn't in any position to worry about the ability of a machine body. Decorum required that I give this competition my all.

I found that a grin was crossing my lips, which Alice returned.

"It does remind me...of the first time we met in combat, in the garden on the eightieth floor of the cathedral."

"And you destroyed me back then. It won't go so well for you this time."

We didn't have a judge to give us a cue to begin—but our smiles vanished at the same time anyway.

Without breaking our stances, we began to inch closer to each other. The air positively crackled between us, and the buzzing of the cicadas out in the yard grew distant.

The silence grew louder and denser by the moment, until it was truly painful.

Alice's blue eyes narrowed.

There was a flash deep within their core, like a glimpse of lightning—

"Yaaaaah!!"

"Seeaaaaa!!"

We unleashed piercing battle cries in unison, and I found myself dumbfounded by the sight of that golden hair whipping as the knight's sword cut down at me.

Vweem!! Her actuators roared at max output, and a tremendous shock ran through my hands. A dry smack filled the dojo. The two *shinai* fell out of our hands and clattered left and right, spinning away over the floorboards.

Alice and I had failed to neutralize the force of the impact, so we collided and toppled to the right. Out of pure instinct, I rotated so that I fell first.

My back hit the floor. Two dull impacts came afterward: The

first was Alice's forehead hitting my forehead—and the second was the back of my head against the wooden floor.

"Aaah……," I grunted.

Alice looked down at me from inches away and grinned. "I win. The clincher was my ultimate technique, Steel Headbutt."

"I've…never heard of…"

"I've just invented it," she said, giggling with delight. Her pale cheek descended and pressed against mine. Her voice was in my ear like a spring breeze.

"I'm fine now, Kirito. I can survive in this world. No matter where I am, I will be myself as long as I can swing a sword. I've just realized that…my fight isn't over. Neither is yours. So I will look forward, and only forward, and keep moving."

That night was a tense, nerve-racking affair, for reasons different than our impromptu duel.

We held a family party to celebrate my hospital discharge, a gathering so long in the making that I couldn't remember the last time we'd done so—with one extra-special guest.

Suguha and Alice were already friends in *ALO*, and they got along quickly on this side, too, bonding over kendo. Alice found it easy to relate to my mom by telling stories about things I'd done.

On the other hand, there was a terrible tension between my dad and me on the other side of the table. My adoptive father, Minetaka Kirigaya, was almost the polar opposite of me in every regard. He was serious. Hardworking. Talented. He graduated from a top college and went to business school in America, then found work at the largest securities business there. He'd barely spent any time in Japan the last several years. It was a wonder that he didn't have any issues with my rather outgoing mother—if anything, they still seemed to be madly in love.

Despite having had plenty of beer and wine, Dad didn't seem any different from his usual self. He gave me a serious look and got right to the most important topic of the night.

"Kazuto, there's lots to talk about, but first of all, there's something I need to hear directly from you."

The left side of the dining table suddenly went quiet. I set down the chicken wing I was eating, cleared my throat, and stood up. I placed my hands on the edge of the table and lowered my head.

"…Dad, Mom, I'm sorry for putting you through all this heartache again."

My mother, Midori, just beamed at me and shook her head. "We're used to it by now. And it was a really big, important thing you did this time, right, Kazu? When a person takes on a job, they have to see it through to the end. If you say you're going to write a novel, you write it. If you say you're going to stick to a deadline, you do it!"

"Mom, you're taking that in a more personal direction," Suguha teased. Things relaxed briefly before my dad tightened the screws again.

"Now, your mother says that, but while you were missing, she was under an incredible amount of stress. The people from the Oceanic Resource Exploration & Research Institution explained the situation, and from that young lady's presence, it's clear that you played a big role in this, but you mustn't forget one crucial question. What are you, Kazuto?"

It would've felt good to say, *A swordsman!* But that wasn't the right answer for this situation.

"A teenager in high school."

I was deflated, a child being lectured by his parents. I could sense Alice's stunned gaze on my cheek, and it stung. After all the tremendously powerful foes I'd fought in the Underworld, this was my truth in the real world.

Dad nodded and continued sternly, "That's right. And therefore, it should be clear where the brunt of your effort should be going."

"…To studying and focusing on getting into college."

"You're at the summer of your second year. Your mother told me you want to study abroad, in America. Have you been making progress toward that end?"

"Ah...well, about that," I mumbled, looking at Mom, then Dad. I bowed again. "I'm sorry. I want to change my focus."

Behind his metal-framed glasses, Dad's eyes narrowed. "Explain," he commanded.

I steeled myself and revealed the goal that I'd told only Asuna about so far.

"I want to enter an electrical engineering program at a Japanese school...preferably Tohto Industrial College. Then after that, I'd like to get a job with Ra...with the Oceanic Resource Exploration & Research Institution."

Ka-thunk!

Alice bolted upright from her chair.

She had her hands clutched together before her, and her eyes were wide open. I glanced briefly at those blue pools and gave her the tiniest smile.

A long, long time ago—or two months, depending on how you measured it—I'd told Asuna that I wanted to go to America to study brain-implant chips. That was because I'd thought BICs were the proper evolution of full-diving that began with the NerveGear. I had a familiarity and an attachment to classic polygonal 3-D modeling spaces, rather than the STL and its fundamentally different Mnemonic Visualizer system.

But...the time I'd spent in the Underworld had totally flipped my perception around.

I couldn't drift away from that world now, and I had no intention of doing so. I'd finally found the theme I could make my life's work.

The melding of the Underworld and the real.

Alice stared at me, smiling like a blooming flower, then turned to Dad and said, "Father..."

That earned a shocked look from Suguha.

"My father never did give me his blessing to become a knight. But I no longer have any regrets about that. I made what I felt clear through my actions, and I believe that my father understood that. Kirito—I mean, Kazuto—is someone who can do that, too.

He may only be a student in this world, but in the other world, he is the mightiest swordsman of them all. He fought bravely and valiantly to rescue the lives of so many. He is a hero."

"Alice…," I said, trying to stop her. I knew that talking about knights and battles wasn't going to mean anything to the man.

But to my shock, there was a tiny smile on his stern lips. "Alice," he said, "his mother and I both know that already. Kazuto's already a hero in this world. Isn't that right, Black Swordsman?"

"Ack…" I grimaced, pulling away. Had they both read *Full Record of the* SAO *Incident*, as full of hearsay and nonsense as they were?

Dad's smile disappeared, and he fixed me with that American-style direct stare. "Kazuto, deciding your path, studying, taking tests, advancing to college, and getting a job are only a process you go through, but at the same time, they are the fruit of life. You can be unsure and change your mind, but make sure you live your life without regrets."

I closed my eyes, took a deep breath—and bowed a third time.

"I will. Thank you, Dad, Mom." I lifted my head and smirked a bit. "It's not exactly payment for that valuable advice…but if you happen to have any stock in Glowgen Defense Systems or their affiliates, I would sell them as soon as possible. I hear they gambled big and lost."

It was a tiny bit of payback, but the only response my dad had was a little twitch of an eyebrow.

"Ah. I'll have to keep that in mind."

I guess this is how ordinary life gets back to being ordinary, I thought, rolling back onto my bed.

Our little home party was over. Dad and Mom retired to their bedroom on the first floor, and Alice slept in Suguha's room upstairs. Imagining what they might be talking about together was frightening, but at least they were getting along. It was a good thing for Alice to get used to the real world like this, one step at a time.

Summer vacation would be over soon, and second term would begin.

I was over two and a half years away from high school classes in subjective time, so I was going to spend the last two weeks of vacation in study boot camp with Asuna. It was time to overwrite all those memorized sacred arts from the North Centoria Imperial Swordcraft Academy with equations and English vocab.

Despite what Alice had said, I probably wasn't ever going to engage in a true sword fight again. It was time for me to expend all my time and energy on fulfilling my goals in the real world. I had to study, graduate, and get a job—whether my first choice or not—in as straightforward a path as I could.

That was a very important battle, too. Even if it left me feeling a bit lonely.

The years of my youth were always going to end someday.

By the time I was able to recognize the precious nature of my teenage years with their sunlight and breeze, cheers and excitement, adventure and the unknown, they would already be in my past, never to return.

I was probably a very fortunate child.

How many alternate worlds had I raced through, heart pounding, sword in my right hand, blank map in my left? So many memories, like precious jewels, that my soul could barely contain them all.

Outside my window, somewhere in the distance, the final train of the night crossed the metal bridge.

In the grass of the yard below, the insects sang the song of summer's end.

A chilly breeze blew through the screen, rustling the curtain.

I breathed deep of the scents and sounds of the real world and shut my eyes.

"...Good-bye," I murmured.

Bidding farewell to a passing age.

8

Or so I had thought.

Up until the moment I drifted off to sleep in my bed, late at night on August 17th.

"...Kirito. Wake up, Kirito."

Someone was shaking my shoulder, pulling me back from a bittersweet sentiment.

".........Mm...," I grunted, my eyelids rising against my will.

Right in front of me were pure-blue eyes framed by golden lashes. I froze atop my sheets.

"Fhwah...?! A-Alice?!"

"Shh, don't raise a fuss."

"L-listen, I don't know what you're thinking, but this isn't really appropriate behavior for..."

"What are *you* thinking?" she said, pulling on my earlobe until my brain began to function properly at last.

Blearily, I looked over at the clock next to my bed: It was just past three in the morning. The moon was still round and bright, high in the sky through the window.

I looked back to my room.

Under the dim moonlight, Alice knelt at my bedside, dressed quite inappropriately in a plain blue T-shirt and nothing else.

Her white legs extended from its long hem, so bright that they seemed to be giving off a light of their own. With as dark as it was, I couldn't see the seams in the silicone skin, and it was impossible to believe that those graceful lines were man-made.

"D-don't stare at me like that," she said, pulling the shirt hem lower. I jerked upright, breath catching in my throat. I forced my eyes to rise, but that only revealed a rising curve through the thin fabric and, above that, shining hair like molten gold. Altogether, the sight dulled my ability to think.

In fact, my flustering was so obvious that it started to embarrass Alice. She pouted and turned her face away. "You may not remember this, but we slept in the same bed for half a year. You needn't be so self-conscious after all this time."

"Wha…? W-we did?"

"Yes, we did!!" she shouted, then covered her mouth with her hands. I hunched my neck, listening for sound from the adjacent room; fortunately, Suguha didn't seem to have woken up. She was the kind of person who could sleep through an earthquake or a typhoon, provided that it was more than thirty minutes before the time she usually woke up for morning practice.

Alice cleared her throat and glared at me. "I haven't been able to get to the point because you keep acting strange."

"Oh…s-sorry about that. Um, I…that is…I'm fine now."

She sighed, got to her feet with a faint motor whir, composed herself, and announced, "Roughly five minutes ago…I received a message via remote relayed arts—or what you would call, er… 'the network'—with most alarming content."

"An e-mail, you mean? From whom?"

"There was no name. As for the content…I suppose it would be faster for you to read it yourself."

She turned and looked at the printer sitting atop my desk. To my disbelief, the printer's exhaust fan suddenly whirred to life. Alice had just given it a remote signal to print. When did she learn to do such a thing?

But the shock of that revelation was knocked clean over the

horizon when I picked up the piece of paper the printer spat out and saw what was actually written on it.

Written horizontally on the white sheet was the following:

Climb the white tower, and ye shall reach unto yon world.

Cloudtop Garden.Great Kitchen Armory.Morning Star Lookout.Holy Spring Staircase Great Hall of Ghostly Light

For at least five full seconds, I could not process what I was reading.

As my half-working brain continued getting up to speed, I finally understood why Alice had called this "alarming content."

The first part was one thing.

But the big problem was the second. It was a string of place names...that I recognized.

Cloudtop Garden...Morning Star Lookout...these were the names of floors in the Axiom Church's Central Cathedral, the main feature of Centoria, human capital of the Underworld.

But then, who had sent this message?

There were only two people in the real world who had intimate knowledge of the inner details of the cathedral: Alice and me.

Rath personnel like Kikuoka and Higa could monitor the names of organizations like the Axiom Church from the outside, but they had no way of knowing the names of individual floors of the building. And there were many VRMMO players who'd logged in to help in the fight to save the Underworld, like Asuna and Klein, but they had all been in the Dark Territory, miles and miles from Centoria, and had logged out there as well. None of them would have even gotten a chance to glimpse that structure for themselves.

But...

When I read through the message again, I noticed something even more bizarre.

Near the end of the second part was the name *Holy Spring Staircase*. I couldn't recall having passed such a floor. That meant that whoever had sent this e-mail had written information even I didn't know.

I glanced at Alice, who looked nervous, and asked, "Is this... Holy Spring Staircase a place in the cathedral?"

"Yes...it absolutely does exist," the knight confirmed. She wrung her hands with nervous energy. "But...it is a hidden place. It's a structure from long before the cathedral was a hundred-story masterpiece—back when it was only a tiny three-story church! It was sealed below the great stairs on the first floor, so it was almost impossible to ever see. The only people who ever even knew about it were Uncle, me, and...the pontifex, Administrator..."

"Wha...?" I gaped, even more stunned.

Alice stepped forward and clutched my hand. Her fingers were actually trembling, possibly a malfunction of her electroactive-polymer cylinders.

"Kirito...you don't think...you don't think...she's alive, do you...? That half goddess...the pontifex...?"

Her voice shook with deep, deep fear.

I put a hand to her delicate shoulder and squeezed. "No...that's not possible. Administrator is dead. I saw her and Chudelkin get blasted into light and dissipate. Here...look at this," I said, lifting the printout to show her.

"This is what the first part says: 'Climb the white tower, and ye shall reach unto yon world.' The white tower is Central Cathedral, and I assume that 'yon world' is the Underworld. If Administrator was sending this, she wouldn't write 'yon world'—she would write 'my world.'"

"That...is true, I suppose. I can confirm that," Alice said, her face so close to mine that her golden bangs nearly brushed my cheek. "But then...who would have written this...?"

"I don't know. There's too little here for me to guess. My suspicion is...that if we crack the meaning of the message, we'll understand who sent it..."

"Meaning...?"

"Yeah. If you look closer, there are a couple odd things about it."

I motioned for Alice to sit next to me on the bed, then traced the printed message with my finger.

"It says to climb on the first line...but then the second part doesn't make sense, does it? It starts with Cloudtop Garden— that's the floor where you and I first fought. That was really high up there. But next it says Great Kitchen Armory. I don't know what this kitchen is, but there was an armory way down at the bottom, on the third floor. And then the next item is the Morning Star Lookout. That was the floor where we climbed back up the outside wall and finally got back inside the cathedral. That was practically at the top of the building. So the order is going back and forth."

"Yes...that's right...Ah, so many memories...I seem to recall that when we were hanging from a sword on the outside of the tower, you called me an idiot about eight times."

"Y-you don't have to hold on to details like that, you know," I muttered, hunching my shoulders.

Alice smiled, though. "It actually meant something to me. That was the first time in my life I ever truly argued with someone with all of my being."

Her smile was so pristine, so transparent, that I couldn't help but stare. Was it my imagination, or were those sapphire-lensed eyes actually moist?

It took all my willpower to tear my eyes away from those deep pools. I resumed my explanation, my throat a bit hoarse.

"And then there's the location of the periods—that doesn't make sense. Why is there no dot between 'Great Kitchen' and 'Armory,' or 'Holy Spring Staircase' and 'Great Hall of Ghostly Light'?"

Alice looked back to the sheet, her fine motors whirring. "I don't suppose...they merely forgot them..."

We inclined our heads at the same angle out of curiosity, but no ideas came to us.

Eventually, I gave up and took a small device off my wall rack so that I could summon a helper who was extremely good at cracking codes.

The black half sphere, small enough to fit in my palm, was a very high-quality network camera called an AV interactive communication probe. I mounted the probe on my shoulder, powered it on, tested that it had a wireless connection to my desktop PC, then spoke into it.

"Yui, are you awake?"

Two seconds later, a sleepy-sounding voice came through the probe's speaker.

"Yesh...Good morning, Papa." Then the camera inside the little dome swiveled to catch the person sitting next to me. "Good morning, Alice."

"Oh...g-good morning, Yui."

It was Alice's first time seeing the probe, but she'd spoken with Yui several times in Alfheim. Alice must have figured out that the device on my shoulder was Yui's real-world body, because she smiled right away.

Yui's camera rotated back and forth a few times, and when she spoke again, her voice was grave.

"Papa...what am I looking at?"

"T-trust me, it's nothing out of the ordinary. Nothing suspicious here. At all."

"The time is 3:21 AM, and you are alone in your bedroom with Alice. I cannot identify a scenario in which this would be considered a normal set of circumstances."

"W-well, we...All right, I'll admit, it's not normal, but it wasn't something I asked for...," I protested desperately.

Instead, Alice stepped in to explain, trying to hide a gleeful smile. "Yui, it's really nothing. I received a strange missive—an 'e-mail'—and I asked Kirito what it could mean."

"If you say so, Alice, then I will record it as such. But, Papa, you shouldn't keep secrets from Mama."

"Why, of course," I agreed, relieved. Alice held up the sheet of paper so that Yui could see it, then explained its contents.

Watching them interact gave me a very strange, indescribable feeling.

Yui was a top-down AI, a program made possible by pushing traditional computing architecture to its limits. And Alice was a bottom-up AI, a model of the human brain built into a totally new kind of architecture called the lightcube.

Two artificial intelligences, created from completely opposite approaches, interacting naturally and enjoyably. It seemed like an impossible miracle...

The two girls exchanged ideas and comments, totally ignoring the fact that I was getting a little teary-eyed. Eventually, Yui picked up on something.

"Oh...I'm noticing that the spacing of the first and second parts is a bit different."

"What, really?" I leaned over the paper in Alice's hand to stare at the teeny-tiny black spots.

Yui was right. There was a comma *and* a space after the word *tower* in the first part. But in the second part, the three instances of periods separating different items were squished in there, with no space. It was almost like they weren't periods, but dots or pixels.

Pixels......

"Oh.........*Oh!!*" I gasped, rising from the bed. "Th-that's it. The cathedral only goes to a hundred floors...and that's why they stuck two together...which makes this..."

I felt around my headboard for a pen, popped the cap off, and asked in a voice high-pitched with nerves, "Alice, what floor was the Cloudtop Garden?"

"...Have you truly forgotten? The very place where you and I first fought?"

"N-no, I didn't forget. It's, uh..."

"The eightieth floor," she replied, sounding a bit peeved.

I wrote the number on a blank part of the paper. "Right, right, of course. And...the Great Kitchen?"

"Tenth floor."

I wrote each number down in order, filling up the blank space.

"And the lookout was...And then...the Holy Spring Staircase was the first floor...and the Great Hall..."

When I stopped writing, there were four numbers in a row, separated by three dots.

It wasn't just a familiar structure. It was a particular kind of written protocol that people like me were used to seeing just about every day.

Yui recognized it at once, too. *"Oh...Papa, that's an IP address!"*

"Yes, it's gotta be."

It wasn't an IPv6 address, which nearly everything had switched to using by 2026, but the older IPv4 protocol. It was still possible to use v4, however, so...

In other words, this e-mail was pointing us toward a server somewhere in the real world.

I got out of bed and sat in the mesh chair at my desk, grabbing the mouse. When the monitor popped out of sleep mode, I opened the browser and tried to reach the address via http first, then FTP. Both methods refused access.

"Maybe RTSP...or telnet...?" I muttered.

The next step would be to open up the command prompt, but at my shoulder, Yui suddenly warned, *"Papa! Remember the content of the message again!"*

"Huh...?"

Alice held out the paper. When it was within Yui's view, she said, *"The 'white tower' to be climbed would seem to be indicating the address in the second part."*

"Uh-huh."

"And once climbed, it leads to 'yon world.' Which would mean that this address points to..."

"Oh...! Th-that's it...of course!!" I said, feeling my fingertips going cold and numb. I spun around. "Alice, this is the way... This is the path that leads to the Underworld!!" I hissed.

Her eyes were wide with shock. "The path...that leads...In other words, this is how we can go—I mean, get back. To that world...to *my* world...," she whispered. I nodded, sure of my answer.

Alice's actuators buzzed to life as she leaped straight toward me. I caught her in my arms. There were sobs in my ear, and a wet sensation on her cheek where she touched me, but that was probably just an illusion.

Her body of metal and silicone wasn't capable of producing such things.

Neither Alice nor I had the patience to wait for a more sensible hour to take the next step. So I liberally interpreted four AM as "early morning" rather than "middle of the night" and placed a call to Dr. Rinko's phone.

Fortunately, she was staying at the Roppongi office. At first, she seemed totally bewildered by what I was telling her, but once I got to the end of my explanation, she practically shrieked into the phone, "*Is this t-true?!*"

"It is. I don't think we can trace the source of the message, but the contents tell me that it has to be real."

"*Oh…oh. In that case, we should get to the bottom of this at once,*" the scientist said.

I promptly said, "Please let me and Alice be the ones to test it."

"*What…?*" She let out a breath that sounded like half shock and half exasperation. "*Kirigaya…after what you went through…*"

"If I was going to learn my lesson from that, I would never have agreed to work with Rath in the first place!" I protested.

She exhaled again. "*No…I suppose not. And it's that nature that helped you do what you did and that same nature that will help confront what lies ahead. But this time…please get your parents' permission.*"

"Of course, don't worry. But…I do need to confirm something first. If Alice connects to the *Ocean Turtle* from over there, will she need to use an STL?"

"*No, it won't be necessary. Alice's lightcube package combines the exact capabilities of your biological brain and the STL together. All she'll need is a single cable.*"

"Ah, that's good. In that case…um, hold on a moment." I glanced over at Alice, who was wringing her hands nervously.

"Alice, I know this is asking a lot, but…do you mind if we bring Asuna along, too?"

One of her eyebrows twitched and rose. Instead of a sigh, there was a quiet motor buzz.

"*…I suppose not. If something unforeseen should happen, there is no harm in having extra power on our side.*"

"Th-thanks, that's great…Well, you heard her, Doctor…"

After a few more comments, the call was over. I got in touch with Asuna, waking her up so I could explain the situation. All I had to do was tell her that we'd found a route to connect to the Underworld for her to understand what was going on.

Within a minute or two, we were done talking. I took the probe off my shoulder and looked into the lens. "I'm sorry, Yui…We still haven't found a way to take you into the Underworld."

My daughter listened patiently…but a bit sadly, too. "*Yes, Papa, I understand. Please be careful.*"

"We'll find a way to take you there someday," I promised, placing the probe on the desk. Next to it was a stack of manuals and textbooks that I'd been planning to look through later today. Sadly, they would have to wait a little longer.

I pulled a blank sheet of paper from the printer tray and scribbled on it with the pen. Alice went over to Suguha's room to get her uniform. We turned our backs to each other to get dressed, then snuck out of the room.

When we got down to the living room, I left my note on the table. Then I carefully, quietly slid open the old-fashioned door, and the two of us headed out into the chilly air of early morning.

To avoid causing too much noise, I pushed my 125cc motorcycle a good distance away from the house before straddling the seat. Suguha's helmet went onto Alice's head, and I put my own on before starting the engine; it kicked to life nicely for having been abandoned for three months.

Then I revved it a little and called out to my tandem rider, "Hold on tight! I'm gonna gun this thing like a dragon!"

Alice put her hands around my stomach and said, "Who do you think I am?!"

"Ha-ha, of course, Miss Integrity Knight. Then...let's go!!"

The note I left in the living room said, *Dad, Mom, Sugu: I've got one little adventure left. I'll be back right away. Don't worry about me.*

The roads were empty before dawn. We headed down Kawagoe Highway, then Kannana-Dori Avenue, then Route 246 in quick order. When we got to Rath's Roppongi branch, Asuna had already arrived via taxi.

She started to wave with a big smile, then froze when she noticed that Alice was riding behind me.

"...Kirito...what exactly does this mean?"

"W-well, uh...To put it briefly, some things happened...but nothing happened...The end..."

"Define 'some things' and 'nothing.'"

I'd known this was going to happen. I'd known it would, but I'd shown up here without a plan anyway. There was no innocent way to explain the situation.

"I'll explain everything later, I promise! We'll have plenty of time...when we're old and sipping tea...," I murmured, parking my bike in the employee lot.

When I turned around, what I feared was already coming to pass.

There was Asuna, hands on her waist. Alice had her arms folded. The air crackled like lightning between the two of them.

Very, very carefully, I said, "Pardon me...but I thought you two were past that...You know, at the Human Guardian Army's campsite..."

"It was only a cease-fire, nothing more!"

"And a cease-fire signals an intent for the battle to resume!" the two women said before glaring at each other again.

I observed the two warriors, their hostility and rivalry blazing—and did the one thing that I could do in this situation.

I made myself as small as possible, backed away, and tried to evacuate into the building. But when I submitted my ID card, fingerprint, and retinal scan at the door's security terminal, it let out a high-pitched beep, drawing their attention.

"Ah! Hey! Kirito!!"

"You shall not run from us!!"

But I was already rushing into the building. Asuna and I arrived at the STL room sweating and out of breath, and while Alice had no respiratory system to speak of, her mechanical body was giving off more heat than usual. Dr. Koujiro looked at us with alarm.

"I understand that you want to hurry, but you didn't have to sprint here. The Soul Translators and Underworld aren't going anywhere in the next few minutes," she said, a bit annoyed.

I flashed her a very snarky smile. "Oh, gosh, we just wanted to get connected without a moment to waste! After all, whether or not we can successfully dive will have a huge influence on the future security of the Under-*wuaaa!!*" Asuna pinched me hard on the side.

After that, I retreated to the nearby changing room so I could get into the sterilized robes for diving with the STL—and not just so that I could avoid a follow-up attack from Alice.

As a matter of fact, what I'd told the scientist was my honest opinion. The *Ocean Turtle* was still anchored out at sea in the Izu Islands, and its future was uncertain, to say the least. At the moment, there was only one strategy for ensuring its operation and independence.

We had to promote exchange between the artificial fluctlights of the Underworld and humans from the real world and breed friendly relations. If we could get a majority of people in the real world to accept the Underworlders as human beings, countries and corporations would not be able to simply have their way with the tech.

But…while it was extreme, there was another way as well.

Seizing actual defensive power. Arming the *Ocean Turtle* with the lightcube-bearing unmanned fighter drones that the nation was already developing, so that it could go independent as its own nation.

For now, that was just a pipe dream. How would the *Ocean Turtle* get the UAVs? How would they fund basic functions and be self-sufficient? How many months—if not years—would it take for Underworlders to transition from flying their dragons to properly operating supersonic jets? There were just too many challenges to overcome.

In either case, one absolute requirement for continued existence would be a high-capacity wireless connection aside from government-owned communication satellites. Only then could the Underworlders dive into the brand-new world of The Seed Nexus and allow people of the real world to understand them. Whether this would be possible depended entirely on the IP address written down on the paper in my pocket.

I finished changing, left the room, and held the memo out to Dr. Rinko. She hesitated for a moment, then lifted her hand and took the piece of paper.

"...I'm guessing *he* has something to do with this," she murmured. I gave her a little nod.

I didn't know how he knew about the names of the various floors of Central Cathedral. But there was only one man who could have set up a secret connection to the Internet from the *Ocean Turtle*.

Akihiko Kayaba…Heathcliff.

In a sense, my battle couldn't end without a direct confrontation between him and me. Heathcliff had passed very close by the STL where I slumbered, then vanished back into the darkness of the network. He would show himself again, though. He would gather all the fragments born of that floating steel fortress to one place and bring a conclusion to it all.

I faced away from Dr. Koujiro, who was setting up for the dive, and booted my smartphone. "Yui, have you figured out anything about that address?"

Her cute little face shook side to side on the screen. *"The location of the server is in Iceland, but I think it's only a relay point. Its defenses are very strong, and I can't search for any route beyond that."*

"I see…Thanks. Were you able to trace the source of the message to Alice?"

"Well…I spotted traces that resembled it on Node 304 of The Seed Nexus, but I lost the signal there, too," she said, drooping her shoulders.

I rubbed the touch screen with a fingertip. "No, you've done enough. If it's in the three hundreds, that would be the United States…You don't need to search any further. Even for you, making direct contact would be dangerous. He's essentially the same kind of being as you now."

"Well, I'm better!" she protested, puffing out her cheeks.

I smirked and poked her. "At any rate, I'm going now. This time it's not going to involve all these dangers…I think."

"If anything happens, I'll come to help you at once!"

"And I'm counting on that. So long."

She held up a tiny hand on-screen, and I brushed it with a finger, then turned off the device's power. Alice and Asuna were just emerging from the women's changing room at that moment. Fortunately, they seemed to have forged a second cease-fire; their faces were shining with expectation.

I shared a look with each of them in turn and said, "Remember, two hundred years have passed. We can't begin to guess what the human and dark realms look like at this point. That's shorter than the three centuries Administrator ruled over things, of course, so it probably won't be *dramatically* different, but…"

Alice's head bobbed. "At the very least, it seems certain that Central Cathedral will still be standing. So I think we can assume that the Human Empire will be the same."

Asuna brushed Alice's arm and grinned. "And we have to go and wake up Selka first thing."

"That's right!"

We shared a moment of firm resolution—then headed over to the two STLs and one reclining seat. I lay back against the chilly gel bed. Dr. Rinko operated the control that lowered the large headblock down over the top of my head.

"All right...here we go," she said.

The three of us replied in unison. "Right!"

The enormous machine began to hum. My fluctlight—the light quantum network that constituted my very consciousness—split off from my flesh, removing me from my bodily senses and gravity.

My mind was translated into electronic signals and thrown into a vast network without boundaries.

I flew at ultra-high speed down a high-capacity optical line, soaring toward another familiar world I considered home.

Into a new adventure.

Into the next story.

First, I saw a light.

A tiny little speck of white that stretched and grew into rainbow gradient, until it covered my entire vision—and beyond.

Within it a space of pure dark appeared.

I dived straight through the tunnel of light toward the darkness.

But it was not, in fact, total darkness.

Black was only the background, with a frightening number of colored dots that quietly flickered against it.

They were stars. A night sky......

But not quite. No, because...

"...Aaaaah!!"

I screamed when I looked down at my feet.

Because there was no ground beneath them.

I flailed and swung my legs, but the bottoms of my boots touched nothing. The boundless starry sky continued in every direction—sides, top, bottom. Stars, stars, stars.

"Eeeeek!!"

"Wh...what is this?!" said other voices to my sides.

Other hands grabbed my outstretched ones. On my right

floated Asuna, dressed in the clothing of the goddess Stacia: pearl-white half armor and skirt and a beautiful rapier.

On my left, Alice was in her golden breastplate and long white skirt, with a white whip and a golden-yellow longsword at her sides.

Both of them were in a panic, gazing wide-eyed at the endless sky of stars before us.

But in truth…this was not even a sky.

"…Outer space…?" I mumbled, hardly daring to say it.

Suddenly, I was aware of a ferocious chill. Alice and Asuna both sneezed spectacularly. The temperature was so low here that I could easily feel the rapid decline of my life value by the moment.

The fact that I could hear their voices meant that we weren't in the actual vacuum of space, but it must have been very close. And we were simply floating there, without protection.

I focused hard, generating a defensive wall of light elements in a sphere large enough to surround all three of us. Once the thin shining layer was enveloping us, that piercing chill finally began to subside.

Once the immediate danger was behind us, I looked around at the stunning sight before me again. A tight belt of stars ran from the upper right of my field of view to the lower left. It was like the Milky Way—but no matter how I tried to connect the brightest stars, I couldn't find a single familiar constellation.

This *was* the Underworld.

But in that case, where was the land…and where was the sky over it?

I felt a terrible chill steal over me and shivered.

It couldn't have…vanished, could it?

After two hundred years, had the very earth that made up the human realm and the Dark Territory simply run out of its own life? Had the tens of thousands of people who lived on it all ceased to exist when it happened…?

"No way…It can't be…," I murmured in a trembling voice.

Suddenly, Alice squeezed my hand so hard it creaked. "Kirito… look there."

I turned to my left. The golden knight had turned herself around to look behind us. Her arm was outstretched, gesturing toward a single point.

Breathlessly and oh so slowly, I turned to see.

There was a star.

Not a true stellar star, like those twinkling in the great distance—but a planet, vast and close, taking up a large part of our view.

The upper half of the sphere was sunk into thick darkness. But around the middle, the black transitioned to navy, then to ultramarine and azure. And on the lower half of the sphere, right at its lip, the planet shone bright blue.

The blue was steadily growing brighter and brighter. A white orb bulged from the center of the curve, spraying rays of light in a straight line.

It was dawn.

The sun—Solus—hiding on the far side of the planet was coming into view.

I shielded my eyes from its brilliance and examined the surface of the planet again. The parts of the curve that had been deep navy blue before were transitioning into brighter hues already.

Through scraps and trails of white cloud, I could see the outline of a continent.

It was shaped like an inverted triangle, wider across than it was from top to bottom.

At the upper right of the continent was a concentrated mass of lights. At the top left, an even larger spread of light.

This was a clear sign of civilization. And upon further examination, there were several glowing lines extending from those two central sources, grids stretching farther downward.

From the locations of the cities on the continent, I instantly knew exactly what I was looking at.

The city on the right was Obsidia, capital of the dark world.

The city on the left was Centoria, capital of the human realm.

That continent—the planet it was on—was the Underworld where I'd lived and fought for so long.

I tore my eyes from the planet and looked over at Alice. The only thing I saw in her face was deep shock and profound awe.

Then her eyes bulged. She let go of my hand and rummaged in the small pouch attached to her sword belt, then drew out two eggs small enough to fit in the palm of her hand.

One was faint green, while the other shone blue. The light they gave off pulsed stronger and weaker in two-second cycles. Like breathing. Like a heartbeat.

Alice clutched the two eggs to her chest and closed her eyes. Tears ran silently down her cheeks and fell free, floating as little droplets.

I could feel tears coming to my own eyes. I looked over to the person still holding my right hand and saw that Asuna's eyes were damp, too.

As the two of us watched, Alice took one step forward across the sea of stars. She held the two eggs in her left hand and reached toward the vast planet with her right.

Her eyes the same color as the dawning star and sparkling with unlimited brilliance, the golden Integrity Knight called out in a voice pure and crisp and regal, "Hear me, land!! Underworld where I was born and land that I love!! Is my voice reaching you?!"

The stars in the endless universe trembled, and the blue planet below briefly shone brighter, as though taking a breath.

I closed my eyes and listened well.

I listened to the words that ushered in a new era, carving them into my memory for all eternity.

"I have returned to you! ......I am here!!"

PROLOGUE III

STELLAR YEAR 582

"This is *Blue Rose 73*. I have confirmed atmospheric escape. Transitioning to interstellar cruising speed," said Integrity Pilot Stica Schtrinen into the voice transmitter near her mouth, pushing the control rod forward with her left hand.

The dragoncraft's silvery form shuddered. Its widespread wings began to shine a faint blue. It was collecting the scarce resources of the vacuum of space and transferring them to the drive mechanism.

The eternal-heat elements locked in the core of the mechanism screamed in response, sending white flames from the primary thrust apertures on either side of the craft's long tail. She felt her body being pressed back against the pilot seat. The sensation of powerful acceleration was something she couldn't experience within the planet's atmosphere, and it put a smile on her face.

"Blue Rose 74, *affirmative*," came a brief response from the transmitter. She looked at the auxiliary visual board on the right. Her number two was following to her side, jets burning bright.

The pilot of the second craft had been Stica's partner since they'd been ordained together, Integrity Pilot Laurannei Arabel. She was silent most of the time, and when piloting her dragoncraft, she was even less chatty.

But even Stica's addiction to speed paled in comparison to hers. Stica grimaced and warned her, "You're going too fast, Laura."

"You're too slow, Sti."

Oh yeah?

The rules of the Underworld Space Force were absolute, but even their drill instructor couldn't see them out beyond the atmosphere. And it was a whole three-hour journey to reach the companion star of Admina. That meant there was room for a little error.

Stica gave the control rod another push, pulling away from the second craft just a tiny bit. She leaned back in her seat, grinning.

When her eyes drifted upward, she caught sight of the detailed art relief on the canopy of the cramped pilot's chamber.

Two vertical swords, white and black. Blue roses and golden osmanthus flowers entwined around them. The insignia of the Star King, a figure now turning into legend.

Thirty years had passed since the Star King and Queen left their palace of Central Cathedral on the main star, Cardina.

Stica and Laurannei were only fifteen years old, and four years into their service as Integrity Pilots, so they never had the chance for a royal audience. But they'd grown up on the stories their mothers, also pilots, had told them about the royal couple. And those mothers had heard plenty of stories from theirs, and so on.

The Schtrinen and Arabel families had served as Royal Pilots—originally called "knights"—for all two hundred years of the Star King's long reign. Seven generations ago, the knights Tiese Schtrinen and Ronie Arabel protected the Star King before he was king, and they achieved great deeds in the battle against the four emperors who sought power on Cardina's First Continent. The imperial families and higher nobles' corrupt and abusive power was stripped from them, and the common people enslaved on their private property were freed.

After that, the king developed the first dragoncraft and used it to fly over the Wall at the End of the World, which surrounded the continent and rose all the way to the edge of the atmosphere.

In the uncharted lands he found there, the king patiently negotiated with the ancient god-beasts and occasionally defeated them in singular battle, taking and developing their fertile lands, then giving them over to the goblins and orcs, who had suffered prejudices under the label of "demi-humans," so that they could have their own nations.

Once the king had traveled all of Cardina, he set his sights on the endless universe above.

The dragoncraft were improved again and again, until they were capable of leaving the atmosphere altogether. He found the companion planet that orbited Solus with Cardina, and he named it Admina.

Then he created large interstellar dragoncraft capable of undertaking regular routes, established the first colony city on Admina, and was urged to take on the role of the Underworld's first Star King.

Under the rule of the king and queen, who possessed eternal life without aging, the two stars prospered—and would do so for eternity, all thought. But one day, the two of them left behind a prophecy and entered a long sleep. Thirty years ago, without ever returning to face their people, they vanished from the world.

Since then, governing had been conducted by a council of representatives from the military and civilians. With no enemy to fight at this point, the ground force and the space force were shrinking, but in accordance with the king's prophecy, pilots underwent the same fierce training they always had since ancient days.

This was the king's last message:

One day, the gate to the real world will open again. When it does, a great upheaval will come to both worlds.

Stica couldn't grasp this event in practical terms, but it was said that when the gate to the other world was opened, it would usher in a time when the continued existence of the Underworld itself would come into flux. They could not just hope for coexistence and brotherly love. They would have to prove their strength in order to maintain their pride and independence. Otherwise, the five human races of man, giant, goblin, orc, and ogre would suffer a tragedy even greater than the Otherworld War of two centuries past.

But Stica was not afraid.

No matter what world she might visit and what age might

arrive, she would fight valiantly as long as she had the wings of her dragoncraft.

I'm a member of the proud Integrity Pilots, maintainers of a tradition stretching back to the days of creation, she thought, looking up at the insignia on the roof again.

Without warning, red blazed on the bottom of the main visual board. Both a written message and an alarm indicated the detection of an element agglomeration of abnormal scale.

"Wh-what?!" she yelped, sitting up again.

Over the voice transmitter, she heard Laurannei say nervously, "Blue Rose 74, *detecting the approach of an ultra-life-form of darkness! Element density…twenty-seven thousand?!*"

"It's the mythic spacebeast…the Abyssal Horror…"

Even as she spoke its name in the sacred tongue, an empty darkness covered the right edge of the main visual board, like a pot of ink had been dropped there.

Of all the known spacebeasts, the Abyssal Horror was the most dangerous. It was over two hundred mels at its largest, with its twelve huge tentacles fully extended from its spherical body. That was twenty times the size of a single-seat fighter dragon.

Its vast body was made entirely of high-density darkness elements, meaning that it shrugged off essentially all types of attacks. The reason it was so dangerous was something else, however.

Unlike many of the other god-beasts, the Abyssal Horror refused to engage in any communication with humans. It seemed to run solely on the impulse to destroy and slaughter. When it spotted any dragoncraft on an interstellar journey, it would pursue them directly until it devoured them.

The Star King was said to have treated all the god-beasts with respect—but when he heard reports of the large passenger dragoncraft destroyed on the way to Admina, he attempted to destroy this particular creature. But even the king, whose powers were greater than an entire army's, could not completely destroy the Abyssal Horror.

Through careful observation, they learned that the spacebeast orbited between the two planets on a fixed speed and trajectory. The best they could do to minimize its threat was to restrict interstellar flight so that they could safely avoid its path.

Naturally, Stica and Laurannei had taken off from Cardina at a time that the spacebeast would have been on the far side of Admina. It didn't make sense.

"Why…? It's appearing too early…," Stica murmured, hands trembling on the control rod. She recovered her spirit quickly, however, and shouted into the transmitter, "Left turn, one-eighty degrees, then withdraw at full speed! Retreating to Cardina's atmosphere!"

"*Affirmative!!*" Laurannei replied, a spike of nerves in her voice.

Stica steered the craft left and pulled the rod as far back as she could. White flames shot from the stabilizing thrust apertures, pressing her body so heavily into the seat that she could barely breathe. The stars in the visual boards blurred from points into lines toward the bottom right.

When the turn was complete, the main visual board featured the blue shine of the planet Cardina, which she'd left less than an hour before. It felt close enough that she could reach out and grab it yet devastatingly far away.

She put on maximum acceleration, praying. The eternal-heat elements screamed and roared.

But the speedometer's needle came to a stop five whole pips short of its maximum value. The Abyssal Horror was taking resources from such a vast range that the resource-collection tanks in the dragoncraft's wings couldn't reach their maximum potential.

The rear view on the auxiliary vision board made it clear that the spacebeast's black form was much larger than before. She could even see its writhing tentacled appendages already.

Soon the ends of two especially long arms began to glow a faint bluish purple.

"*Sti, it's going into attack position!*" advised her second.

She acted instantly. "I see it, too! Deploying rear light shield!!"

She hit one of the buttons on the control board to her left. The craft's pelvic armor opened with a series of clunks. Stica took a deep breath and focused.

"System Call! Generate Luminous Element!!"

Through the conducting channels within the control rod in her hands, ten light elements were shot out of the craft's wings into space. They followed Stica's mental command, transforming into a circular defensive wall.

Right then, the spacebeast's arms hurtled past the bright, purplish light they were harboring. With a shriek like tearing metal, the blasts of darkness roared through empty space.

Just three seconds later, they made contact with the light walls.

"Aaaah!!" screamed Stica when the dragoncraft shuddered with the impact. She could hear Laurannei screaming through the voice transmitter, too.

The two blasts broke through the light shield Stica had deployed as though it were paper, tearing deep into the rear side armor of the craft. Instantly, her instruments glowed red. Something went wrong with the resource conducting channels, and her speed slowed noticeably.

Through the auxiliary vision board, she sensed the Abyssal Horror, which was no more than an amorphous blot of darkness, somehow leer at her.

On the auxiliary vision board, the second craft was missing a wing and rapidly dropping in speed. "Laura! Laura!!" she shouted, and she was relieved to hear a response.

"…It's all right. I'm fine. But…she won't fly anymore…"

"We won't have any choice but to eject out of the crafts. We'll have to find a way to get back to Cardina with just the thrusters on our pilot suits…"

"I can't! I mean…I won't! I can't leave her behind!!" shouted Laurannei. Stica couldn't tell her anything to the contrary.

A dragoncraft was not just a steel construction the pilot sat inside. It was your one and only partner, a piece of your heart.

Just like the flying dragons that the Integrity Knights of the distant past were said to ride.

"...No. No, I suppose not," Stica murmured, carefully squeezing her control rod. She took a deep breath, smiled, and said, "Then let's fight to the end. Make another turn, then fire main cannons at maximum power. Will that suffice, Laura?"

"...*Affirmative.*"

Her last transmission was short and brusque, just like she always was.

Still smiling, Stica pulled back on the rod, leading her wounded dragon into another one-eighty turn. The main visual board displayed the massive oncoming beast. Eight of its writhing tentacles were glowing with its next round of blasts now.

Ooooooooohng, the Abyssal Horror roared. Or perhaps it was laughing.

At least let me give it a good stinging as I die. Anything to prolong the time until it attacks this route again, Stica thought, pushing the red button on top of the rod halfway in.

The main cannon on the tip of the dragoncraft clanked into position. Normally she would generate whatever the most effective element was for the target, but since the Abyssal Horror's bodily form was thin at best, even its opposite element of light would do very little damage.

Instead, she decided to go with a frost-element attack, her best type.

The dragoncraft's jaws glowed a clear blue. She glanced over at the other craft—its cannon was glowing red. Laurannei had chosen heat elements.

The spacebeast was just a thousand mels away now. It stretched out its eight tentacles, preparing to attack.

Stica inhaled, ready to give the command to fire. But instead...

"*W-wait, Sti!! What's that...?!*" Laurannei gasped into her right ear.

What could it possibly be now? she wondered.

But then Stica saw it, too.

A shooting star.

Just above the main visual board, a shining white light was approaching at incredible speed.

For an instant, she thought it was a dragoncraft. But she ruled that out right away. It was much too small. It was less than two mels, only the size of a human being…

In fact, it *was* a human being.

What she'd thought was a star was the shine of a spherical wall of light elements. On the inside, she could clearly make out a black shadow in the shape of a person.

The figure came to a stop about a hundred mels in front of the two dragoncraft. At nearly the same moment, the Abyssal Horror bellowed and unleashed eight light blasts.

Before she could even grasp the shock of seeking an unprotected person in the freezing chill of outer space, Stica was shouting at them. "What are you doing?! Hurry—get away!!"

But the person did not budge at all.

The end of their long coat flapped violently as they remained stationary, arms crossed boldly. That thin defensive wall was going to be less useful than wet paper against the Abyssal Horror's blasts. Stica could already imagine the figure transforming into a spray of blood and flesh as soon as it made contact with the roaring purple blasts.

"Run awaaaaay!!"

"Watch out!!" she and Laurannei shouted together.

Eight bursts of purple light roared closer, each one nearly three mels in size.

They stopped in the middle of nothing, as if colliding with an invisible wall and bouncing off in random directions.

Space shook.

Before Stica's stunned eyes, the stars seemed to waver, like the surface of a pond struck to produce ripples. The shock wave reached her dragoncraft, rumbling and vibrating it. Speechless, she glanced at the little gauge on the right end of the main visual board. It had instantly shot all the way to its top.

"No way…Th-that's impossible…"

Stica had never seen the Incarnameter swing as much as 20 percent at a time. With fear in her voice, Laurannei said, "I don't believe it…Such incredible Incarnate strength…As though the entire universe is shaking…"

But there was no denying what was happening before them. The small, unprotected human being, without an elemental wall, used his Incarnate power—the greatest technique of the Integrity Knights of yore—to deflect the spacebeast's attack.

Ooooooooooooh…, roared the Abyssal Horror in the distance. But was it in anger or in fear?

The beast seemed to sense that its remote darkness blasts would not work, so it began to charge, thrusting its multitude of appendages forward.

The small figure reached his arms behind his back and pulled loose the two longswords that were equipped there.

"He's not going to fight it…with *swords*, is he?!" Stica gasped, leaning forward and placing her hands on the vision board.

The Abyssal Horror was over two hundred mels in size. And its body was an amalgamation of darkness without form. No little sliver of metal less than a mel long could do anything to a monster like that.

But the mysterious swordsman calmly, easily pointed the white sword in his left hand toward the mammoth creature.

He shouted something.

Through the vacuum of space and the thick armor of the dragoncraft, Stica somehow heard his voice loud and clear.

"Release Recollection!!"

A bright light flashed, covering her main vision board. When she could see again a moment later, there were many beams of light shooting from the swordsman's blade toward the monster.

They looked as tiny as threads compared to the huge spacebeast, but as they pierced through and tangled around its shadowy form, the creature clearly began to lose speed. The twelve appendages writhing on their own stiffened—as though they were freezing solid.

But that wasn't possible. The Abyssal Horror was designed to thrive in the ultra-cold region of outer space. There couldn't possibly be any chill colder than that.

Stica's shock didn't last long, however; Laurannei's voice in her ear obliterated it.

"That technique...isn't that a Perfect Weapon Control art...? No, a Memory Release art...?"

"What...? Only Supreme Integrity Pilots should be able to use that!"

"But...I can't see how it could be anything else..."

A third roar from the spacebeast cut them off.

Awoooooooooh!!

Its tied-up body trembled, and three new tentacle arms appeared. They became like great spears of night, bearing down on the mysterious swordsman.

But the man remained calm and composed, drawing his right-hand sword this time.

Again, he shouted, *"Release Recollection!!"*

The blade erupted with dense darkness, deeper and heavier than that of the spacebeast's arms. A preposterously huge blade over fifty mels long met the three appendages. When the two sides made contact, there was another shock wave, which seemed powerful enough to bend space itself. The dragoncraft rocked, and purplish lights crawled about in empty space, lighting up the vision boards.

Stica could no longer put her shock into words.

There were only seven Supreme Integrity Pilots, and this man was using their greatest power—multiple times at once. Not even a fleet of destroyer craft could handle the Abyssal Horror's full power, and he was handling it all—just a single man.

Even her own parents back in Centoria wouldn't believe her if she told them about this swordsman.

But the true shock was yet to come.

"Sti!! There's a...another person!!"

Stica looked around until she saw, coming from the same

direction that the mysterious dual swordsman had come from, another human figure arriving.

This one was smaller. Through the defensive layer of light elements, she could see long hair and a skirt. In her right hand was an incredibly delicate-looking rapier.

The swordswoman raised her arm—then swung it down to point forward.

A rainbow aurora appeared in the blackness of space, flickering and wavering in beautiful fashion. There was also a very strange sound that accompanied it, like a chorus of countless voices singing at once.

Laaaaaaaaaaaa!

The needle on the Incarnameter rattled and vibrated at its upper end.

A star appeared.

More accurately, a truly massive meteor came out of nowhere, passing just overhead with fire wreathing its surface.

Any dwarf planets that had existed between Cardina and Admina had been obliterated decades ago. But the sense of gravity that shook the entire dragoncraft could not possibly be an illusion.

The Abyssal Horror roared, sensing the huge rock plummeting toward it. It generated two more new appendages, holding them out to catch the satellite.

The impact was silent.

The tip of the burning meteor instantly obliterated the spacebeast's arms and sank easily into the center of its enormous body.

The beast that was an agglomeration of condensed darkness turned to dust in a single blow.

Ooooooooooooooo......

Its death scream overlapped with the explosion of the meteor; the combination rattled across the universe. Stica's eyes stung at the sight of resources exploding outward, from white to red to purple.

"D...did they beat...that monster......?" she whispered, her voice trembling.

But...

"Oh...no! Not yet!!"

Her second craft pilot always seemed to keep her cool and spot things a moment before Stica did.

The fragments of the Abyssal Horror, which had appeared to be obliterated and burned into nothing by the explosion, were now moving. Each one was only a portion of a single mel in size, tiny pieces of the original whole. They wriggled and wandered away like a swarm of flies.

According to the records, the Star King had pushed the beast to this point, too.

But he was unable to eradicate all the thousands of pieces of the Abyssal Horror as they escaped. So the beast fled to the ends of the universe to escape until it could heal its wounds and attack the stellar route again.

This was only going to be a repeat of that legend.

"No...you can't let it get away!! You have to burn all those things!!" Stica found herself shouting.

But the dual swordsman and the fencer did not seem capable of moving yet. And no wonder, after the tremendous exhibition of Incarnation they'd just managed.

The shards of the Abyssal Horror squirmed away, seemingly mocking the humans.

And yet—suddenly the swarm of flies scattered. They buzzed and fled, disjointed, all in a panic.

Stica held her breath and touched the main vision board, magnifying its image.

She saw golden light.

Something was there, shining bright and pure like a tiny Solus. She magnified it further.

"......A person......"

Yet another swordsman.

Hair like flowing gold. Armor of the same color. A brilliant-white skirt. And eyes that stared down her foes with the color of the blue sky.

......*I know her.*

"I...I know this swordswoman...I mean, this knight," Stica whispered. She heard Laurannei whisper back, "*Me too.*"

The golden knight looked exactly as she was painted in the huge portrait hung in the throne room on the fiftieth floor of Central Cathedral. She was one of the greatest Integrity Knights in history, who'd achieved great feats in the ancient Otherworld War and disappeared in the midst of the fighting. In fact, her name was...

"...Alice...?"

The knight's hand moved, almost in recognition that her name had been called. She drew a longsword from her side with a smooth motion.

The yellow blade reflected the light of Solus to an almost blinding degree. In their fear, the minute fragments of the spacebeast lost whatever controlling force they might have had, fizzling away in random directions.

The knight held the sword before her body. She called out in a voice like wind that blew through space. The dragoncraft's Incarnameter burst right off its mount.

"*Release Recollection!!*"

The sword blazed even brighter. Its body made a sound like scraping metal and fragmented into a million tiny pieces.

The hilt was still in the knight's hand, however, and she swung it easily. The fragments spilled forth into the void, spreading like flower petals on a light breeze.

It turned into a golden meteor shower.

Each and every little bit of light exhibited frighteningly precise aim, piercing the fleeing scraps of the dark beast. Each bit of darkness, once shot through, was burned away into nothing by the brilliance of the golden line.

"......Incredible..."

It was all that Stica could find the words to say. You could line up every last craft in the Integrity Pilothood, fire all their main cannons at once, and not hope to exhibit this much precision and power.

When the last little scrap of the Abyssal Horror, the deadliest spacebeast in all of the Underworld, succumbed to a golden arrow, it let out a scream that put all its others to shame.

Gyeeeiiieeeooooo.........

And with that, the creature was finally, truly gone.

Stica watched, dumbfounded, as the golden swarm of shooting stars gathered at the knight's hand and returned to being a whole sword again.

But if the golden knight really was the very Integrity Knight Alice of old, then who were the other two people? On the vision board, the knight returned the sword to her sheath and flew through space toward the warriors in black and pearly white.

The three had a brief discussion, then turned to face Stica and Laurannei.

They were too far away for Stica to see their faces clearly. But she could tell that all three of them were smiling.

Then the swordsman with the white and black swords put them behind his back again and waved to the pilots.

In that moment, Stica felt some tremendous emotion she couldn't describe piercing her heart deep, deep inside its core. A kind of lonely pain that took her breath away.

"Ah...ahhh...," she murmured.

Quietly, Laurannei murmured, "*Sti, I know him. I know who that is.*"

"Yes, Laura. So do I...so do I."

She nodded again and again.

It wasn't something she knew because she'd seen his portrait in the throne room. It was something else.

Her heart. Her fingers. Her soul knew him.

She felt the scent of honey pie, sweet and fragrant, tickling her nostrils.

A calming breeze blowing across the field. The warm light of the gentle sun.

Faint laughter in the distance.

In a daze, Stica put on her airtight helmet and pulled a handle on the right side of the pilot's seat. The temperature-controlled air squeaked and escaped. The layer of armor protecting the dragoncraft's control seat moved away, revealing the sea of stars overhead. Her second was opening her own cockpit as well.

Stica stood up in her seat, staring at the three warriors standing thirty mels away, waving at her.

But in fact...

...there was another.

Stica's maple-red eyes beheld the figure of a fourth person flickering into existence.

He stood just to the left of the one in black, smiling gently. He was wavering like heat haze, translucent and fragile, like he might vanish if she took her eyes off him for an instant.

The flaxen-haired young man looked at Stica and nodded firmly, just for her.

She felt tears burst from her eyes.

The warm liquid trickled down her cheeks, spilling into her airtight helmet.

In time, the sight of the young man melted away into the light of Solus as it appeared around the edge of Cardina.

At that moment, the young Integrity Pilot understood: This instant, *right now*, was the starting of the new age that the Star King had prophesied.

They were messengers, appearing from the past to open the door to the future.

Starting from here, the world was going to change.

The door to the other world would open, and the tide of a new age would rush through it.

That would not be the arrival of an age of paradise. This would be a time of revolution and turbulence in the Underworld, an age that none of them could imagine.

But Stica was not afraid.

She couldn't be—not when her heart was leaping with joy.

This encounter was something her soul had been dying to experience.

She blinked the tears away and stared straight ahead.

From a standing position, she reached to tilt the control rod forward.

The damaged dragoncraft wing took on a blue glow.

The eternal flame elements breathed, putting a tiny bit of life into the craft.

She looked over to Laurannei, and the two of them shared a knowing glance.

The girl of the Underworld, Integrity Pilot Stica Schtrinen, gently flew her dragon along.

Onward toward the unfamiliar strangers waving at her.

Toward the door to the new era.

Toward the future.

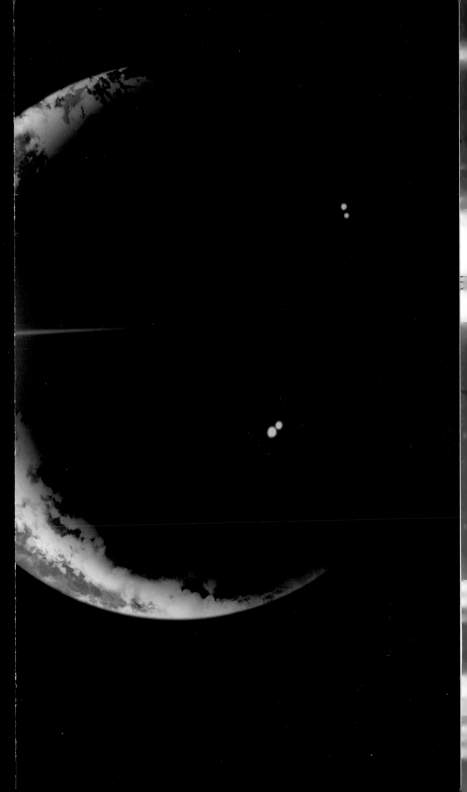

But as of this moment, all possibilities are merely bobbing along in flux, flickering beyond a field of fluctuating light.

Thanks to good fortune for bringing us together...

《Comic Unit》
Tamako Nakamura
Minamijyujisei
Tsubasa Haduki
Neko Nekobyou
Kiseki Himura
Koutarou Yamada
CSY

《Animation Unit》
Tomohiko Ito
Shingo Adachi
Tetsuya Kawakami
Yu Yamashita
Takahiro Shikama
Tetsuya Takeuchi
Yoshikazu Iwanami
Yasuyuki Konno
and more...

《Producer Unit》
Atsuhiro Iwakami
Nobuhiro Osawa
Shinichiro Kashiwada
Jun Kato

《Voice Actor Unit》
Yoshitsugu Matsuoka
Haruka Tomatsu
Ayana Taketatsu
Miyuki Sawashiro
and more...

《Artist Unit》
LiSA
Eir Aoi
Runa Haruna
Yuki Kajiura
Takeshi Washizaki

《Game Unit》
Yosuke Futami
Yasukazu Kawai

and you.

AFTERWORD

Thank you for reading *Sword Art Online 18: Alicization Lasting*. And a huge, heartfelt thanks to you for following along with all ten volumes of the Alicization arc, starting with Volume 9.

To repeat something I wrote in the afterword of Volume 1, the story of *Sword Art Online* (*SAO*) was originally something I wrote in the fall of 2001 to submit for the Ninth Dengeki Novel Prize. I finished it by the deadline in spring of 2002 but was far over the page limit, and because I didn't know what to cut out, I gave up on submitting it.

In other words, when I started writing *SAO*, the only thing in my head was the Aincrad story—just the few weeks before the game was beaten on the seventy-fifth floor, in fact. But when I set up a website after that and published *SAO* as an online novel, I was fortunate enough to hear from many readers asking for more of the story. I wrote Fairy Dance as the second arc and Phantom Bullet as the third arc (titled Death Gun in the online version), with shorter stories sandwiched in between them. I remember starting the fourth arc, Alicization, in January 2005.

Writing this now, I cannot actually recall why I decided to leave the boundaries of VRMMOs I had been writing about to tackle concepts like bottom-up AI, drone weaponry, quantum brain theory, and simulated reality. All I can remember is writing and writing in a daze, hitting walls, and finding ways around them.

It was in July 2008 that the Alicization arc's online publication concluded.

About the same time, I was writing a story called *Chouzetsu Kasoku Burst Linker* for a novel-submission website. After six years' more experience, I decided to try my luck with the Fifteenth Dengeki Novel Prize, and I was lucky enough to win. I changed the title from *Burst Linker* to *Accel World*, and that was my debut as a professionally published author. When I put the notice about this on my website, my editor, Kazuma Miki, saw it and sent me an e-mail saying that they wanted to read *SAO*.

I sent over all the data files I'd compiled over eight years of writing to them. Between their editing duties, they managed to read it all in a week. I still vividly remember when they said to me, "Let's publish this with Dengeki Bunko, too."

At the time, Miki said, "Let's make it our goal to get to the end of the Alicization arc." It seemed like a total pipe dream to me. If you converted the word count from the online version into a book manuscript, it would be over fifteen volumes. Even going at a pace of three books per year, it would need to capture reader interest for five whole years to get to that point.

I wasn't thinking about getting all the way to the end of the Alicization arc. I didn't think that my career as an author was going to last that long. But Miki's passion for making books, his work in recruiting abec to provide clean and powerful illustrations, and of course, the support of so many readers made it possible for the series to continue. Now, in August 2016, about seven years after Volume 1 came out, I've been able to release the final volume of the Alicization story.

As a matter of fact, there was a lot of added writing that went into the Dengeki Bunko version of *SAO*. This book is the eighteenth volume—the twenty-second if you include *Progressive*. It's the forty-fifth if you include my other series. It's been seven and a half years since my pro debut, and about fifteen years since I started writing *SAO*. It feels impossibly long, and it feels like it passed by in the blink of an eye.

Now that I've reached the end of it, what I'm left with in my chest is a vague question of *why* I wrote *SAO*, and this Alicization story in particular.

Because I liked online games and the idea of games turned deadly? That was probably all it was at the start. I don't know what would've happened if I'd turned in my Aincrad story to the Dengeki contest the way I'd planned, but I do feel it's likely I would have put just the Aincrad story on my website in installments and called it a day. The scene I really wanted to write fifteen years ago was Kirito and Asuna sitting in the sunset, watching Aincrad collapse, then going back to the real world, where Kirito would start off in search of Asuna.

But I didn't stop there. I wrote Fairy Dance, Phantom Bullet, and Alicization, and perhaps the engine that kept me going was not just all the people visiting my website, but the story itself—the characters who laughed, cried, and fought together. I kept following, pacing behind Kirito and Asuna as they sought out new worlds and new adventures, until it brought me to today, I think.

If I stop typing and close my eyes right now, I feel like I can still see the backs of Kirito and his friends as they run toward the distant light. Their journey will not end, and I'm certain that many adventures still await them, in *ALO* and the rest of The Seed Nexus, in the sealed-off Underworld, and in the real world.

A part of me wants to follow along with those new stories, of course. But at the same time, the map of the future is so vast and uncertain, a part of me is hesitant. Before I step into the next world, I want to think about what the lengthy story of Alicization meant to Kirito, Asuna, Alice—and me—and soak in that feeling. That's my plan.

Over the course of the *SAO* series, I've come into the debt of a great many people.

Those who have handled the manga adaptations: Tamako Nakamura, Minamijyujisei, Tsubasa Haduki, Neko Nekobyou, Kiseki Himura, Koutarou Yamada, Shii Kiya.

Those who have taken part in the animation series: director Tomohiko Itou, character designers Shingo Adachi and Tetsuya Kawakami, action-animation director Takahiro Shikama, all the people from A-1 Pictures, producers Atsuhiro Iwakami, Nobuhiro Oosawa, Shinichirou Kashiwada, Jun Katou, Masami Niwa. Kirito's voice actor, Yoshitsugu Matsuoka; Asuna's voice actor, Haruka Tomatsu; Leafa's voice actor, Ayana Taketatsu; Sinon's voice actor, Miyuki Sawashiro; and all the other cast members. The singers for the theme songs: LiSA, Eir Aoi, Luna Haruna. Sound director Yoshikazu Iwanami, sound designer Yasuyuki Konno, composer Yuki Kajiura.

Those who made so many games: Yousuke Futami, Yasukazu Kawai. Takeshi Washizaki, who did promotion on the radio and at events.

My editors, Kazuma Miki and Tomoyuki Tsuchiya. Tatsuya Kurusu, who drew my little maps and such. abec, who brought the story to life with such beautiful illustrations.

And lastly, to all you readers who followed along with the story to this point, my undying gratitude.

Thank you all so much. I hope you'll continue to love the *SAO* series.

Reki Kawahara—July 2016